PRAISE FOR THE NOVELS OF LAUREN BARATZ-LOGSTED

A Little Change of Face

"Baratz-Logsted offers a clever twist on makeover fiction."
–*Booklist*

"Has something to say about how women look, and are looked at by others, but it says it with a whip-smart, funny voice."
–Christopher Moore, author of *Lamb* and *Fluke*

Crossing the Line

"Baratz-Logsted has a great voice.... Entertaining, and the message she sends about unconditional love is touching."
–*Romantic Times BOOKclub*

"Chick lit with a twist!"
–Meg Cabot, author of *The Princess Diaries*

The Thin Pink Line

"Wonderfully funny debut with a fine sense of the absurd and a flair for comic characterization."
–*Kirkus* (starred review)

"...hilarious and original."
–*Publishers Weekly*

D0557362

How Nancy Drew Saved My Life

LAUREN BARATZ-LOGSTED

RED
DRESS
INK
™

HOW NANCY DREW SAVED MY LIFE

A Red Dress Ink novel

ISBN-13: 978-0-373-89591-5
ISBN-10: 0-373-89591-7

NANCY DREW is a registered trademark of Simon & Schuster, Inc., used with permission.

www.RedDressInk.com

Printed in U.S.A.

For my mother, Lucille Baratz, one of the world's greatest ladies, and the woman who gave me my first Nancy Drew. Mom, if I keep putting off dedicating a book to you, will you stay with us forever?

No book is ever written in a vacuum, even if it feels that way at times, and this book is certainly no exception, so here come the curtain calls.

Thanks to Margaret O'Neill Marbury, Rebecca Soukis and the whole RDI team, with special thanks to Keyren Gerlach for going above and beyond.

Pamela Harty is in a line all by herself for restoring my faith and giving me my shot, all in one go—thank you forever.

Thanks to the Friday night writing group: Greg Logsted, Jerry Brooker, Andrea Schicke Hirsch, Rob Mayette, Lauren Catherine Simpson. What I want to know is: Who's bringing the wine next week?

Thanks to the Monday night reading group: Irene Clarke, Anita Hannan, Cheryl McCaffrey, Jacquie Pugsley, Rebecca Tate and my longtime friend Jeannine Fagan. I'm a better reader, writer and mother because of all of you.

If I lived forever, I could not thank Sue Estabrook enough for making me a better writer and a better person.

And if I listed all the friends and family I'm grateful for we wouldn't be here all day, but we would be here for quite a bit, so suffice it to say you know who you are and by now, you ought to know what you mean to me. That said, I would be beyond remiss not to thank those who are under my roof as I write this:

Thanks to my niece, Caroline Logsted, for bringing so much unlooked-for joy into our lives; thanks to my daughter, Jackie, who makes me marvel every day, not merely that I have a child, but that I have this child; thanks to my husband, Greg, for being the greatest man who ever lived. Without the three of you, I would be both less sane and less insane; certainly, I would be less loved.

prologue

People think it must be easy for you, when they see you out here on the wire.

They think you don't know fear.

But what they never stop to consider is that you know fear better than anybody and your greatest fear is *not* being here, not taking the chance, not living this life.

Some people think it's brave to fight in wars and I suspect it must be true. Some people think it's brave to go after your career dream and while I wish it were personal experience talking here, I suspect that must be true, as well. But the bravest thing of all, to me, is to love another human being, to take the chance of being disappointed, to risk having your heart broken.

That's the wire I'm talking about, the only wire that really matters in the end.

In spite of everything that happened to me, I still believe this to be true.

chapter 1

You know, none of this ever would have happened, were it not for that Maureen Dowd column in the *New York Times*. After all, it's not like grown women over the age of twenty think very much about Nancy Drew, is it? Besides which, as a young girl, I'd not been much of a Nancy Drew fan. Sure, I'd seen the shelves of her books in the libraries and bookstores I frequented whenever I got the chance, but she'd seemed so other-timely, outdated, so *retro* in a way that would never be fashionable again.

At least that's what I thought.

Anyway, the article had one of those oblique angles, as these things so often do, but it was generally about Iraq and the Osama bin Laden Presidential Daily Briefings. The tie-in with Nancy Drew was that we really needed someone brash and intrepid like her involved, and questioned where all the brash and intrepid people had gone.

As for me, at the age of twenty-three, I no longer felt brash and intrepid, since events had conspired to rob me of those feelings.

I had committed the cardinal sin of many a young woman before me, something Nancy Drew would never do: I had fallen in love with a married man—named Buster, no less; with two kids, no more. I know it was a foolish thing to do, inexcusable, too, and I know it sounds lame to say he *made* me fall in love with him.

Except that's the truth.

I would have been content to admire him from afar, but he drew me in, came at me like a freight train, convinced me his wife neither loved nor understood him and they hadn't had sex in forever—I can hear you laughing at me now!— and I was the only woman he'd ever really been in love with, that no other woman had ever been as smart or as sexy or as funny or as wonderful and nothing better had ever happened to him in his life than loving me. He convinced me it would be a crime against the universe were we not to reach for this rare chance so few people ever know in this life: to be with someone, not because both parties are settling or desperate or fooling themselves, but because all the crossed stars in the firmament had deemed it should be so.

And I fell for it.

He was like a master glassmaker, building a floor underneath me, sheet by sheet of perfect glass, laid one next to the other like the most sparking tile in the world. And he led me out to the center of that amazing floor, had me stand right in the middle waiting for my Cinderella moment. But before I got my chance to dance with the prince, the craftsmanship turned into a game of Don't Break the Ice. You know the game, where you take turns using little red and green plastic mallets to knock the cubes of white plastic ice one by one through the red plastic frame until one poor sucker dislodges the catastrophic piece that sends the little red plastic figurine at the center thudding through to the floor. Well, it was just like that, with me playing the part of the little red plastic figurine.

Only it was so much worse.

Buster got me right where he wanted me, out on that amazingly gorgeous crystal dance floor, constructed solely for me, and then he began smashing those glass tiles he'd made for me, one by one, until at last I fell through the floor, flaying my skin, shredding my soul and breaking my heart in the process.

I had always believed there are keys to the inner workings of every person alive. When love is wrong or insufficient, people jealously guard those keys, preferring to play games instead, making the other person guess at what is required, knowing the other person will fail miserably. When love is right, good, you gladly hand over the keys; you trust, and let the other person know exactly what makes you tick, for good or ill. I gave Buster so many of my keys, I let him inside me. I thought I had his keys, too, and he just ransacked the whole fucking place, like the Grinch paying a call on Cindy Lou Who the night before Christmas, and left me with no more than some picture-hanging wire and a few nails sticking out of the walls. I should have seen it coming, but still…how could he do that to me? How could he do that to me in the way in which he did it?

I could go into all the gory details, but why bother? These stories always end the same. Suffice it to say, I was the only one destroyed, certainly not Buster.

I don't think his wife ever knew.

I sincerely hope she did not.

Not that she was any great shakes as a human being herself.

I'll tell you one thing for damn certain: Nancy Drew never would have fallen in love with a married man.

In the wake of my bust-up with Buster, I moved temporarily back in with my aunt Bea and her three kids. It wasn't so much that I wanted to be there, and it was sure as rain that the four of them didn't particularly want me back there, but I was feeling too emotionally fragile to strike out on my own right away. Plus, for one thing, my exit from Buster's household had been too abrupt for me to find something right away—slim chance to find a decent apartment in New York City on the same day as one starts looking. Two, I didn't intend the situation to be permanent, just long enough until I could make up my mind and clearly decide what to do next. Three, last but not least, despite that I had some savings from my long-ago glory as a commercial child star, it would dwindle with alarming speed if I took up residency for a few months—the optimum time needed, I figured, to recover from a major heartbreak—in a New York City hotel room.

Thus it was, in the wake of my breakup with Buster and having moved back in with my aunt, that I saw the *Times* article that led me to Nancy Drew. It was in that same edition of the *Times* that I found my next nannying position, for I had indeed been the nanny to Buster's own two kids, in his Manhattan penthouse on the Upper West Side.

The classified ad read:

WANTED!
NANNY
Full-time position.
Applicants must be willing
to travel to Reykjavik.

It said the job would not start for another two months, but since there had not been any other listings in the recent weeks since I'd been checking—indeed, the recession we were supposedly *not* having had dried up even the nanny market—I figured it was Reykjavik or bust for me. Now, if only I knew where Reykjavik was....

It is indeed possible to be widely read, as I am, and still have black holes in one's knowledge. So, although I'm a nanny by profession, my sense of geography sucks. I'd thought St. Louis was in the state of New Orleans—well, wouldn't it be better if it was, both places being great for jazz, and I used to get Las Vegas and Los Angeles mixed up on a regular basis.

Don't even get me started on where Michigan should really be.

After the part about the delayed start date, the ad listed a fax number for sending résumés.

I pulled a copy of my résumé from out of the stack in the folder on my dresser—I might not be feeling intrepid anymore, but a member of the Mary Poppins profession is always prepared—and went in search of Aunt Bea to see if she would let me use her fax machine.

Given that I'd lived in that household, a Greenwich Village town house, off and on since my father moved to Africa when I was three—more on him and my mother later—you would not think I'd still have to obtain permission for such minor things. Oh no. I'm guessing you never lived in a household like Aunt Bea's.

I found her in her king-size brass bed—nothing about Aunt Bea's desire for luxury was ever small—huddled under the frilly bedsheets, a can of SlimFast with a straw on the night table, the TV tuned to *All My Children;* another thing we differed on, to her unending horror, as I was a *Days of Our Lives* fan, born if not bred, just like my late mother.

Aunt Bea at fifty looked about ten years older than she needed to. Not that she didn't make every vain effort to look younger, at least as far as clothing choices and makeup, but she'd spent so much of her life frowning that she was as in need of Botox as a shar-pei.

But she was scared of needles.

And botulism.

I had learned over time, through many trials and a whole slew of errors, that the best way to get something out of Aunt Bea was to appeal to her sense of her own needs. Certainly, appealing to her sense of *my* needs hadn't gotten me anywhere.

"Excuse me?" I coughed.

"Can't you see Erica's about to have one of her big scenes?" Aunt Bea didn't even look in my direction.

It seemed to me that Erica was always having big scenes and that her big scenes were never as big as Marlena's big scenes, but what did I know?

I sucked it up and plowed on.

"There're almost no want ads anymore in the *Times*," I said woefully.

"But you have to get a job," she said, eyes still glued to Erica. "You can't stay here forever."

"True, true."

I let that rest for a minute. Then:

"In that whole big paper today, there was only one job I'm qualified for. And you know there haven't been any other ads for nannies in weeks…"

"What job?" She looked at me sharply.

I produced the ad from behind my back, holding the résumé in reserve.

"Here," I said. "But look, it's all the way in Reykjavik." I wrinkled up my nose. "Do you know where Reykjavik is?" Usually, the nose-wrinkling is an affectation on my part, but not this time. "Isn't it in Yugoslavia somewhere—is Yugoslavia even still there?—or Poland? Cities in those countries always end in 'k,' right?"

"Reykjavik doesn't ring any strong bells?" Aunt Bea asked.

I shook my head.

"Reagan?" she prompted.

"I know who he was," I admitted cautiously.

"Gorbachev?" she prompted some more. "Big summit there? Reagan proposed complete disarmament and the Pentagon went crazy because, at that time, the USSR had a huge conventional military superiority over NATO and the West needed its nuclear deterrent? Still nothing?"

I shook my head.

"What year was this?" I asked.

"Nineteen eighty-six," she snapped, as though only a fool, or someone like me, wouldn't know the answer.

"It was kind of before my time," I said. "I'm fairly certain I was still mostly preoccupied with my Little People Farmhouse back then."

"You don't know anything," she said, disgusted.

I shrugged. Maybe I didn't.

"It's in Iceland," Aunt Bea said.

Crap, Iceland sounded cold. Oh, well.

"Oh," I said. "I was kind of worried you'd say that."

"You mean you asked me when you knew all along?"

"Let's just say I had my suspicions. I was kind of hoping for mainland Europe somewhere. So," I said. "Iceland."

"Population one hundred and seventy thousand in Reykjavik, last time I checked," she said.

"Ah," I said. "Puny."

"Whole country doesn't have more than three hundred thousand, I don't think," she said.

"You wonder why they bother," I said.

"So," she said, handing the paper back to me, "what are you planning to do about this? Reykjavik is nice and far away…"

There was that Aunt Bea gleam, the gleam of the aunt who loved me so well.

"Well, it does have a fax number for résumés here…"

"What are you waiting for?" Aunt Bea demanded.

Your permission, I thought, *since we both know that if I had used the fax first and asked later, no matter what the good cause, even if it had been to help starving children in the Third World, you'd have done something insane like deny me hot water for a month.*

Home may have been the place where, when you're desperate, they have to let you in. But some had creepy red rooms that were like mental torture chambers in the upstairs and some homes still sucked.

"Get going!" Aunt Bea shooed me.

I went, having gotten my own way the hard way.

I may have been down and out, but I was still perky and resilient. That's one thing you should know about me: even when I'm not feeling at all brash and intrepid, I've always been perky and resilient.

As I fed my résumé facedown through the fax machine, I thought about what was on the business side of it: my name, Charlotte Bell; my address, here; my early schooling, unspectacular; my two years of business college, entered into upon and completed at Aunt Bea's insistence, since she thought I'd never amount to much and wanted to make sure I embarked on a path that would ensure this would be so. After that, of course, there was my three years in Ambassador Bertram—Buster to his friends—Keating and Mrs. Keating's home as nanny to their two kids.

I'd gotten the Keating job through an agency. Upon receiving my business-college certificate and having decided that I didn't want to do anything remotely business related, and having Aunt Bea at my back pushing me to get a job that would earn me enough money to get me out of the house, I'd decided to kill all the birds with one stone: I'd take a job that would, by definition, get me out of the house twenty-four hours a day.

I'd be a live-in nanny.

How hard could it be?

Perhaps I'd read too many gothic novels as a young child

and was romanticizing the job, but I pictured young children looking up to me and me loving them; I pictured feeling competent.

Okay, obviously I wasn't thinking about anything by Henry James.

The way I figured it, though, being a nanny would be the perfect confidence-building thing to get me out of Aunt Bea's house. And, so long as nobody noticed the gaps in my knowledge, like geography, everyone involved would be better for it.

I looked again, ruefully, at the résumé I was faxing.

Since the only job I'd ever held of any substance was in the household of a man I'd made the mistake of sleeping with during most of my three-year stint there, and since being an adulteress hardly qualifies one in the eyes of the world as being good for much of anything other than more adultery, you would think I'd be trepidatious at the notion of my future riding on so little.

But if you thought that, again you would think wrong.

And isn't it amazing how close intrepid and trepidatious are when you look at them on the page like that? Hard to believe they could be such different things and that at different points in my life I was destined to be one or the other.

One thing I was sure about: Ambassador Buster would give me the greatest reference the world had ever seen, if only to get me out of town, so that he could stop feeling so damn guilty and stop worrying that I'd turn all *Fatal Attraction* on him, sneaking into his house and boiling a rabbit in his pot.

In addition to football, Buster also watched a lot of

movies. Really, once TiVo had entered the picture, it was a wonder he got any ambassadorial work done at all.

Nope, I was more Buster's worry than he was mine and, really, the one thing you never want to do is piss off the nanny.

Like I said, I'm nothing if not perky and resilient, even if I'm still a far way from intrepid.

chapter 2

Fax faxed, I took myself down to my local Barnes & Noble, a three-story building I treated like a second home, attending as many author readings there as I could, haunting the stacks for new books like a crack addict searching for her next fix.

Since I had read as many literary novels and commercial truffles as I could stand for the nonce, and since Maureen Dowd had put Nancy Drew on my mind, I made my way to the children's department and looked around until I found the originals in the series: small jacketless hardcovers, with their bright yellow spines and blue lettering, the original old-fashioned artwork still on the front.

Feeling pluckier already, I plucked the first one off the shelf. It was *The Secret of the Old Clock*. I turned it over, expecting there to be some description of the plot of the book, but all there was was some kind of all-purpose blurb about the series—"For cliff-hanging suspense and thrilling action…"—and a listing of the first six titles in the series, followed by the promise, "50 additional titles in hardcover. See complete listing inside."

Fifty-six seemed like an awful lot of titles to have to live up to "cliff-hanging suspense" and "thrilling action," particularly if they featured the same character time and time again. How good could Nancy Drew be? Was she really that exciting or was someone pulling the young consumer's leg?

As I'd said before, I'd never read much Nancy Drew as a young girl, could only remember liking *The Witch Tree Symbol,* better known to whoever compiled that comprehensive list at the back of the book as #33.

I plucked #33 from the shelf, flipped through it, the memories flooding me. There was Nancy climbing on top of a tabletop, holding a lantern up to a ventilator and passing one hand in front of the light at intervals such that the S.O.S. signal would be transmitted, over and over again. (I'd have just screamed for help and then died before anybody came, because help was too far away to hear a scream but it could see a well-planned S.O.S. signal.) There was the young detective, at the end of the book, not thinking about what she'd just been through but rather turning her mind to the next mystery, with a ham-fisted authorial plug for *The Hidden Window Mystery, #34.*

I put the book back on the shelf. It all seemed so…*kitschy.*

But suddenly I found myself curious, curious to know what had attracted generations of readers. Even if I had always assumed her to be too retro for my tastes, year after year the books had kept selling. And, surely, if Maureen Dowd was touting her as the answer to the world's problems…

It took several scoopings, but I scooped up all fifty-six

books, everything from #1, *The Secret of the Old Clock*—and that clock on the cover really did look old, with Nancy sitting there on the ground at night, looking all intrepid in her green dress and sensible watch, legs tucked ladylike to the side as she prepared to do something unladylike to that clock with the handy screwdriver in her hand—to #56, *The Thirteenth Pearl,* with its vaguely pagodaish cover. So #56 was the last one? I thought. God, I hoped she didn't die in the end. Even if I didn't end up liking her any more than I had as a little girl, that'd just kill me after reading about her for fifty-six books. I was fairly sure that after reading all fifty-six books, I'd start feeling attached.

Then I noticed that there were other books on the shelves with "Nancy Drew" on their spines but with different packaging. So she *did* live on!

I hauled my armloads over to the nearest available register and plunked the books down.

"A completist's present for some special young person?" the young man at the counter asked.

"Yes," I said, opening my wallet to pull out the necessary cash. "Me."

He raised a tastefully pierced eyebrow.

"My childhood wasn't so good and adulthood hasn't been much better so far," I said, "so I'm doing a do-over here."

He just shrugged. Apparently, he'd waited on weirder.

Fifty-six books at $5.99 each came to...

"Three hundred and thirty-five dollars and forty-four cents plus tax," he said. "Cash or cre—?"

I handed over the cash.

Okay, so maybe I was an out-of-work and underpaid

nanny looking to become an in-work and underpaid nanny yet again, but I did have cash left over from my commercial child-star days.

So then why, you may well ask, was I living off of Aunt Bea's meager largesse when I could have afforded a place of my own?

Because when Buster had broken my stupid little heart, he'd shattered it completely, despite the justified anger I tried to cling to. I'd been absolutely shattered, having believed I'd found true love, only to have it smashed away—and the only place I'd had the strength to go to was home, such as it was; home to Aunt Bea.

Nancy and I have nothing in common, I thought, *absolutely nothing,* as I read the beginning of #1.

It said that Nancy Drew was an attractive girl of eighteen, that she was driving along a country road in her new, dark blue convertible and that she had just delivered some legal papers for her father.

Apparently, her dad had given her the car as a birthday present and she thought it was fun helping him in his work.

It went on to say that her father was Carson Drew, a well-known lawyer in River Heights, and that he frequently discussed puzzling aspects of cases with his blond blue-eyed daughter. Smug, I thought, Nancy was pleased her father relied on her intuition.

Nancy was nothing like me. She was five years younger, for one thing. She also drove, a convertible no less; I couldn't even drive a donkey cart, had never even bothered getting my license. Who needed a car if you'd lived all your life in the city? It would only be a nuisance here, even a convertible in the summer. Besides, I was kind of terrified of driving, would rather poke a needle through my own eye than be responsible for powering a vehicle.

Nancy also had a father who trusted her to help him with things, while all I had was Aunt Bea to trust that I would fuck everything up and a father in Africa whom I rarely saw. I seemed to remember Nancy being motherless, like me, but somehow I doubted we'd lost our mothers in the same fashion.

Finally, there was that whole thing about her being blond and blue-eyed—wasn't she supposed to be famously titian-haired? I seemed to remember that, too, and remembered thinking the word sounded glamorous but then thinking it icky when I'd learned the Webster's definition of it was "of a brownish-orange color," which hardly sounded attractive—which was in direct opposition to my own curly black hair and brick-brown eyes.

I hated her already.

The bitch probably didn't even have any cheesy cellulite on the backs of her thighs. It would be nice to be able to say I was too young to worry about cellulite, but genetics will out and mine had outed itself post-puberty in an unpleasant way. Oh, nothing too major, just enough to make the idea of appearing on a beach in a bathing suit somewhat less than confidence-building.

Feeling more disgusted than I'd expected to feel, I put aside #1 and picked up #56, the one with the pagoda on the cover, and turned to page one again.

Nancy was discussing some drink called Pearl Powder with friends Bess and George.

I remembered being confused by George when I was a

little girl. Obviously, George was a boy's name, and yet whenever there were pictures of the girls with Nancy's boyfriend Ned in the book, I'd *always* think Ned was George and wonder where Ned was and who was that other girl? It was years before I sorted George's androgyny out.

I grumbled. I didn't have any friends.

Before Buster, I'd had a few friends, at least people to do things with and people to talk to when times got rough. But after I succumbed to Buster's charms, I committed the other cardinal sin that girls make: I made the man not just the center of the universe, but the entire universe, and I let everyone else drift off to different galaxies.

So maybe I messed up that metaphor, but so what, because in that moment, I realized I no longer had any friends, not like Nancy did, not even a friend of not-readily-determinable sexual orientation like George.

You could say I felt sorry for myself. I knew my own choices and actions had led me to where I was, but I still felt sorry for myself.

If things had somehow worked out with Buster—not that I'd ever been able to define for myself, even before the bust-up, what would constitute things "working out" with a married man plus two kids—would I still be feeling sorry for myself at this point?

Probably, I figured. Because I would have still reached that critical state in a relationship where you realize you've let all your friendships die and all you have left is the one relationship.

Not that I'd had any other experience with relationships.

Come to think of it, I'd had limited experience with friendships, too.

I glanced down that first page of #56 and saw that—omigod!—*Nancy was still eighteen!* How was such a thing possible? I was pretty sure that even Sherlock Holmes, over the course of his many adventures, had aged a few years. So how had Nancy managed to age not one year over the course of fifty-six mysteries? I quickly did the math.

Okay, I went to find my calculator.

Figuring it wasn't a leap year—because what are the odds? Something like one in four?—I did the division. Let's see…365 divided by 56 is…6.5178571. 6.5178571??? This…*teenager* was solving mysteries at the rate of one every six and a half days? What kind of a girl was she? Oh, *man,* was I sooo not her.

Talk about an overachiever.

But then, after I was annoyed for a really long time, I started to think, *How cool!*

Imagine having one incredibly long year, the most stretched-out year imaginable, with enough time to get right everything a person needed to get right. What would I do with such a year? I couldn't change the past. But maybe in changing my present, I could change my future?

I looked at the calendar on the back of my bedroom door, kittens in Greece, the sole present I'd received from Aunt Bea for my birthday: it was April 26. So, calculator time again, I had already lost 116 days so far that year—it wasn't a leap year—meaning I'd already blown the chance to solve 17.846153 mysteries. But hey, there were still 249 days left, so there was still the opportunity for me to solve the remaining 38.153847 mysteries.

Whatever they were.

If only I could get up to speed real fast.

Actually, I was beginning to think that even *I* should be able to solve .153847 mysteries. It was the 38 part, I suspected, that would be the problem.

For the remainder of the two months until it was time for me to get on the plane to Iceland, I could read a book a day of Nancy Drew, leaving me five days at the end for shopping, packing and biting my nails to the quick.

Except for the day I went for the job interview, of course. Even someone desperate for a nanny who was willing to leave her life and go to Iceland wasn't going to hire that nanny without first meeting her in person.... No matter what kind of wonderful things Ambassador Buster had said about her.

chapter 3

Then came the call. It was by one Mrs. Fairly, definitely a Mrs. who would never allow herself to be addressed as Ms., who requested I come to her master's—*master's?*—Park Avenue home for an interview. Clearly, this was a step up from Ambassador Buster Keating's home, where I'd originally been interviewed and hired by his disinterested wife. I was now to be hired by a minion, which I figured meant I was moving up in the world.

Trying to answer that ever-popular euphonious question, WWNDD—What Would Nancy Drew Do?—I searched my practical wardrobe for the perfect persuasive costume to wear. Rejecting the casual allure of slacks and the confidence-inducing appeal of a dressy dress, I at last settled on a sensible plaid skirt and short-sleeved turtleneck I found in the back of my closet. I had no idea where these garments came from, could not for the life of me remember purchasing them, but when I looked in the mirror I saw they were doing the trick. Adding my mother's pearls and unassuming flats to the picture, even though the flats gave me none of the height I so badly needed, I was ready to roll.

But first I had to run the gauntlet of Aunt Bea's children.

"You look boring," said Joe, the oldest at fifteen. "I'd never date you."

"That's a hideous combination," said Elena, thirteen.

"Who would ever wear pearls with plaid?" sniffed Georgia, nine.

I was tempted to tell her that I was pretty damn sure Nancy Drew would wear plaid and pearls on an interview—hell, Nancy, who always wore gloves when she went out, but for entirely different reasons than why I ever did, would have undoubtedly worn gloves, too—but I didn't want her to think I was crazier than she already clearly thought me. Plus, I still awaited Aunt Bea's verdict.

She looked at me long.

"I...like it," she finally said.

And that scared the shit out of me more than anything that had gone before.

When someone whose taste you don't respect thinks that whatever you are wearing is the bee's knees, chances are you're making a fashion faux pas from which your image is unlikely to recover.

I grabbed a leather bag, black with brown suede trim, that was more satchel than purse, and was gone.

The living room I was led into by an actual liveried servant was big enough to fit Aunt Bea's entire first floor into and it was quickly obvious that someone around here had an overly enthusiastic appetite for French furniture. Not that I'm particularly heavy, carrying no more extra baggage than the obligatory all-American extra ten, but when the servant indicated a Louis-something chair to me, and I felt the skinny legs wobble back and forth on the slippery marble floor beneath me, I found myself wishing for something more sturdy.

Mrs. Fairly turned out to be as old as Aunt Bea looked, with a staid black dress and her own pearls on—ha! Thank you, Nancy Drew!—that somehow reflected back the glow of her bluish white hair. She also carried an extra twenty pounds to my ten and was shorter than me, which is always a shocker.

I've spent my life thinking of my height more in terms of the technical—"I am a short person"—rather than in practice, because I've always felt taller and indeed all my life have been told, except by my family, that I don't look that short, and that I have a much taller personality, whatever that means; even people who remember the commercials I made as a child, upon meeting me, never fail to comment, "You didn't *look* like a short child!" Again, whatever that means.

"What religion are you?" she asked.

I would have guessed it was against some kind of law to ask a prospective employee about religious affiliation, unless of course you were hiring a bishop or a rabbi, but questioning the legality of her business ethics right off the bat hardly seemed the best tactic to secure me the position I wanted.

"Jewish," I said.

"I see," she said.

I wondered what she was seeing, endeavored to at least look like I was waiting patiently for some kind of elucidation.

"It's just that," she hesitated, "Iceland is such a...not-Jewish place."

"Is that a problem?" I asked, wanting to kick myself even as the words were leaving my stupid, stupid mouth. Did I want the job or didn't I? Why raise the issue, why say the word *problem* for her? Let her do it if she was going to do it.

"Oh, no, no," she pooh-poohed. "I mean, after all, with that hair alone, not to mention the lack of height—" she eyed me up and down in no time at all "—you're bound to stand out."

This from a woman who was shorter than me *and* had blue hair?

But I kept my thoughts to myself.

"Challenges can be good," I said, "for me and for Iceland."

She smiled for the first time.

"You're a little plucky," she said, "aren't you? I kind of like that."

"Are Icelanders prejudiced?" I couldn't stop myself from asking.

"Not at all," she said. "They're just all tall. And blond. And not Jewish."

Until she'd brought up the subject of my religion, it hadn't occurred to me to wonder that it might be strange to be a short, dark-haired Jew in Iceland. Maybe I hadn't thought about the last so much because Judaism had never been a salient feature of my existence and was more like one of the less prominent lines on my résumé, like my high-school job at Dunkin' Donuts.

In fact, it wasn't until I was eight that I even learned I was Jewish and even then it was by accident.

Aunt Bea had just given birth to Joe, her first, and they were getting ready to baptize him. I was curious about the process, having never seen one before.

"Why would you know anything about it?" Aunt Bea had asked me in a rare unguarded moment. "Your mother was Jewish."

I had known so little about my mother, other than that she'd died while having me. Women aren't supposed to die in childbirth anymore, all the books tell you that it just doesn't happen, but sometimes it does.

A decade before, I'd been a fan of the TV program *E.R.,* until one night when I saw an episode called "Love's Labors Lost." It was about a woman who goes into the hospital to have a baby and everything goes wrong, one thing after another, until the woman dies. It was like they were playing the story of my birth, and after that I could never watch the show again, had no interest in any medical show or movie of any sort.

After my mother's death at the moment of my birth, my father raised me until I was three. It was at that point that the constant reminder I represented to him of my mother, whom he had loved dearly, became too much for him. I was sent to live with Aunt Bea and Uncle Thornton, while my dad departed for Africa where he pursued work as an archaeologist. He wrote often, and came to visit a couple of times a year, his visits always initially having the forced formal feel of royalty calling. I cherished those visits, kept what warm moments transpired during them locked in a special treasure chest in my heart. But it always seemed that no sooner had we got used to one another once more, he was off again.

Uncle Thornton was kind to me in the ways that Aunt Bea was not, but when he died not long after their third child was born, I was left without an ally in the household. Aunt Bea was of a mind that I needed to earn my way there and the form that earning took was in helping to care for her three spoiled children. The upside was that in caring for them, I learned a trade that would help me care for the children of others, like now.

Still, finding out I was Jewish had come as a surprise, not necessarily an unpleasant one, but a surprise nonetheless. Once I knew, I clung to it as the only remaining legacy, other than the pearls, of my mother. Aunt Bea tried to shrug it off as some kind of obstinate whim I had taken into my head, and there was no one to teach me about my religion, but I clung to it all the same. I might not practice it very much, might not know enough about it, but it was a part of who I was, where I came from, who I'd always be.

Mrs. Fairly wanted to know some more about my experience with children, so I told her about my years helping Aunt Bea raise her three, neglecting to mention the parts about those three abusing me in every way their evil little minds could come up with.

At least, I thought, there had never been any red bedroom for them to lock me in.

"Children can be a wonderful challenge," I told Mrs. Fairly. "I like challenges. I like wonder, too."

If she thought that last was odder than something most people would say, she didn't let on.

"Would you like to meet Annette now?" she inquired.

I looked at her questioningly.

"You did realize," she said, "when you applied for a nanny position, that you'd be caring for a child…didn't you?"

Apparently, she had her own plucky side.

"Annette," she told me, "is the little girl you'd be caring for."

When I nodded my consent, Mrs. Fairly summoned the liveried servant who in turn summoned an older woman in a tweed skirt and sweater set who entered the room holding the hand of a small girl, about age six, who was dressed in an old-fashioned pink dress that had puff sleeves with a white apron on it. The girl had dark curls, not so different from my own, and a spark of mischief in her dark eyes that would not be quenched, I suspected, no matter how serious those around her might get.

Annette quickly curtsied when she was immediately before me and tilted her head to one side as we were introduced by Mrs. Fairly.

"What kinds of things will you teach me?" she asked. "Are you good at geography? Math?"

I wondered how the little imp had read my mind so quickly and seen into my shortcomings.

I shook my head slowly, twice.

"I'm afraid that neither of those things is my strong point," I confessed.

"Good," she laughed, "since I am not good at them either and I would hate to have a nanny who was going on all the time about places and numbers. But…what *are* you good at?"

"Words," I said. "I'm very good with words, language. Anything to do with reading, writing, I'm your girl."

She laughed again, apparently delighted at the idea of me being her girl rather than the other way around.

I was puzzled though. Even though Mrs. Fairly had neglected to introduce me to the woman accompanying Annette, I knew instinctively this woman was not the child's mother and must in fact be her nanny. She was too stereotypically caretaking to be anything else.

Apparently, though, I was in a houseful of mind readers, for Mrs. Fairly said next, "Sylvia has no wish to go to Iceland. That is why the master has had me look for a replacement."

I did so wish she would stop referring to him as "the master." Give her a humpback, crooked teeth, make her a man and put her in a castle, change her accent, too, and I'd swear I was sitting there with Dr. Frankenstein's assistant.

"That will be all, Sylvia," Mrs. Fairly said, indicating they could go.

I was curious: Why wouldn't Mrs. Fairly, who seemed to be an *uber* competent woman, take care of Annette in Iceland? Was she perhaps staying behind in New York?

"Oh, no," Mrs. Fairly answered after I voiced my questions aloud. "My job is to see to the general running of the household. I couldn't possibly also be expected to be solely responsible for a small child myself. What sort of person could do both jobs at once?"

It was on the tip of my tongue to answer "a lot of mothers," for I had read of such creatures in books and seen the role acted sometimes in that way on television and in movies, but I doubted snippiness would win me the job; pluckiness, perhaps, but not snippiness.

"I do hope you are chosen to come to Iceland with us," Annette said, turning at the door. "We could have a lot of fun together."

I somehow doubted that Mrs. Fairly's greatest concern was that the new nanny be "fun." Indeed, I somehow suspected that such a feature might prove a detriment in her eyes, for hadn't she presumably hired the stern Sylvia? But at least she must be able to tell, obviously, that Annette and I would get along, which must surely be some kind of selling point when one is entrusting a precious young charge into the hands of a new nanny.

Mrs. Fairly studied me curiously once the other two were gone.

"Don't you have any questions for me?" she asked. "Usually, it is normal for prospective employees to have some questions."

Shit! I wanted to appear normal, but what to ask, what to ask…

I was sure if Nancy Drew were sitting in this wobbly chair, she'd know exactly what to ask. Of course, if she were sitting in this chair, I doubted it would have the audacity to wobble under her.

Nancy Drew would probably ask sensible questions: what her responsibilities would be, what was expected of her. She'd probably leave off asking to last—but she would definitely ask, being a practical girl and the daughter of a lawyer—about things like benefits, if they covered dental. Of course, if an injured carrier pigeon suddenly flew into the room, Nancy would undoubtedly wire the International Federation of American Homing Pigeon Fanciers in order to give them the number stamped on the bird's leg ring since, as she'd pointed out in *The Password to Larkspur Lane* (#10), all homing pigeons are registered by number so their owners can be traced. Then she'd feed the bird water with an eyedropper, fill a box with wild bird-seed and notify all and sundry that carrier pigeons had been clocked at a mile a minute from Mexico City to New York. How did she know all these things? Was it just good instincts?

"Who is my employer and what does he do?" I blurted.

"His name is Edgar Rawlings..." She smiled, as though I should know whom she was talking about. "He's to be the new United States ambassador to Iceland."

Crap! I thought. *Not another ambassador!*

What were the odds? Then I remembered that the first time I'd found myself in the employ of an ambassador, an agency had placed me there. This time, on the other hand, I'd found the ad in the paper all on my own. I thought about the oddness of the coincidence, reeled at the notion of putting myself through this déjà vu. It was like the universe was playing a perverse trick on me, forcing me to repeat parts of my past. I supposed I could always turn down the position, provided it was even offered to me. But I had really liked Annette...

Mrs. Fairly misread the cause of my dismay.

"Don't all countries have an ambassador? Surely," she said, "even Iceland needs an ambassador, doesn't it?"

She was asking me? I didn't even know anything about Iceland. I mean, I knew that it was supposed to be completely dark there part of the year, completely light another part, but I had no idea what part I'd be flying into or if I'd indeed be flying into anything, if I indeed had landed the job.

"And is there a Mrs. Ambassador Rawlings?" I asked.

"Oh," she said sternly, "you don't need to know about her."

Well, *that* sounded ominous.

"Now, then." She leaned forward in her chair. "Why don't you tell me why it was you left your last position."

chapter 4

Icelandair must be the greatest airline in the world. The flight attendants wear these soothing uniforms that are kind of cool, they're actually nice to the passengers and they give you real food, none of that "here's your one-ounce bag of peanuts you'll never be able to open and four ounces of soda and don't you dare ask for the whole can, what else could you possibly need?" crap.

I was just getting ready to tuck into my salmon and grilled baby vegetables when my aisle mate, an elderly gentleman with not much hair, steel glasses and a lot of polyester recognized me.

This still happened occasionally, even though it had been sixteen years since I'd made the last commercial. It was the hair, the unruly black curls, and the quirky curve to my smile the few times I still smiled. At age three, right after my father had left me with Aunt Bea, that quirky curve had been deemed visually precocious, hence the casting director's decision to select me as the face to represent Gubber Snack Foods. I was the Gubber Snack Foods Kid, had been spotted for my potential when Aunt Bea and I had been squashed next to the casting director on the subway.

"That child has amazing hair!" the casting director, Mort Damon, had enthused.

"If you like lots of hair on a little girl," Aunt Bea had said.

"And that smile!" Mort Damon continued as he had begun. "It's like looking at the Mona Lisa if she were a dwarf!"

Mort had given Aunt Bea his card and Aunt Bea had reluctantly accepted it.

"Don't let this go to your head," she'd cautioned after we'd answered the formality of a casting call and been called. "But this will be a way for you to earn your education. Not that I don't think your father would be willing to pay, but you never know what might happen with an archaeologist."

Gubber Snack Foods was supposed to be the perfect organic alternative to the overprocessed, oversugared foods for kids that lined the supermarket shelves. And a new generation of moms, working harder all the time both in and out of the home, had gratefully reached for it.

My big line, the one I intoned at the end of each commercial, having made sixteen commercials for various products in the line from the time I started until the time I turned seven, the words bubbling out of my organic chocolate-smeared mouth?

"It's *Gubber*licious!"

Four years later, at age seven, despite the fact that I was small for my age, I was deemed too old to hawk the prod-

uct. Personally, I think it was because I stopped being cute.
But whatever the reason, I counted myself lucky. Unlike
other child stars who had difficulty adjusting to a life where
they were no longer treated as special I had never been allowed by Aunt Bea to be treated as special in the first place
and so I had no overinflated ego to recover from.

The commercials were still aired occasionally, appealing
to audiences in a nostalgic way, and I still received the odd
residual check.

As I say, people still sometimes recognized me, based on
the hair and curvy smile. It by no means happened often,
but at least a couple of times a year, some stranger would
say, "I know I've seen that smile before! But where…?"

As far-fetched as it might sound, that people could recognize you just from a smile, I understood it from firsthand
experience. Home sick with mono for a month in high
school, I'd watched more old movies than I'd ever watched
in my life or would ever watch again. On my first day of
freedom, I'd been walking down Broadway when I caught
the eye of an older woman, meaning someone lots older
than me, traveling in the other direction, and she smiled.

"I know you!" I'd shouted, unable to come up with a
name.

If she'd been someone truly recognizable, like Meryl
Streep, I would never have stopped her. I mean, how
mortifying!

She stopped on the street, smiling indulgently.

I racked my brain, trying to place that familiar face.

"Toothpaste commercial?" I tried.

She shook her head, smiled wider.

It was that last smile that nailed it.

"*Animal House!*" The way I jumped up and down, clapped my hands, you'd think I'd just beat Ken Jennings on Final Jeopardy. "You were the girl who was twelve but looked eighteen!" I shouted, talking to her like I was telling her something she didn't know. "You passed out at the frat house!"

She smiled again, nodded.

"Well," I said, winding down now that the glitch-in-my-memory itch had been scratched, "that's just great. Thanks. And, hey, you really do have the best smile."

I'd continued on my way, never even learning her real name. It wasn't until later that it occurred to me to wonder how often that happened to her.

I have to confess, I wasn't as consistently gracious as she was with me when confronted with the whole "I know I've seen that smile before! But where…?" situation. If I was in a good mood, I shyly answered, "Gubber Snack Foods." If I was in a bad mood, I said, "It must have been when I body-doubled for Julia Roberts."

They'd look at my non-tall, non-lithe body in confusion and say, "No, I don't think *that* was it…"

The reason I plucked Julia Roberts's name out of the air was no accident. It was because she had that same kind of smile: you could block out the rest of her face and with no other clue guess, "That's Julia Roberts!" Julia Roberts and I shared nothing else in common, but we did share that one thing: block-out-the-rest-of-your-face smiles.

Indeed, even Mrs. Fairly had recognized me, once she'd seen the Gubber Snack Foods gig on my résumé.

"*I* used to buy Gubber Snack Foods," she'd said, just like everybody always says it, like they've performed some kind of accomplishment you should be impressed by and not the reverse. "Oh, not for myself," she'd gone on, "but in a previous post, I'd had more direct responsibility for the children of the household. I tasted one of those Gubber Snacks once…" She leaned across conspiratorially. "Revolting."

Indeed. But the checks had been good at least.

Now the man in the seat next to me, George Cranston from Staten Island, was saying pretty much the same thing, all of which I'd heard a thousand times before, or at least fifty.

"I can't wait to get home after my trip and tell my grand-kids I sat for seven hours next to a beautiful somebody who used to be on television."

And, for some reason, I was not in the mood to spend seven hours reminiscing about my years as the Gubber Snack Foods Kid. With my luck, he'd make me say my famous line, the line that other kids had teased me about at every phase of my schooling, once they'd figured out who I was.

"I'm not who you think I am," I said impulsively.

"No?" He looked crestfallen. "Are you sure?"

"Quite."

"Come on," he said. "Say, 'It's *Gubber*licious!' for me just one time. I'll bet you're her."

"No, I'm not," I said firmly. "I'm…I'm…I'm her doppelgänger. People just confuse me with her all the time, but I'm really not her. Hell, people probably confuse her with me all the time, for all I know."

George Cranston from Staten Island pulled back at my use of "hell," but he was curious enough that it didn't stop him for long.

"So," he said, arms crossed, "who are you that people

should confuse you with *her?*" He said "her" like the Gubber Foods Kid was Madeleine Albright or something.

"I'm a *writer,*" I countered the challenge without thinking.

Shit, where did that come from? I asked myself timidly as soon as the words were out of my mouth.

Actually, I kind of knew where that had come from. Back when I'd been interviewed by Mrs. Fairly, I'd even intimated as much, shyly confessing a newfound ambition to one day write.

Well, I had to do something with my life, didn't I?

"Why would you want to do that?" she'd asked, stunned.

It's amazing how, if a person has no inclination to do a thing themselves, they have trouble understanding the attraction/fascination it might hold for others.

I recalled for her an article I'd read once in the *New York Times*—it's amazing how much trouble being an avid devotee of the *Times* has gotten me into—that said that eighty-one percent of people polled said they thought they had a book in them. What other career could boast that kind of attraction? Surely lots of people might say they want to be doctors, but it was more for the BMW and the nebulous help-humanity aspect of it than the desire to be up to their elbows in O.R. blood, I was sure of it. And surely eighty-one percent of people were not lining up to be systems analysts. I'll bet not even that many people wanted to be actors, despite the glamour, what with public speaking being the number-one phobia, up there ahead of death and spiders.

And yet so many people wanted to write, and not necessarily because they saw it as an easy path to fame and fortune, although surely there were those who thought that.

So why the high statistics?

It was, I thought, because of the almost universal desire to be heard.

I wanted to be heard, too.

But since I couldn't even hold my own interest with the scribblings in my diary, I knew I had my work cut out for me if I wanted to take steps in that direction.

I wondered at my own audacity, the notion that I might have something worth saying. But I also knew that enough had happened to me—the death of my mother, the absence of my father, the whole sorry affair with Buster—to infuse my voice, however naive it might be at times, with a precocious wisdom.

Even if I only wrote for myself, but seriously, it might give me the catharsis I needed.

Apparently, George took my avowal of being a writer at face value.

As he droned on with an idea he had for what I should write next, a story he was too lazy to write himself but that he felt someone should tell, I found myself wishing Mrs. Fairly were in the seat next to me instead, but she'd flown on to Iceland a few days before with Annette, saying it would be best if they got situated and the master grew accustomed to having two more in the new Iceland house before adding me as a third.

George seemed offended I didn't jump at his novel idea, even though I suspected he would have sued me penniless if I'd ever dared to try.

"So," he said, still enormously miffed, "if you're not going to write *Travels with George* for your next novel, then what the hell are you going to write?"

What, indeed?

And, more importantly, WWNDD about my annoying companion?

Reading all fifty-six of those books, I'd fast learned that people always started telling Nancy everything…just as soon as they met her! And, before long, Nancy could always read their minds. She was like the ultimate Mistress of Empathy.

So, WWNDD?

She'd be nice to the nosy old geezer, she'd listen to every boring thing he had to say, she'd answer his questions with complete politeness without giving anything important away.

"I'm not sure what I plan to write," I said honestly. "That's part of what I'm going to Iceland to find out."

And it was.

Ever since I was a young girl, I'd flirted with the idea of being a writer, had even written a long story, *Diary of the Wicked Aunt's Girl,* a roman à clef if there ever was one. Writing, mostly in my journal, was my way of making sense of the world. More importantly, perhaps, it was a way of getting outside of myself, of living the lives I was not smart enough or talented enough or brave enough to live. I might not be able to sing on key, but maybe one day I could write a character who was an opera singer or a rock singer, beset by trials and tribulations but finding love where and when it mattered most. Best of all, if I were a writer, I could write my own endings, whether I was in the mood for tragedy or joy. I could kill those who deserved to be killed, I could kill those I loved best in my fictional worlds just for the sake of creating great drama, I could love without fear.

The only problem was, I had yet to come up with an idea that moved me. Even *Diary of the Wicked Aunt's Girl,* once

I'd read it through for the twelfth time, didn't seem like something anyone else would ever pay good money for, unless it was because they wanted an example of writing that was howlingly awful.

I burned it in the fireplace, but I never forgot the one great line of my young heroine, Carly Bongstein: "If I ever get out of here alive, with God as my witness, I'll never eat pork chops again."

But I knew in my young heart I was destined to write something far more important than *Diary of the Wicked Aunt's Girl,* even if it turned out to be the kind of book that sold meagerly, the critics raving or ranting for naught. It wouldn't matter, because I would have written something true, something that really mattered, if to no one else, then to myself.

The only problem was, I had no idea what that book might be about.

And that was part of why, at age twenty, I'd applied for the position of nanny at Ambassador Keating's house. I thought it might be good for my would-be writer's soul to seek out low-level employment, cocooning as it were, until I knew what to write about.

And now, having not been able to come up with the inspiration for My Great Novel during my years in the Keating household, I was winging my way to a new household in Iceland in the hopes that a change of scenery would finally do the trick.

But I still hadn't a clue as to what I would write about and had said as much to Mrs. Fairly, said as much to George now.

Mrs. Fairly had taken it better than George.

George seemed to be of a mind that I was holding out on him, that I was some kind of paranoid freak, fearful he might steal my ideas and use them for lucrative gain, just as he undoubtedly imagined I wanted to steal his.

"Well, if you want to be *that* way about it," he huffed, reaching into the pocket hanging from the back of the seat in front of him in order to retrieve the reading material he'd stowed there earlier as insurance against the boredom of our long flight.

When he'd first put his reading material there earlier as we'd been settling in, I hadn't bothered to take note of the specifics, concerned as I was at the time with arranging for my own comfort. Contacts out and glasses in to prevent dry eyes? Check. Shoes off to give my feet maximum comfort until such time as I might need to use the restroom with the no doubt urine-stained floor? Check. My copy of Shirley Hazzard's *Transit of Venus,* the brass Poe bookmark— "Those who dream by day are cognizant of many things which escape those who dream by night," the brass of which had set off the metal detector at airport security— firmly lodged at page 52? Check.

But now, for some reason, I was dead curious as to what George would deem appropriate in-flight reading material.

I stole a surreptitious glance.

It was Nancy Drew, #47, *The Mysterious Mannequin.*

He must have heard me gasp, because he looked up.

"Something wrong," he asked, "*Ms.* Writer?"

"It's just that…"

"Yes?"

"Oh. It's just that I didn't expect to see…"

"See *what?* Someone reading Nancy Drew on the way to Iceland?"

I hesitated, nodded.

"Ha!" he snorted, turned back to his book. "Shows how much you know."

"What does that mean?" I pressed.

But my aisle mate was no longer interested in engaging in polite discourse with me. Apparently, I'd somehow managed to offend his delicate sensibilities one too many times.

"It's just that," he finally answered, not even deigning to lift his eyes from the dark print on the page, "if you'd ever been to Iceland before, you'd know better than to wonder about such things."

I tried to immerse myself in Ms. Hazzard, but it just wasn't cutting it. At the right time, I knew I'd love what I was reading, admire it intensely. But I was on a plane to Iceland, for God's sake, had no idea what I was getting myself into, and probably the only reading that might have worked for me right then was brain candy.

Quickly, I learned that the *SkyMall* magazine was not the answer, either. And so, for a brief time I tried to read Nancy Drew over George's shoulder, but he caught on fast, protectively hunching over the book and cradling the page with his right arm, like we were in grade school and he was the smart kid preventing the unprepared kid—that would be me—from cheating.

Sighing, I wished once again that Mrs. Fairly were my aisle mate instead of the dyspeptic George. True, they'd both recognized me as the Gubber Snack Foods Kid, although I'd successfully deflected George into believing I was not—some success!—but at least Mrs. Fairly had remained cheerful about it throughout the whole thing, whereas George...

Of course, Mrs. Fairly had only been peripherally interested in me as a former commercial child star. Yes, more than her interest in me as that had been Mrs. Fairly's interest in me as the woman who used to be employed by Ambassador Keating.

What had been the story behind my employment? What had it been like there? Why had I *left?*

As I mentioned earlier, I had sought out employment in the Keating household as a refuge from both my claustrophobic situation in my aunt's house and as a way to bide my time until a novel grew inside my brain.

My interview with Mrs. Keating had been far different than the one I'd more recently survived with Mrs. Fairly. Mrs. Keating, a tennis-playing tax attorney staunchly committed to loopholes and her weak backhand, had drilled me like she was a member of the Senate Foreign Relations Committee and I was someone who had applied for the job of, well, *ambassador.*

Alissa Keating was pretty enough, but only in the way of women who have enough time and money to ensure they look that way. Without the bells and whistles and bows, she'd have just looked like anybody else who wasn't really such a much.

Not that I'm trying to be catty here, just stating fact.

Anyway, Alissa needed a new nanny for her two kids because the last one "had left under unpleasant circumstances."

Her face got all pinched when she said that, kind of like a golden raisin, and I suppose I should have questioned her further on it, but I just assumed that my predecessor had been a thief or incompetent or both. Since I was not a thief, and hopefully not incompetent, I figured I would suit the Keatings just fine.

Then Alissa brought in the kids for me to meet them.

Stevie, the girl, named for the sultry singer from Fleetwood Mac, who Alissa claimed her husband adored, was five at the time and was cute and bouncy, all blond curls and laughing glee. Children of neglectful parents—and I would indeed come to learn over the next three years that the Keatings were neglectful parents—are often sad little creatures, cynical before their time. But I'd long known there was the rare exception to that rule, kids who remained perky and resilient despite a cruel or indifferent upbringing. I knew these characteristics, could recognize them in another, because I possessed them myself.

The boy's name was unfortunately Kim, ill advisedly named after the Kipling character by his mother, who obviously had not stopped to think that her literary pretensions might get the crap beaten out of her son later on in life. Kim was three at the time, a dour towhead with sad blue pools for eyes with too-long lashes who had not managed to become as resilient as his sister.

I liked the kids well enough on first meeting and they seemed to like me, with even Kim allowing a single tentative smile in my direction, like maybe he thought, *Okay, so you're being nice now, but how long will that last? How long will you last?*

Alissa said I'd be expected to make sure the kids ate breakfast and dinner, make sure they got off to school okay and to all their extracurricular activities—there was a lot of ballet and soccer and that early-violin thing all the rich New York kids go to that I can never remember the name of, Samurai or something—and that when at home, she did not want them watching TV; she wanted me teaching them more important things all the time.

"Um, I'm not very good with math or geography," I confessed, figuring it was best to get that out of the way so she could decide against me without wasting any more time.

That brought her up short for a minute, but only a minute, since three years earlier a good nanny had been hard to find, unlike now when a good position was hard for a nanny to find.

"I suppose that could be okay," she finally said. "They can get some geography from their father. I'm pretty sure he keeps a map of some kind in his office. And they're already the genetic recipients of good math from me."

Alissa stressed that she wanted someone who would live in, that she needed someone seven days a week because she and her husband went out a lot and she did not want to disrupt the children by having them handed off to different sitters all the time.

I said that would be fine and it was. I wanted to get out of Aunt Bea's house but, despite my own money, did not feel ready to live on my own. At least in the Keating household there would be the distraction of a job to do. Plus, I loved children.

"I don't want a nanny," said Alissa, "who is more interested in her own social life than in taking care of my children."

I could have said that it seemed that she was more interested in her own social life than in taking care of her kids, but I held my tongue in an effort to come across as employable. So instead I said:

"That won't be me. I have no social life."

She gave me a once-over that said she was hardly surprised, for I had indeed worn the most sensible clothes plus no makeup for the interview, but then all of a sudden she *did* look surprised, snapping her fingers three times, as if she was trying to come up with something.

"The Gubber Snack Foods Kid, right?" she accused, pointing to me on the last snap.

In the instant after Alissa snapped and pointed, it was clear from her look that she thought I'd come down in the world, lookswise, since my last commercial. Well, that had been sixteen years ago.

"I guess they have someone come in and do makeup and stuff for those things, huh?" she said, in words that could have implied sympathy but didn't.

I just shrugged.

But I could see in the next minute, by the acquisitive gleam in her eye, that if nothing about my résumé had clinched the job for me earlier—surely my lack of geography and math hadn't exactly won me points, nor had her children's immediate liking of me seemed to make an impression on her in any way—*this* had. Alissa Keating would enjoy nothing more than having friends and colleagues learn that she kept a former child star—even if all I'd done was make a few stupid commercials—as a subordinate in a tiny bedroom in her household.

I could just hear her at the tennis club now.

"Can you believe it?" Alissa would ask. *Thwack!* "'It's *Gubber*licious!'" *Thwack!* "Yup! I've got her right up in my attic!" *Thwack!*

And, okay, I hadn't actually seen the tiny bedroom at that point, but I could certainly guess.

Not long after her victorious gleam, the master of the household entered the kitchen where she had been interviewing me, walked by us without a glance, retrieved a

foreign beer from the refrigerator and, with one testos-
terone-charged flick of the wrist, used a bottle opener to
shoot off the cap. Turning, bottle to his lips, he took me in
for the first time and I him.

It's no overstatement to say that Buster Keating was the
most beautiful man I'd seen in person up until that life-
changing moment of my life. The rich dinners he'd undoubtedly consumed at diplomatic get-togethers had done
not a trace of damage to his tall, muscular physique, and
whatever tennis he himself played had only served to
strengthen the structure into hardness, like a da Vinci
model—I'm talking about the carved men of the sculptures
here—every line and sinew defined. He had a shock of dark
hair that defied the well-trimmed look one would expect
in a diplomat, instead giving him the perpetual appearance
of someone who had just climbed out of bed, a bed in
which he and whoever his lucky partner was had no doubt
had great sex. His brown eyes were to die for, his jawline
like something a superhero couldn't dent. When he smiled,
the flash of white was almost obscene, both in intensity and
implied invitation.

Of course, Buster was about twenty years older than me,
but that didn't matter. Why should it? Anyone could see
that he was in a league I could only dream about, a league
I'd never even seen before.

"Hey, *you're* new," he said before taking a slug of his beer.

It never occurred to me, in that moment, that his reaction could be anything more than that of the habitual
flirt. I'd met people like Buster Keating before. Not necessarily bisexual, they couldn't help themselves from flirting with every single person they came across, man,

woman or animal. He probably flashed that same smile at his secretary, whether she was hot or not, at the carrier boy who delivered important papers to his office, at the schnauzer on the corner. For him, such a thing was merely a Pavlovian response; I was sure of it. There was nothing special to be read in his reaction to me; I was sure of that, too.

Alissa Keating was apparently sure of it, as well, for, without even turning to look at her husband, she said, "That's right, Buster. Charlotte is the new nanny."

And so it started, both my job in the Keating household and my ruinous affair with Buster.

Oh, I don't mean to imply that it started right that minute. The onset took much longer than that. But, really, it kind of did.

The first several months there, I had hardly any contact with Buster at all, nor with Alissa for that matter. Since Buster spent a large part of every year either in Washington or at the foreign embassy to which he had been posted, he was mostly at home only on weekends and sometimes not even then. As for Alissa, she was too busy being everything but a mother to be a mother; that's what she had me for. And so, most of my dealings with them were through the daily notes Alissa left for me on the butcher block in the kitchen, a knife always stuck in the top of the note so that no stray wind could ever blow her precious words away, notes filled with instructions on nutrition and scheduling recommendations for Stevie and Kim.

"Five fruits and vegetables each and every day, Charlotte. Even with your math-challenged mind, you can count that high…right?"

"Fifteen minutes of TV in the morning and fifteen at night. That's it. They don't call it the idiot box for nothing…right?"

"That last piece of chocolate cheesecake is mine…right?"

There were times I thought there must be better uses for that sharp note-stabbing knife than the purpose it was being used for.

And so, before another day had passed following my interview with Alissa, my life began to be filled with the education of small children, with shopping for birthday parties and making sure granola bars and juice boxes were in backpacks, with tutus and Samurai violin lessons.

It didn't take many more days to pass before I started to fall in love with those kids. It wasn't so much that they were particularly charming, certainly Kim wasn't, but there was something so vulnerable about their orphans-within-a-two-parent-household circumstances. If their parents would not pay enough attention to them, then I would let Stevie play with what little makeup I owned, I would learn how to play games involving balls and things so I could teach Kim how to play, too.

It may not have been anybody's idea of the Ideal Life, but it had become *my* life and it was sufficient.

The bedroom they gave me was in the far corner of the penthouse, a tiny box of a room—see? I had guessed that would happen!—that I suspected had been meant as an extra storage closet. It wasn't so bad, though, not like what I imagined would be the airless, lightless, spiderweb-infested lodgings of any nanny living in the suburbs. I had a bed, a lamp to read by, there was even a TV, if I were so inclined, which I rarely was. So what if the room was a shade of yellow I detested; I was too timid to complain.

All households with small children have their routines. But the Keating household really didn't have a routine that involved both parents and children for six out of the seven days of the week.

The only thing Alissa could be depended upon to do with her children was to take them out on Saturday afternoons. They invariably left at 1:00 p.m. and would remain gone for three to four hours, no more, never less. Their routine was also invariable: lunch at a kid-friendly restaurant like Rumpelmeyer's, a visit to the toy store FAO Schwarz when it was still there, the big Toys "R" Us when it replaced the other and a final stop at some educational place, the planetarium or the Museum of Natural History.

The first few Saturdays that Alissa took the kids out for their afternoon outing passed unexceptionally. Even though I had told myself I would spend my three hours off a week working on writing something, anything, I instead met my own friends for lunch and shopping, Helen and Grace, my closest girlfriends.

Take care of kids for 165 hours; eat, shop for three. Take care of kids for 165 hours; eat, shop for three. If nothing else, the routine that I was forced to follow was improving my math skills.

But then a Saturday came when I woke with a stomach bug, leaving me no choice but to complete the remaining three of the 168-hour weekly cycle in my room, with no more than golf on the tiny TV to keep me company.

Then a knock came at the door and I suddenly had company.

"May I come in?" Buster poked his head around the door. "I didn't hear you leave today so I thought you might be in here. Are you unwell?"

It seemed such a formal way to phrase the question— "Are you unwell?"—formal and utterly charming.

And when he came all the way around the doorway, the tray in his hands containing a Lenox bowl of chicken soup and a SpongeBob SquarePants plastic glass with a straw in it, he needed to do no more to sweep me away.

Even if I was lying down, he still swept me away.

"I just figured that—" he smiled sheepishly like a wolf "—even the girl who takes care of everyone else needs someone to take care of her sometimes."

See what I mean?

When I had trouble sitting up, he set the tray gently on the floor and even more gently helped me, arranging the pillows behind me.

He even fed me with the spoon.

"Shh," he said when I started to protest.

It just seemed so unseemly, my ambassador boss treating me with more tenderness than I'd ever seen him show to, well, his own children. It was inconceivable that he'd ever behaved so with Alissa.

"One day, when you're feeling better, maybe I'll let you take a turn and you can feed me."

Combined with my feverish state, the image he'd put in my mind of me feeding him caused me to snort, which in turn caused the chicken soup that had been in my mouth to spray out my nose.

I must have seemed a charming companion.

Red-faced, I finished being fed in silence.

Afterward, he dabbed at my mouth, then eased me back down upon the pillows, smoothing the sheet over me.

"Would you rather be alone," he asked, then paused before adding hopefully, "or would you like some company?"

All of a sudden, I hated the thought of being alone in that yellow room with nothing but golf, which I could neither stand nor understand, for company.

"Some company would be okay," I said tentatively, "I guess."

Aside from the narrow twin bed, the only other seating in the yellow room was an uncomfortable armchair with unpredictable springs that I only used late at night to sit at my desk, trying to convince myself I could someday be a writer.

Buster looked the question "May I?" And before I knew it, he had pulled the uncomfortable seat up alongside the bed, settling himself into it, despite that he dwarfed the thing.

"Do you know much about golf?" he asked.

I shook my head.

"It's a silly game," he said. "Useful, though. Would you rather watch or talk?"

"Talk would be good," I said, "I guess."

The chicken soup and juice had revived me enough so that I was wanting to cringe for having nothing better to say than "I guess" at the end of every response. In fact, I found myself hoping that I'd be interesting enough to command the attention of a handsome ambassador, even a married one.

He got up, switched off the set—there was nothing so exotic as a remote control for the nanny, certainly not one that worked—and sat back down again.

And then we talked.

Mostly, he talked, I should say, about his exciting career, about the books he liked to read. And yet, even though he did most of the talking, it felt as though we talked a lot about me. He would ask a question, like, "So what was it like, being on television in all those commercials at such a young age?" And then, when I mealymouthed with, "It was okay…I guess," he amplified my answer with, "I know it must have been surprising. Oh, not that those commercials weren't wonderful, because they most certainly were, in particular the one where you rubbed your tummy as you said your line. But how many people can say they were in a series of commercials? Not many, would be my guess." He'd seen my stupid commercials! What could he have been at the time, his early twenties? What man that age would take note of, and later remember, such insipid commercials?

"Actually," I corrected in a small voice, "television has been around for quite a while, so probably a lot of people could say that. I guess."

He laughed as though I were an incredibly witty person, as opposed to the overprecise geek that I was.

And so we passed our first Saturday together, with him carrying on the conversation for both of us in that same innocuous vein. Just before four o'clock, with Alissa and the kids due back any minute, he picked up the tray, excused himself and said he sincerely hoped he'd made me feel just a bit better.

"You did," I said.

When the next Saturday afternoon rolled around, and I was well enough to go out again, I had my hand on the door before I heard his voice call out to me.

"Charlotte, I guess you must be feeling well enough to do whatever it is you usually do?"

"I guess," I said.

"But it sure would be nice if you changed your mind and decided to stay here," he said with his sheep-wolf smile, "with me. I feel as though we barely got a chance to talk last week."

"I could always cancel my plans," I said, "I guess."

"And I guess that would be finer than fine...." He sheep-wolf smiled again.

And so I canceled my plans with Grace and Helen, canceled my friendships with everyone in the world, never looking back, at least not for a long time.

Over the course of the next several Saturdays, we got to know each other better, always in the yellow bedroom. Even though we had the whole deserted penthouse to range over, we stayed where we had begun. What it lacked in comfort, it made up for in feeling talismanic to what we both felt growing.

At first, we talked about safe subjects. He liked to tell me about his career, seemed to respect that I was intelligent enough to understand whatever he might choose to share. And he was most interested in hearing about my desire to be a writer. Despite my relative lack of experience with men, I'd come to realize that there is a certain kind of man for whom the writing female is an endless source of fascination. Perhaps it's as simple as this: they are curious as to what we write because they imagine we share our characters' bravery and desire. Certainly, if there's any sex involved in the writing, people would assume that you've either done or desperately want to do all the acts depicted; although God knows what they think about people who write serial-killer books with sex scenes involving gerbils. Or perhaps the fascination that writers hold for some people is more complex, like recognizing that the mind that is capable of sustaining a fantasy over a hundred thousand readable words must somehow be qualitatively different than the mind that cannot. They see the creativity as something other, foreign, exotic, those three adjectives having discretely different meanings.

"That's the thing," said Buster at last, one Saturday, "my wife could never be a writer."

There it was: the first time he had brought up her name between us, even though he hadn't named her by name at all, but had merely spoken of her in her assigned role.

That was all it took, though, the watershed after which he felt it safe to discuss his wife's shortcomings at length. It would be easy to characterize him merely as a selfish and philandering husband—indeed, he was those things—but it would be a mistake not to allow the core truth in the things he said.

He said his wife didn't understand him; and she didn't.

He said there was no warmth between them; and there wasn't.

He said she was the coldest of cold fish; and she was.

It was all true. Every accusation he leveled at her carefully coiffed head was true; I'd seen it all with my own eyes.

"I'm feeling overwhelmed by work lately," I'd overheard him say to her one time.

"You just need to be more focused," she replied, not even deigning to look up from her own work.

"Hey, how about a hug for an overtired ambassador?" I'd heard him suggest to her not long after I moved in.

"Not now," Alissa replied. "I just did my hair. Are you really going to wear *that* to dinner with the Carlsons tonight?"

Then there was the time I tried to explain to her that some of the other kids at the playground were bullying Kim over his name, singsonging the cheer "Kim, Kim, he's no Tim! If *she* can't do it, let's get a boy and win!" True, it was a lousy rhyming scheme, but it still hurt Kim. I told Alissa that it might be a good idea to come up with a nickname for him, preferably an "I eat nails for breakfast" kind of name, so he could avoid the taunts until he was old enough to defend himself from such abuse, at least mentally.

"What about Killer?" I suggested.

"What about Kim?" she countered. "Look, Charlotte, I really do appreciate your concern, but you are, after all, just the nanny. Kim needs to get tough. It's a cruel world out there. He might as well learn it at an early age. He'll be all the stronger for it later. One day, he'll thank me for this."

Somehow, I doubted that. What I really thought was that, one day, the overpriced therapist he'd undoubtedly need would thank her for it.

Sure, it was a cruel world out there. Nobody needed to tell me that. But I also knew that there was no need to make it any harder on a kid than it needed to be, just for the sake of toughening a kid up. What, did all of life have to be boot camp? And I also knew Kim's pain, because I was the one who was there for him when the other kids bullied him, I was the one who held him when he cried about it at night.

"Why couldn't they just name me Dirk?" he sobbed.

I had no answer but to hold him tighter.

Alissa and Buster were the kind of couple, not necessarily hating each other but with so little kinship or kindship between them, that when you looked at them and their children, you could only conclude: *Well, at least on two separate occasions, everyone closed their eyes, gritted their teeth and thought of England.*

And, of course, I understood Buster where she didn't; he thought so and so did I. I was never cold. If not completely as warm as I could be yet, I was growing warmer all the time.

It was a few months before he traced the back of my hand with his strong finger; he was that patient.

It was another two weeks after that before we had our first kiss and then it was me initiating it. At this point, I had dreamed about doing so for so long, I could no longer wait for him to decide the matter for me. What if he never did? What if he remained content to have a woman who would listen to him? What if he remained content to have a woman to whom he enjoyed listening?

I'd tell him stories, shyly at first, about growing up in Aunt Bea's house.

"I was eight when Joe was born," I said. "I was so excited about having a new baby in the house. I thought, 'Great! I've finally got a brother!' But Aunt Bea pointed out that he wasn't my brother. Well, of course, he wasn't, not really. But then she said, 'And don't go getting any ideas that you're equal. This is Joe's house, not yours.'"

"Ouch!" Buster said. "What a bitch!"

Somehow, it was the perfect thing to say.

And when I told him about wanting to write, he made me feel understood.

At least that's the part I let myself remember.

And I'd tell him what the kids had been doing during the week.

"Stevie and Kim helped me bake cookies. They said they'd never baked anything before. They were supposed to be chocolate chip, but they ended up being charred chip because we forgot to set the timer and got caught up playing Don't Spill the Beans."

He looked at me admiringly. "You take such good care of them," he said. "We're so lucky to have you," he said.

Sometimes, it felt as though *I* were their mother!

Oh, what a wonderful thing for a woman, any woman certainly but this woman in particular, to be listened to raptly by someone who in turn interested her.

I was in love with him, falling, free-falling through the sky without ever stopping to wonder about consequence.

He said no one would ever say we were bad people. He said two people so rarely fall truly in love, the sin would be in not pursuing our feelings to wherever they might take us. He said that one day—no, not soon, probably, but one day—he and I would be together publicly, as well we should be. He wanted us to have a baby together. Not then, most definitely not then, but someday.

He was shocked to learn I was a virgin. To him, who had been having sex longer than I had been alive, it was a shock to think that anyone over the age of consent could still be a virgin.

But he loved the idea.

You'll laugh when I say I was a virgin, but I swear I was, a twenty-one-year-old virgin. And you can laugh again when I say that I had been saving myself for that one true love that would be worthy of the greatest gift I had left to give.

Perhaps in preparation for an event I hoped would come, I wrote a short story about a young woman's first time and showed it to Helen and Grace on a night out. They, far more experienced than I, marveled at what they called the to-the-bone authenticity of the lovemaking scene.

"Pretend I'm Roger Ebert," laughed Helen, assuming a masculine voice. "'You can almost feel the body fluids.'"

"And I'm the other guy," giggled Grace, also going baritone. "'Better than a modern Harold Robbins—I think I just wet myself!'"

"That's great," I said. "But I don't think those guys review books, too."

"Oh, well…" Helen shrugged. "We don't know any book reviewers."

"But it really is good," Grace said, handing the loose pages back to me. "You must be getting more action than I thought."

Oh, if they had only known how little experience the author of that hotly erotic scene had ever had.

It really is amazing what you can learn in books. From Judy Blume, I'd learned how to deal with my first period. And from countless other books, I'd culled enough to know what exactly I would like from a sexual experience, enough so that I could fake a written simultaneous orgasm with the best of them, powerful enough to make Grace, imitating the reviewer who reviews with Roger Ebert, wet her pants.

I never minded that Buster was so much older than me. I know some will look at these events, set them beside what they know of my childhood and Freudianly conclude, "Ah, it is so obvious—she was looking for a father figure."

But people who would think that seem to me to be the

same kind of people who ironically conclude that sometimes a cigar is just a cigar. A cigar is never just a cigar.

For the permanent record, I did mind calling a grown
man Buster. Hell, I wouldn't want to call a *young* boy Buster.
But the one time I tried to call him Bertram it just didn't
feel right, either. So for better or worse, "Buster" it was.

Making love with Buster, when it finally happened, was
the greatest thing that had ever happened to me. Oh, there
was pain to be sure, but it was so much more than pain. It
was beauty and it was love and it was a closeness I'd only
previously known through writing.

I never felt sorry for Alissa. I could see how cold she was,
had no problem believing Buster that for her it had always
been a marriage of convenience, the cachet of being married to the attaché.

And so the Saturdays piled up, whenever he wasn't out
of town on diplomatic business. The Saturdays piled up
until there were nearly three years of them from when we
had begun. And during those three hours a week, it was like
we were the only two people in the world, a small yellow
world with bad TV reception.

Sleep with someone in haste, repent at your own damn
leisure, I always say. Well, I always say it now, at least.

Long into our third year together, I missed my period. If
I'd been another woman, I never would have panicked so
quickly, being just a couple of days late. But I'd always been
regular, reliable like calling Western Union for the exact
time. If I'd been a more practical and less in-love woman,
I might have concluded that the delay in my period had to
do with the anorexia I'd been flirting with, the lack of appetite brought about by my advanced state of in-loveness

leading to a dramatic weight loss that had disturbed the tides of my regular cycle.

I told Buster, not too trepidatiously. After all, wasn't this what we had been intending all along? Okay, so maybe this was a bit sooner than we would have liked, but did it really matter so very much if we'd jumped the gun by just a smidgen?

And that was when Buster offered me money to go away and have an abortion. I was crazy to think we could do this thing, he said. It would destroy his career, he said. His wife would take him to the cleaners, he said.

How quickly you can go from thinking someone is the greatest person who lived to thinking they don't deserve you, never deserved you in the first place. Sometimes, the freefall out of love is quicker than the fall into it.

I didn't want Buster's money, of course, didn't need it. But I also had no intention of aborting his child. I'm not trying to take a moral stand here on what's right, pro-choice or pro-life, but if you push me I'll tell you I'm pro-choice and only wish that more people, me included, were more careful about their choices ahead of time. But I couldn't see destroying something that had been conceived in what I could still only think of as love. I had loved Buster, Buster had loved me, and any child of ours would have a great set of brains.

Okay, so maybe he or she would suck at math, but with my verbal skills—written, more than oral, "I guess" I'd have to say—and Buster's sense of geography, any child of ours would still have a great set of brains.

Buster was livid, said if I was going to talk like a crazy woman, I should leave sooner rather than later.

And that was when I got the cramp, not a convenient

miscarriage cramp as you might think, just a delayed-period cramp, so severe because of the delay, the buildup.

As soon as Buster realized what it was, he was contrite. Wouldn't I stay? Wouldn't I forgive him? Surely I understood: he had merely panicked at the suddenness of everything. If I hadn't dropped the news on him so suddenly, so out of the blue, he would not have reacted so. If I were to tell him the same thing right now, he would most definitely react differently. Couldn't we just make love to reseal our faith and love in one another? After all, we'd made love while I was on my period many times before…

I packed my things the same day.

It is a truth universally unacknowledged that just because you're sleeping with your charges' father, it doesn't mean you can't be a good mother to kids. But I wasn't a good mother to Stevie and Kim, of course. I was a great mother. And when it came time for me to go, it killed me to leave them behind. I would have liked to stay on long enough to help them grow up all the way—they were eight and six at the time I left. But one of the most important lessons life teaches you is to tell when a thing is over and it's time to move on.

I did not want to see Buster ever again, but I knew he would give me a good reference. After all, he wouldn't want to risk my wrath, not knowing what my wrath might be.

Loving Buster had made me feel spectacular, special, and now I was back to being as ordinary as dirt.

Well, I certainly wasn't going to tell Mrs. Fairly *that*. So instead, I lied.

When she'd asked about the conditions under which I'd left my previous position, I eschewed the pregnant-nanny story and told her instead that it was simply time to move on, that with Stevie now eight and Kim now six, they seemed too old, too involved with their own worlds to need me so much, and the position had become no longer sufficiently challenging.

"But Annette is already six," Mrs. Fairly objected to my reasoning. "Will you find that she too doesn't need you enough, that she is insufficiently challenging?"

"Oh, no," I allayed her fears in cockeyed fashion. "The Keating children were New York children. After a certain point, what more could they possibly need? But Annette will now be an Iceland child. I'm sure she'll need all kinds of things in her new situation and will prove challenging for some time to come."

Well, it worked for me.

What Would Nancy Drew Do?

I was convinced that, in similar circumstances, being the nanny in an ambassador's home, there were a lot of things I did that Nancy would never do. But I was sure she would hug and kiss those two dear children goodbye and tell them she loved them and was proud of them and was only a phone call away should they ever need her, and I did all that. I don't know if Nancy would have cried when she hugged and kissed Stevie and Kim goodbye, but I did that, too.

The flight from New York to Reykjavik takes seven hours, more than enough time for a person to relive the biggest mistake of her life while sitting next to an old man who now hates her guts because she won't tell him what ideas she has for what she wants to write about, because she doesn't know, nor will she steal his.

But all bad things must come to an end.

Or so I thought.

Just as I was envisioning the plane touching down without incident, the copilot emerged from the cockpit, tool kit in hand, as the pilot made an announcement.

"Ladies and gentlemen, we have a slight problem with the landing gear…"

"Slight problem?" George gulped beside me, his old eyes suffused with fear as the copilot bustled past us and proceeded to cut a big rectangle out of the carpeting.

"I'm sure everything is fine," said the pilot, "probably just a malfunction on the landing-gear light."

"Malfunction?" George looked as if he was going to be sick.

I felt sick, too.

Why had I ever gotten on this plane? my mind shrieked. Sure, people said that flying was safer than driving a car, but that was for other people who were not control freaks like me who never felt safe unless she could feel the earth. Besides, I didn't even drive a car!

I was about to go into a panic, like most of the people around me, when I saw how truly upset George was, silently praying to himself as he watched the copilot disappear down into the plane.

What Would Nancy Drew Do? I wondered frantically.

I pictured that titian-haired retro girl and suddenly I knew exactly what she'd do: she'd remain calm on the outside, no matter what thoughts were going through her head, and she'd offer comfort to anyone who needed it.

I put my hand over George's wrinkled one.

"It's going to be okay," I said.

George was still muttering, saying tearful goodbyes to his grandchildren.

"Really," I said. "I've been through this kind of thing a hundred times."

That stopped him. "You have?" he asked.

"Yes," I lied, wondering if Nancy Drew ever lied to make someone else feel better. Probably not, I figured: one, she was probably morally against lying; and, two, with fifty-six cases under her belt, she really *had* been through everything a hundred times!

"Yes," I said again, "and it always turns out okay in the end."

"It does?" George asked, wanting to believe.

"Of course," I said. "You'll have an exciting story to tell your grandkids the next time you see them. Why, you should just look at this as material for that story you'll one day write."

"Ha!" he said, regaining some of his former spirit. "I thought *you* were the writer!"

Still, he clung to my hand right up until the copilot emerged from the bottom of the plane.

"Everything's fine," the copilot announced to cheers. "It was just as the pilot said—must have been a malfunction with the light."

Even still, it was treated as an emergency landing, fire trucks screaming beside the plane as we hit the runway.

"Thank you," George said so softly I almost couldn't hear him over the sirens. "You made me feel better."

And I realized that while I'd been busy making him feel better, I forgot about feeling scared myself.

After the plane came to a complete halt without incident, I managed to remove my carry-on bag from the overhead bin without giving myself a concussion, and I was on my way to my new life.

In Iceland, I would reinvent myself.

In Iceland, I would become a new person.

"I hope you figure this place out," George said in parting. I thought that he was wishing me well, but then I saw from the look in his eyes that he'd forgotten about clinging together when we thought we were going to die and had now reverted to resenting me for being The Writer Who Refused To Tell His Story. I became sure of it when he added, "Not that I think that's likely."

What do you say to something like that?

"You know," George said, studying me, "some people don't deserve a helping hand."

Now, where did that come from?

Then it hit me and I snap-pointed at him. "*The Bungalow Mystery,* #3! You're quoting *The Bungalow Mystery* at me!"

He gave me a look of grudging respect. "Got it in one," he conceded.

chapter 5

I surprisingly hadn't brushed up on my knowledge of Iceland before flying into the country. It was an adventure, right? I should just be winging it rather than overplanning it, right?

Just before leaving JFK, feeling a frisson akin to guilt that I should at least prepare in some way, I'd purchased a couple of guidebooks—Lonely Planet's *Iceland, Greenland and the Faroe Islands,* Fodor's *Scandinavia* and a series that was new to me, *Hanging Out in Europe.*

Then I'd shoved them in my bag and proceeded to spend the entire flight bumming about George and taking my scenic trip down Bad-Memory Lane.

Maybe I was in denial. Maybe I was in denial because I'd left a rarely beautiful, crystal and completely non-humid midsummer New York day for…

RAIN!

I heard it before I saw it, pelting the tiny windows of the plane as I waited in line to debark. In a sudden panic over my own unpreparedness, I rifled through my bag—passport, money, cigarettes, just in case I needed to become a smoker again—and whipped out Lonely Planet.

Index.

Let's see…climate, climate, climate…

It said this time of year I could expect a daily temperature of 10.6°C. Great to know, but not fucking helpful. I was a Fahrenheit girl. Who made Lonely Planet, the Europeans?

I reached for the Fodor's instead. They seemed like reasonable people.

Climate, climate, climate…

Ha! This one said 14°C—the guidebooks couldn't even agree with one another on average daily temperature! I mean, it's not something like a restaurant review, which would be subjective—"The lutefisk rocks!" "The lutefisk sucks!" It was weather, for crying out loud! Wasn't that supposed to be an exact science? Then my eyes saw that in the Fodor's, they gave average daily highs and lows and the high was 14°C, while the low was 9°C, which was closer to the Lonely Planet listing. So maybe the Lonely Planet people were pessimists. Then my eyes shifted to the right and I finally saw a Fahrenheit listing. Daily high: 57°F.

In summer.

I switched to *Hanging Out in Europe*. They didn't bother with Celsius at all, which kind of made me like them more: 58°F.

It also said that during summer months, now, *the warm season*—ha!—the nights stay incredibly bright with sunlight, with the sun only dipping below the horizon for a few hours every day, the sky never getting completely dark. *Hanging Out in Europe* seemed to be the optimist in the bunch and this didn't sound too bad, but then they spoiled the effect by saying the weather changes rapidly and that a beautiful summer day could be wiped out in an instant by cold rain and high winds.

I switched one last time to see what the pessimists had to say about the weather beyond their mean and meaningless 10.6°C. Lonely Planet said that, "Periods of fierce, wind-driven rain (or wet snow in winter) alternate with partial clearing, drizzle, gales and fog to create a distinctly miserable climate. It's mostly a matter of 'if you don't like the weather now, wait five minutes—it will probably get worse.'" It said that in the month in which I was living, just one single fine day was considered to be the norm.

What in God's name was I doing here?

I'm a Jewish girl. We *hate* being cold! It is a *mistake* to let us get wet!

I hadn't even brought any kind of rain slicker.

"Oh, yeah," George crooned from behind me. "You're doing just great so far, aren't you?"

What Would Nancy Drew Do?

She'd have read the damn guidebook, she'd have read all available information, she'd have done *research* before coming here.

Screw it.

Of course, she'd also still be nice to George, no matter what he said to her.

Screw that, too.

The first thing that struck me about the terminal at Keflavik Airport was all the duty-free shops. Everywhere I looked, there were these shops and the chief product they were all selling was chocolate, chocolate in massive industrial-size bags that were bigger than anything I'd ever seen in my own supersize-it country. You would think that with all of that chocolate, Icelanders would be the fattest people on the planet, but everywhere I looked, with the rare tourist exception, there were tall and beautiful and blond people making their graceful way through the airport, as though they were peopling the Scandinavian equivalent of Stepford, toting their duty-free booty.

One of the nice things about being employed by an ambassador is that there is a car and driver to meet you at the airport: I realized this as soon as I saw the man standing there holding a placard that said Nanny Bell. As George, who was waiting in line for the bus, shot daggers at me— I was sorely tempted to stick my tongue out at him, our brief flirtation with being friendly already a thing of the past—I let Lars Aquavit take my bag and lead me out to the embassy car at the curb.

Actually, his name wasn't really Lars Aquavit, but I doubt I could spell and certainly cannot pronounce the name he gave me, so let's just leave it at Lars Aquavit.

Lars was tall, blond and beautiful, and I was quickly realizing that those three adjectives were going to soon grow redundant for me. Oh, well. Maybe to these people I would seem exotic and they would crown me Miss Iceland and send me off as their emissary on an all-expenses-paid trip to the next Miss Universe Pageant.

Yeah, right.

Lars also had a slim silver cell phone glued to his ear. I would have thought this rude, but everywhere I looked, all the other beautiful Icelanders were doing the same. It seemed to be a cultural thing, even more than back home.

Somehow, Lars managed to use his cell-phone hand to also juggle an umbrella over our heads, so what had I really to complain about? At least I wasn't getting wet.

The other cultural thing about Icelanders that I noticed right away was that a lot of people seemed to be smoking. Back home, where smoking had replaced being a witch as the number-one reason to burn someone at the stake, I'd been forced to slowly quit over time and, of course, I'd certainly never smoked around the Keating kids. After all, what kind of an adulterous nanny would I be if I both slept with their father *and* smoked within sniff of their button noses?

But once Lars had me seated comfortably in the back seat and climbed behind the wheel, he lit up, drawing long and hard on his slim cigarette, and that curling smoke sure looked tempting.

Weren't Icelanders supposed to have the highest life expectancy on the face of the planet? I seemed to recall reading that somewhere several years back. Maybe those statistics—Best This, Best That—were revised every year and maybe some other country had outlived them, but still, I distinctly recalled the article saying the average Icelander lived eighty-four years. Eighty-four *healthy* years. So how come they could smoke like chimneys and we couldn't?

"Um, excuse me?" I called up to Lars.

"Yes, Ms. Bell?"

"Your cigarette," I said.

"Oh, I'm so sorry." He reddened, moved to stub his cigarette out. "I forgot how much you Americans detest—"

"NO!" I stopped him. "I was just wondering…"

"Yes?"

"Could I maybe bum one of those off you?"

"'Bum'?"

"Borrow, obtain, get. I can pay you for it." I reached in my bag, looked for my wallet.

"Don't be silly," he laughed, handing the pack back over the seat, the flip-top lid open, a slim cigarette sliding out. I felt like I was in the middle of a Newport commercial, only the brand wasn't one I recognized. "Please help yourself."

I helped myself.

"I'm sure," said Lars, "that Ambassador Rawlings would want you to have every comfort you need, so smoke as much as you like."

I could get used to this, I thought, lighting up, but I still wasn't going to smoke around Annette.

Lars Aquavit was chattier than I would have expected an Icelander to be. Weren't these people supposed to be reserved or something?

Perhaps "the master"—more likely, Mrs. Fairly—had told him that it was part of his job to make me feel at home and that "at home" for an American meant gabbing up a storm until the cows came home on the range.

"Did you know," said Lars Aquavit, "that Iceland is so small in population that we all feel as though we know one another?"

As I looked out the window, and saw pairs and groupings of people walking companionably with one another, it looked as if it might be true.

"It's true," Lars Aquavit nodded at my reflection in the mirror, as though I'd somehow tried to deny it. "And some of us really *do* know everybody!"

"That sounds wonderful," I said, wondering even as I spoke if I really meant it.

Would it be great to know everybody? Would it be great to have everybody know you? I had my doubts.

"Tell me something," Lars Aquavit said, in what sounded to me to be an uncharacteristically challenging tone of voice, "in your country, if you wished to meet the president to discuss some small matter with him and you just tried to call him up on the phone, what kind of response would you get?"

"You mean before or after the FBI and CIA came knocking on my door with questions about what I was really after, perhaps taking me into detention until they could ascertain that I was a harmless nut as opposed to a harmful one?"

He gave the matter some serious thought.

"I suppose," he finally said, "it would need to be after."

"They'd say no," I said. "They'd probably suggest making a campaign donation, but even if I did that, they'd still say no."

"Ah, you see?" he said. "Here it is much different. Here, any citizen can call up the president's secretary and request an audience to discuss whatever they want."

"You're kidding," I said.

"No," he said, "kidding is not something that I am prone to. Why, just last week, I called up the president and we had lunch together the very same day."

What a country. A chauffeur could call up the president and, rather than finding himself in someplace like Guantanamo, wind up with an invitation to eat.

It seemed impossible. I wanted to accuse Lars Aquavit of kidding me again but remembered that it hadn't gone over well the first time.

"Wow," I finally said, "the same day? That's amazing."

He shrugged.

"I suppose it helps," he said, "that, of course, the president is my cousin."

"Your cousin?"

"All right, my second cousin. But still a cousin, of course."

Of course.

What a country. It was like Lilliput, except that everyone was tall.

If I had been less exhausted and less jazzed—I'd left at six in the evening, hadn't slept, and now it was the morning of a new day!—I'm sure I would have looked out the window some more, enjoyed the scenery, taken in my new surroundings.

But I was beat and teetering on the edge of an "I'm starting a new life—HELP!" breakdown. All I had the ambition to do was lean back in the black leather seat, with the driver who was the second cousin to the president of the country steering the way, close my eyes and puff away until the nicotine rush transported me to a heady place. Iceland and I could get to know one another better at a later time.

One other thing I'd noticed at Keflavik Airport, even while rushing to keep up with Lars at the time: in addition to all the big chocolate, all the ubiquitous cell phones, all the superfluous height, all the blinding blondeness and beauty, an inordinate number of Icelanders had been walking around with copies of Nancy Drew books in their hands.

What was up with *that*?

Up until a couple of months ago, Nancy Drew had been no more than a dim memory from my childhood. I'd managed to live basically without her all my life. But now, it was as though she was everywhere!

So, really, what was up with that?

I took another puff and sighed.

I would figure out that mystery later.

The United States embassy was on Laufasvegur 21.

When I walked through the front door, Mrs. Fairly was there to greet me, dressed in what I now assumed was her ever-present black, every single blue strand of hair perfectly in place.

I had opened my eyes long enough on the drive from the airport to note that Reykjavik was a low-lying city, which to me meant no tall buildings like I was used to, and that the houses were all close together, all painted white but with sloping roofs that were painted in bright jewel tones: reds and blues and greens and yellows and purples. It was somehow tropical looking, like what you'd expect to find in the Caribbean, not on a place with a cold and unforgiving climate, one whose name had even been taken from the word to describe what results when the temperature drops below 32°F or 0°C for that matter—ha! I was learning conversions!

As soon as I saw Mrs. Fairly in her black clothes and blue hair, it occurred to me how strongly she must stand out against the foreign landscape we found ourselves in and I resolved, as soon as I had the time and energy, to take to task my own not-too-great wardrobe so that even if my curly black hair made me stand out, I could at least just a little bit fit in.

"Come in, dear…" She opened wide the door, more grandmotherly than she had been upon our first meeting.

"The master is away at one of those weather summits to which he's always getting called away and I think that perhaps is a very good thing."

I entered, looked around: a higher ceiling than expected from the outside, but, other than that, just another entry hall.

"Why do you say that?" I asked.

Lars brushed politely past me and I followed the progress of my bags as he took them up the narrow staircase to an upper floor. I wondered where he was going with them. Wasn't it my naptime yet?

Reluctantly, I turned back to Mrs. Fairly.

"Of course it's a good thing," she said. "You wouldn't want to be meeting the master after a long plane flight, what with you being all jet lagged and everything.

"You'll do much better meeting him," she continued, "after you've had a good night's sleep, preferably two, and have a chance to get acclimated to your new surroundings and responsibilities. It wouldn't hurt, either, if the weather summit were to go well and he returned home in a better mood than the one in which he left."

She made him sound so…charming.

"When do you expect him back?" I asked.

It was then Tuesday.

"Ohhhh—" She pressed her lips together, furrowed her brow and thought long and hard on it. "I would guess that *Thursday* would be soon enough."

Her lack of enthusiasm for his return should have been another red flag, but then Annette came in, bursting with six-year-old energy, grabbing my hand and pulling me along behind her.

"Miss Charlotte!" she cried in a voice that tinkled like the upper scale of a piano. "Come and see your new room!"

She kept tugging and pulling until I was hurrying to keep up with her as she led me up the stairs.

If Mrs. Fairly looked no different than she had in Manhattan, Annette was like a new little girl here. Gone were the puffy pink dress and white apron, the frilly trappings of overcuteness. Oh, she was still cute, but what with her sturdy jeans and vivid knit sweater, in varying shades of Paris green and lilac and salmon, she looked ready to brave both the elements and adventure. With her dark head of curls, she looked as if she could have been my daughter, outside of the fact that she seemed braver than I felt.

The room she led me to at the far corner of the upper story—how well I knew far-corner rooms from my time at the Keating household—had walls that were a match for the lilac in her sweater, the trim painted in a high-gloss white.

"And look at the bed!" she cried.

It, too, was a bright white, painted over simple yet elegantly curved pieces of wood, far larger than my bed in the Keatings' had been. It had a lacy blanket that looked as though it had been crocheted for a bridal trousseau, the whole looking more like the dream bed of a girl with princess aspirations than the mean lodgings one would expect for the nanny.

Annette plopped herself down on the edge of the bed and proceeded to bounce. She got quite a lot of action going before she stopped herself, her expression one of dismay.

"What's wrong?" I asked.

"Is it okay that I do this?" she asked.

There was always something vaguely French about Annette when she spoke, an unnaturally precocious stiltedness for a little girl, as though her father's previous posting might have been in mainland Europe.

"I suppose," she went on, "that I should have asked your permission before I commenced to bounce on your bed."

"It's quite all right," I laughed.

There was also something about Annette that made a person's spirits soar, an unrepressed joy about her that led you to believe she'd never known an unhappy day, despite some of her more seriously earnest speech patterns and the fact that her father, "the master," sounded as if he might be a stern taskmaster.

"You can bounce away," I told her. "It's what some beds are for, I think."

She bounced a little longer, tentatively at first, then with more energy, then she let it die down.

"Look what else!" she cried, jumping up and running over to a glossy white desk and chair, set up in one corner of the room facing a wall, but at an angle such that someone sitting there could see through the filmy white curtains to the view beyond.

Annette pulled back the curtains, showed me the side-by-side long narrow panes of the window with their latch in the center. She climbed up on what was to be my chair, turned the latch and pushed one of the windows outward, letting in a gust of wind so powerful it slammed the window shut almost immediately. She let the curtain go, sat back down in my chair.

"Mrs. Fairly says you wish to be a great writer," she said, "so I told Papa he must make sure you had a great desk!"

I was surprised at…*everything,* really: the consideration

for my comfort, the fact that my new employer had done any of this at all, the fact that the genesis of it had obviously come from this small and delightful child.

Everything about the room was perfect, even the cream braided rug on the dark-stained hardwood floor, especially the absence of any distracting TV. For I had come to realize that the reason for my lack of productivity in the Keating household had been due to too much golf.

I liked the room; loved it, in fact.

"I knew that lilac must be your favorite color!" Annette exulted.

Impulsively, I hugged her, missing Stevie and Kim even as I did so, hoping, knowing that I would one day love her as much.

"How did you know that?" I asked.

"Because it is mine!" she said, turning to laugh at her own reflection in the long antique mirror that occupied one corner.

Mrs. Fairly had interrupted us, calling Annette away, telling her that she needed to give me some breathing room to unpack and begin the process of acclimating myself.

I was both sorry and not sorry to see Annette go: she was great company, but she also had more energy than Stevie and Kim combined. And it had been months now since I'd been responsible for the care of small children. It would take me a bit to get up to the speed of a speedy young person again.

Mrs. Fairly perched on the edge of my bed, watching as I unpacked and put away my things in the large white wardrobe. It made me feel uncomfortable to be watched so, as though she was judging every fashion decision I'd ever made in my life and finding me wanting. And it made me wonder: where was my breathing room?

"It looks like you brought things for a Manhattan summer," she said, eyeing my shorts and tops with a critical eye, "not an Iceland one."

"I suppose—" I shrugged "—when I get some time off, I can shop for more appropriate things."

"Time off?" she said. "Yes, I did want to talk to you about your schedule now."

"Good," I said, removing a sheer snow-white linen nightgown, floor length, with long lace-edged sleeves and a tie at the neck, that I favored for sleeping in summer. At home, it had been the perfect thing to wear in the overly cool atmosphere of Aunt Bea's excessively air-conditioned house. I knew it was old-fashioned, but I loved that nightgown.

Mrs. Fairly tut-tutted.

"Another inappropriate garment," she said. "You'll freeze here at night in that."

"I'll put another blanket on then." I smiled.

I was beginning to like the facility with which I was turning all of her negatives into positives. It wasn't like me at all to parry so well and I liked that just fine.

Of course, I hated being cold, but I tamped that unpleasant thought down. After all, I couldn't very well be squeamish about little things if I was determined to be plucky.

"Suit yourself," Mrs. Fairly said.

"Thank you," I said.

"Now, about your schedule…"

"Yes?"

"It probably won't be as arduous as what you were accustomed to in the Keating household. I believe there you were expected to be on call seven days a week?"

"Yes," I said.

"With only three discretionary hours to use as you would on Saturday afternoons?"

"Yes," I said, trying not to think about what I used to do with those three hours, unable to stop from thinking about it all the same, those time slots I'd spent with Buster.

"Well," she said, "I think you'll be pleased to find then that Ambassador Rawlings is a far more reasonable master, at least in that regard. He won't be expecting you to be a slave."

Nice, I thought, *a master who won't be expecting someone beneath him to be a slave.*

"Oh, of course," she said, "you'll need to take charge of Annette's schooling."

"Wait," I said. "You mean to tell me she won't be going to the school here?"

Mrs. Fairly looked shocked.

"Whyever would she do that?" she asked. "And why would we ever hire a governess, only to send the little one to school?"

"But your ad said nothing about hiring a governess. It said you wanted a nanny."

"They're not the same thing?" she wanted to know.

"Not exactly," I said.

I had thought I would only be supplementing Annette's education, not providing all of it.

"Will that be a problem?" Mrs. Fairly asked.

I couldn't see where I could back out now.

"No, of course not," I said.

"Good," she said. "Now, as to your schedule—you'll be expected to be with Annette on weekdays from breakfast time at eight-thirty through dinnertime at six-thirty. After that, if her father is at home, he'll want her with him until her bedtime. If he's not here, it'll be your job to keep her entertained."

"All right," I said.

"The extra time really isn't that much," she said. "The little one goes to bed at eight o'clock sharp, so you'll still have some time afterward for whatever you might want to do. You can even go out if you'd like. I'm always here at night, plus Cook, so we'll always be around should Annette need anything."

"All right," I said again.

"On weekends, you'll have alternating days off: one week you'll be off on Saturday, the next week you'll be off on Sunday."

"All right."

"On the Sundays you work, you'll be expected to take Annette to church."

That sounded so…un-Jewish.

"Church?" I said.

"Yes, is that a problem?"

I shook my head. In for a penny, in for a krona, or whatever the currency was here.

"It's a nice church," she said, "called Hallgrimskirja."

"That's a mouthful," I said. "What kind of church is it?"

"Who knows?" she laughed.

That startled me.

"I just assumed," I said, "that it must be whatever denomination the Rawlingses belong to."

"Oh," she laughed again, "Ambassador Rawlings doesn't

care about the denomination. He just thinks his daughter should be seen going to church."

How odd.

I wondered what Annette's mother thought of those nondenominational arrangements.

Then I wondered about Annette's mother, period, remembering that when I'd asked about her during my interview in New York, Mrs. Fairly had said something obscure to the effect about me not needing to know about her.

I decided to try again.

"What religion does Mrs. Rawlings belong to?"

Now it was her turn to look startled.

"Whoever said anything about a Mrs. Rawlings?" she demanded.

Who, indeed? Had Annette's mother died? Were they divorced?

But I could see that she wouldn't say any more on the subject and so I resolved to wait for a time when she might be more forthcoming.

"I guess you've told me everything I need to know about my schedule," I said, placing the last pair of socks in the bottom drawer of the wardrobe. "I guess I'll go find Annette and get started."

"Get started with what?" she asked.

"Why, with my work with her," I said.

"Don't be ridiculous," she said. "What kind of cruel people do you take us for?"

Well, they had advertised for a nanny when what they really wanted was a governess, a far more difficult job. And the head of the household was referred to as "the master," causing the Marquis de Sade to dance sugarplums in my

head every time I heard him referred to thus. I wanted to
say those things but, this being my first day, I didn't.

It didn't matter. Mrs. Fairly was of a mind to answer her
own question.

"You can have the remainder of today to acclimate yourself," she said, "tomorrow, too. I've kept Annette busy this
long and I suppose I can keep her busy a while longer.
There'll be time enough for you to start Thursday morning, get a full day in before the master returns for dinner.
In the meantime, you might want to do some of that shopping you mentioned earlier—" she looked at my shorts
pointedly "—and get the things you'll be needing here."

I was suddenly tired of company. After months of being
almost entirely left alone in Aunt Bea's household, where
the four principal members would rather not talk at all than
talk to me and only spoke to me when they were in the
mood to insult my wardrobe, between George, Lars and
Mrs. Fairly, I was unused to so much talk directed at me in
one day. But I knew so little as yet of my new employer
that I convinced Mrs. Fairly to stay for a bit, in the hopes
of drawing her out a bit more.

But she was not to be drawn.

I asked her, "What kind of man is the...master?"

"You'll be finding out soon enough." She smiled.

That wasn't helpful.

"Yes, I'm sure I will," I said. "But you've known him
far longer and I'm naturally curious. Is he kind? Is he a
tough man?"

At this, she laughed outright. "He is a kind of tough
man," she said when she had at last recovered herself. "Yes,
I suppose you could safely say that of him."

I had to ask: "Do you think he and I will get on?"

"You will no doubt please him in some ways," she said, then regarded me, making me feel as though she was regarding everything about me, for a long moment. "In other ways, undoubtedly, you will not."

This was hard for me to hear. Like most women, my chief concern was in being liked, loved, having approval. It is a peculiarly defensive posture to live like that. Suddenly, hearing my words to her and her response, I rejected that posture. I wanted to no longer live a life where I worried if the world approved of me; I decided to reverse the tables so that what should matter most was whether or not I approved of the world that surrounded me.

"And what of the reverse?" I asked her boldly. "Do you think he will please me?"

She herself looked completely pleased with me for the first time.

"I suppose," she answered, "that remains to be seen."

I spent the remainder of the day investigating my new home.

One thing I knew about Nancy Drew, after reading fifty-six books about her, was that she was inquisitive. And, if *she* was inquisitive, *I* was going to be inquisitive.

On the second story, where my own bedroom was, were several other bedrooms—the building was deceptively small from the outside—both for family and staff: Annette's girlish one, not much different from my own, but with the addition of an army of stuffed animals and a legion of pretty dolls, remarkable in that they all retained their heads and limbs, unlike what I was used to from Stevie, who was

known to commence decapitation with each new Barbie
bought for her; Mrs. Fairly's austere room, so austere that
it looked as if she took the word *bed*room seriously, having not much more in it than that; rooms for other ser-
vants; and two rooms with the doors locked. I presumed
one to be that of Ambassador Rawlings. The other, I had
no idea. Turning the handle, only to realize it was to be
part of the no-go zone here for me, I thought I heard an
unrestrained laugh on the other side. I startled at the sound,
but then remembered the wind outside and concluded it
must be that. I mean, really: Why would anyone be unre-
strainedly laughing behind a locked door?

The ground floor was a combination of family living area
and official rooms in which Ambassador Rawlings con-
ducted his business. There was a sunny breakfast room and
a much larger formal dining room, with heavy furniture,
dark painted walls and an ornamental sideboard loaded
with china and silver. There was a recreational room, completely modern with large-screen TV and all the electronic
gadgets anyone could wish for who was of such a mind;
the room could have as easily existed in New York as here.
In the back of the ground floor there was an office for the
ambassador, behind the desk of which were two flanking
flags, one I recognized as my own Stars and Stripes, the other
I assumed to be that of the country I now found myself in;
Mrs. Fairly said I was only to go into that room if invited.

Next to the recreational room was a large library, an ab-
solute dream of a room, as far as I was concerned, with
floor-to-ceiling books on three of the walls; the fourth wall
had floor-to-ceiling books shelved on either end but, in the
center, there was a massive fireplace. Indeed, all the rooms

had fireplaces as though in a land remarkable for its ice, there could only ever be one solution. The furniture in this room was more to my taste than that in the other rooms, being all moody darks and comfortable, but it was the books that were my chief interest. Mrs. Fairly said it was this room in which Ambassador Rawlings liked to receive Annette in the evenings—he hated the TV in the other room, although he recognized it as a necessary evil of modern life—and that I could use this room to my delight when he was not in residence but must leave it to him when he was.

I barely heard her words. Looking around me at all the books, I thought about how happy I would be here.

In the middle of the night, a night that was tough for me to accept as being night because it was still so strangely light out, I woke to a howling rainstorm, the eerie sound of screeching so loud I heard it even in my dreams before I fought my way to consciousness.

One of the windows had come loose—perhaps I had failed to shut it firmly enough when Annette had been with me earlier in the day?—and it took extra strength to fight the wind in order to get it pulled back into its proper place.

As I crawled back beneath the cool sheets, I remembered that screech in my dreams, realized that what sleep I'd gotten had been uneasy.

That screech really was the wind…wasn't it? Surely no human being could make such a sound.

What Would Nancy Drew Do? I wondered.

I got out of bed once more, lifted the side of the mattress, ran my hand underneath to see if someone had left a pea there to devil me.

What can I say? I'd gone almost a day and a half without decent sleep. I was desperate.

But there was no pea there, nothing to explain why, when I should be sleeping like a log, I was sleeping like an insomniac.

I lay back down one last time, punched the pillow more viciously than it deserved.

Damn Nancy Drew!

So far, she wasn't solving squat for me.

chapter 6

Ever since the split from Buster, I had felt myself to be in a state of mourning. It was worse than any loss I had suffered, an extreme form of death. Although I now knew, on an intellectual level, that he was not worthy of me, never had been, his absence left a great hole in my life. When I had believed him to love me, I had been special. Now I no longer was. It didn't matter that what I had believed to be true about us wasn't, it didn't matter that I would never go back to him, having been betrayed, having learned that he wasn't who I thought he was. The hole was still there and nothing could fill it. I no longer thought about him, ached for him every second of the day, but each day since the split, I'd gone to sleep with a sadness and woke the same way. I knew the day would come, had to come, when the Earth would spin on its axis one entire turn without me thinking of him once.

And somehow, in its own way, that day would be the saddest day of all.

But that day still lay in my future and I awoke on my first full day in Iceland with tears in my eyes, the memory of whatever I'd been dreaming about him the night before already drifting its smoke trail into my subconscious, from which it could not be retrieved. Had we been happy in the dream? Was it after he had made me so miserable?

Buster was like a book taken from my personal library, a slot left on the shelf. One day, a new book would be placed there, the others crowding around it to fill the gap.

But again, that day was not this day.

When that day finally came, I would at last be saved from this hell I'd found myself in, a hell created by loss of love. And how would I avoid hell in the future? I asked myself and answered with a laugh: keep putting one foot in front of the other, remember to inhale and exhale, and never love again.

Drying my eyes on the back of my hand, I rose and went to the window. Through the sheer curtains a bright light streamed and I parted them to see a day that glittered like a present. Apparently, the one fine day for the entire month that the guidebooks had promised me would be today, and I wasn't about to waste it.

Behind me, I heard a sound, an animal sound that made me start.

At the end of the bed, curled up in my discarded bed-sheets, was a black-and-white cat.

"Hey!" I said, gently tickling him under the chin. "Where did you come from?"

"Meow!"

"Oh, I see," I said.

He stretched his neck upward, letting me know what he wanted most in this world.

If only human beings were so easy.

"What's your name?" I asked.

"Meow!"

"Fine, then I'll call you Steinway."

"Meow!"

"Too Jewish for you?" I said. "Well, too bad. Then you should have told me your real name when I asked the first time."

American women react to tragedy, particularly tragedies involving loss of love, in one of two ways: either we stuff ourselves, hoping to fill the void, or we try to starve ourselves into oblivion. I had always been a member of the latter group.

And that's what I had been doing since the loss of Buster: starving myself. Had I lived in an earlier century, undoubtedly I would have eventually died of consumption.

Hitherto, for months now, I had experienced no appetite. But as I went down to breakfast, last summer's style of shorts now loosely hanging from my hipbones, I smelled the aroma of warm food and for the first time in a long time, felt real hunger.

I wondered, with half a mind, what had happened to American women to change us so: If previously women had wasted away in times of trouble but now they were split between those who wasted and those who stuffed, what had caused the change in eating fashion?

Mrs. Fairly and Annette were already eating when I entered the sunny yellow breakfast room. And so eager was I to eat, myself, I practically had my fork up before I even sat down.

Outside of the eggs, nothing looked too familiar as being

breakfast food. There were grilled vegetables and some kind of fish I didn't recognize.

I'd never thought of having fish for breakfast before.

Despite the oddness of it, I ate some of everything, quite a lot of everything actually.

"What are you going to do with your day of leisure?" Mrs. Fairly asked when I had at last dabbed at my mouth and laid my linen napkin aside.

What Would Nancy Drew Do?

She'd go out and get appropriate clothes.

Of course, Nancy Drew would have done her research ahead of time and packed accordingly.

I recalled from the fifty-six books I'd read, more than one time coming across the phrase "becomingly dressed" in reference to how Nancy Drew looked when she left the house and, in particular, one time when she had been "becomingly dressed"…to go clothes shopping! In my case, I had to shop because I was never becomingly dressed. Why would someone who was already becomingly dressed ever need to shop? I wondered. Why risk screwing it up?

"First," I said with a smile, "I think I'd better shop. Don't you agree?"

And why was I always so obsessed with what Nancy Drew would do? Because, in the wake of Buster, in a strange land among strange people, she was the most solid thing I had.

I had been offered the car with Lars Aquavit at my disposal, since the master was away, but I declined in favor of my feet and public transportation. Eventually, I would need to find my own way around; might as well start now.

The air was cool against my bare arms, and I rubbed my

skin for warmth, but at least there was no wind today. It took me a while to figure out the bus system, but I eventually was able to use it to get myself to Kringlan Mall.

No, I do realize that a mall wasn't the most romantic destination for my first outing in Iceland—wouldn't small boutiques be more romantic, more glamorous?—but I wanted to be able to get everything I needed at once, under one roof, and have done with it.

And as I mentioned before, I'm an American. When we are not sure exactly where to go, we find a mall. Someday, we earthlings will colonize Mars and as our first official capitalist endeavor, we'll open a K-Mart.

I had lived all my life in a city where I was not a minority, where the breadth of human differences was so vast that no one could be a minority. There were even a few short adults in Manhattan. But here it was as though I were a stranger from another planet. As at the airport the day before, I was so outnumbered in height and blondeness and beauty, it was like I was an alien. With the exception of other tourists, I was a person completely apart from everything around me.

I wondered again what had brought me to such a place in time.

What had I wanted after leaving the Keating household? What did I want in coming here?

I would have said I wanted liberty, liberty from the pain I had acquired in my last post and the vacuous aftermath that had been my half life in Aunt Bea's house.

But then why come here?

I had wanted change, surely I had wanted that.

But why exchange one situation for a remarkably similar one?

I saw then that what I had wanted most to achieve here was neither liberty nor change. I saw now that what I wanted most was another chance, an opportunity to do over the past and make it right again.

Could such a thing be possible? *Would* such a thing be possible?

Pushing away the sense of my own foreignness, I proceeded about the business I had come here for: the necessity of shopping. Unlike most women, shopping has never felt like a luxury to me. It was something I did only when the things I owned had become too worn through repeated washings to withstand any more wearings; or when, being a natural klutz, I had torn some needed garment; or when my underwear had reached the point that to not replace it, should some accident befall me, risked the ambulance driver's embarrassment at my lack of any fashion finesse.

With that mind-set, then, I located a shop that looked as though it would have everything I needed in one convenient stop and entered.

I think the shopgirl was surprised at the quantity of things I selected: most tourists probably only bought one or two items as souvenirs—the sweaters were both the most beautiful and the most expensive I had ever seen—but here I was trying on enough that it would be easy to conclude that I had come to stay. Perhaps she thought I was another irritating patron, that I would try on fifty items only to buy one cheap thing, or perhaps none at all.

She was even more surprised when I came out of the dressing room, a purple sweater replacing my T-shirt—

Annette was right about me and the color purple—and a pair of tailored jeans hanging on my hips, and asked if she had a pair of scissors so that I could cut the tags off, that I wanted to wear the outfit right away rather than having her put it in a bag.

I had picked out jeans that were too large on purpose: recovering my appetite, I thought that if I bought things that fit me today, they might no longer fit me in a month or two…or less, if I ate even more. So my selections were parsimonious insurance against the weight I would undoubtedly regain.

She let me have the requested scissors and I happily snipped away, considering it a small triumph when I showed rare coordination and didn't nick myself in the process.

Ringing me up, she placed my other purchases in a bag: several more pairs of jeans, a few pairs of cords for dressier occasions, a half dozen sweaters, all in the same simple but elegant style, and two weeks' worth of warm socks. When she moved to put my old things in the bag, my T-shirt and shorts, I stopped her, asked her to throw them away instead. I no longer wanted anything from the life I had lived before. I would get rid of the remainder when I returned home.

I was almost out of the store when I saw a rack of dresses I hadn't noticed earlier and remembered Mrs. Fairly telling me that part of my duties would be to take Annette to church every other week. Back home, even though I didn't attend religious services myself, I was aware of a change in the attire of those who did. When I was young, religious services had been a more formal affair, with men and boys in suits, women and girls in dresses. A lot of the women even wore hats, although most of them looked silly, not being Princess Diana. People tried to look their best. But in recent years, when I saw people exiting churches on Sundays and synagogues on Fridays and Saturdays, I'd noticed that there were hardly ever ties or jackets, that the women almost never wore dresses and sometimes you even saw young people in jeans.

But I knew enough to know that respect in terms of dress here would still be more the standard than the exception. With that in mind, then, I reached for the rack of sweater dresses and selected a delicate, off-white one with a cowl neck that, when I held it to me, looked to be about the right size.

"You don't want to try it on first?" the shopgirl asked when I handed it to her along with my credit card for the second time.

"No," I said. "I'm sure it'll be fine, not that it matters."

I knew she must find me puzzling at best, but I didn't particularly care.

Before leaving the mall, I stopped at a shoe store, where I was able to get both hiking boots and a pair of heels to go with the dress, plus a few pairs of stockings.

It wasn't until I was on the bus back to Laufasvegur 21 that I realized I had once again forgotten to get anything to protect myself from that rain that was sure to come again before too much more time had passed.

Back at the house, I had a light meal—okay, so maybe it was more substantial than light; how hungry I was now!—before commencing to decide what to do with the remainder of my last day as a free nonmastered woman.

Mrs. Fairly had plans for me.

"Come," she said. "There's a couple of more things about this house that you have not yet seen."

I thought she must mean the master's bedroom or perhaps that other bedroom door, behind which I'd imagined I'd heard laughter, but that wasn't the case.

Instead, she led me upstairs to my own bedroom.

"What?" I said, looking around me, not understanding: everything was as familiar to me as it had already become in my short time there.

"Look upward," she smiled, looking upward herself.

I followed her gaze.

At first, all I saw was the wide expanse of the high white ceiling. But then, in the corner of the room, above my new writing desk, at which I had yet to do any writing, I saw there was the outline of a trapdoor with a cord extending down from it.

"A secret trapdoor!" I said, charmed.

"Not so secret," she laughed. "It's right there."

How had I not noticed that before?

Again, it was as though she read my mind: "People see mostly what they expect to see," she said, "and only that. You expected to see a regular room with no surprises and that's what you saw."

"Where does it lead?" I asked, my eyes still on that dangling cord.

"Why don't you find out?" she said.

She brushed past me, climbed onto my chair and, reaching, strained to tug at the cord. She pulled and the trapdoor opened, revealing a staircase on the other side that came down to within a foot of the seat of the chair.

Mrs. Fairly had seemed so old to me before, surely not

one to enjoin one to adventure, but she surprised me now, grabbing onto the side railings and placing her foot on the first stair, beginning her short climb.

I hurried to follow behind her, taking care lest she kick me in the face.

When we reached the top of the stairs, I looked around me and saw light everywhere: it was the roof of the house. Stepping upward and out, I found myself on a small, square widow's walk. The size of it would have been claustro-phobic—there was barely enough room, I imagined, for two people to lie down on it side by side—but it was so above everything around me, it made me feel as though I were touching the outside of Iceland for the very first time. I wasn't usually fond of heights, but this was too lovely to turn my back on because of simple fear.

"It's beautiful," I said, looking all around.

"Isn't it, though?" she said. "And it's all yours."

I looked at her.

"How do you mean?" I asked.

"Before you came," she said, "your room was just a sit-ting room, so we all had easy access to this. But now that it is to be your room alone, it would be rude were we to traipse through your privacy without your permission, just so that we might also enjoy the view."

I thought about this for a moment.

"Do you mind very much?" I asked.

"No, dear," she said. "Besides, the weather is hardly ever good enough to enjoy the view."

Just then, the wind kicked up as though it had somehow heard her and wanted to underscore her last words.

I was glad I was getting to enjoy this, however briefly, on

the one good day for the month, since who knew when there might be another such chance.

It was so tranquil up there and I had such a need for tranquillity in my life now. If the wind kicked up no further, I thought I could gladly spend the remainder of my free day up there, just looking around me, at peace in a place where I could see the world but the world could not begin to touch me.

And yet something inside of me stirred.

If I were a man, I thought, the first thing I would want to do in a new territory would be to take action, to have some kind of adventure. Surely a man would not have *shopping* be his first official activity. Why should I be any different?

And Nancy Drew, what of Nancy Drew?

She, who would have undoubtedly arrived prepared, would most definitely be reaching for action and adventure before bothering with anything else.

Impulsively, I turned to Mrs. Fairly.

"If I were just a regular tourist," I said, "what's the most adventurous thing I could still do around here today?"

I dearly hoped she wasn't going to say skydiving.

Of all the adventurous things I've ever wanted to do— I'm really not naturally adventurous at all, so it's not like I've ever been hugely tempted—jumping out of the sky had never been one of them. Living close to the ground, as my short body forces me to do, is a good enough reason for not being too keen on heights.

Mrs. Fairly didn't even need to think about it.

"The ponies," she said. "If you were just a regular tourist, you would go for a ride on one of Iceland's little wild horses."

How bad could that be?

★ ★ ★

I found out, not long after my arrival at Ishestar, the stables from which I was going to do my two-hour guided tour. Surely, the name Ishestar, so close to *Ishtar,* the Hollywood disaster, should have clued me in to what lay in my future.

What can I say? I've never been good at reading signs. If there was an omen to be had, I was sure to misread it.

The Icelandic horse has been around as long as men have walked on that cold island, which is a very long time.

Oh, not the same horse, but you get the idea.

The current Icelandic horse is small yet strong, and is a purebred descendant of its ancestors from the Viking age. An intelligent animal, it has an unusual stepping style, known as the *tolt,* or running walk, which presumably makes the ride it gives smooth. Legend has it that the ride it gives is so smooth, a rider could carry a tray of drinks at full speed without losing a drop. Horse lovers from all over thrill at the speedy speeds of these small animals, who are considered to be exceptionally sure-footed and easy to handle.

Not that any of that did me a whole lot of fucking good.

Fuck! FuckfuckFUCK! my mind screamed as I juddered along in the saddle of this insane creature I found myself on.

I was in a grouping of a dozen people plus two leaders, out for a gentle ride.

I knew that if I really were Nancy Drew, I'd have made fast friends with the other eleven members of my group, especially the two guides.

Nancy was always making fast friends. Indeed, if she

were compelled to seek shelter from a storm in a barn, inevitably someone would show up and offer to iron her clothes, and before long she'd be eating cake with them at the kitchen table of the farmhouse, listening to one of them as she burst into impromptu song, impulsively offering to help the impromptu singer locate a professional voice coach to launch her on her operatic career.

But I was not Nancy Drew…certainly not yet.

I suppose it's remotely possible I might have enjoyed the experience—the feel of beast beneath me, the beautiful scenery whizzing by—were it not for the fact that I was hating every second of it.

I was terrified.

Never one to fear death—of the top three phobias, it had always been public speaking and spiders that terrified me, never death—I was now so very fearful at every second during this hellish ride, I hadn't even a moment's clear thought in which to remind myself of how unfearful of death I was!

Back at the stables, they'd provided us with hard helmets to wear; mine, the smallest they had, was so big it practically covered my eyes. They'd also given the novices rudimentary instructions on how to get the animals to start, go faster, slow down, *stop* and I could have sworn I'd been listening closely, but now that I was astride the little demonic beast, I couldn't seem to do anything to get it to slow down, let alone stop.

When we'd left the stables, I'd noticed the other adults in the party were all normal-size and the two guides were larger than normal, meaning the small horses looked dwarfed underneath them. I was the only one the horse seemed proportionally to fit, a rare feeling that had instilled confidence in me in those first few moments—these small horses had been built by God for *me!*—and yet now I was the only one apparently who had no control.

The others trotted on ahead, farther and farther in the distance ahead of me. Yet, even though I was the laggard, I was going far more quickly than my own comfort allowed.

Oh, well, I sighed, holding on to the reins for dear life. *If I get hopelessly lost back here, surely they will send someone out looking for me. Eventually.*

As the horses and riders grew ever smaller in the distance ahead of me, I heard a noise, an increasing thunder from behind, accompanied by the barking of a dog.

Turning in my saddle—a tactical error, I'll grant you—I saw four riders, the four horsemen of my apocalypse, coming up behind me, a large dog racing beside them.

They were all men, the one in the lead riding without a helmet.

"If you don't know how to ride, you should get out of the way for those who do!" one of the men shouted. I was so surprised at both the content and tone of the message that I was too intimidated to figure out which one of the four had spoken.

Remembering only that the reins were supposed to be like a steering wheel—not that I had any firsthand knowledge of driving cars—I yanked hard to the right.

Another tactical error.

No sooner did I pull on the reins, hard as I could, the horse immediately veering to the right as per my instructions, than I felt that the turn had been too sharp. The ostensible pony tripped over an outcrop of rock, inconveniently placed in my new path, and when it pulled up short, I felt myself sliding out of the saddle, the far foot leaving the stirrup while the near one remained stuck, so that I fell down through the air but caught there like a trapeze artist as my head struck against the rock that had tripped us up.

Thank God for the helmet that had made me look ridiculous.

Even if my brains hurt dreadfully, at least they weren't dashed.

The pony was at least well mannered enough to stand still in one spot, gently grazing—why couldn't the damn thing have been gentle when I was riding it?—as I hung suspended.

My brains must have been at least a little scrambled because it felt like a while before I was able to properly process what was going on around me. When the fog cleared, the first thing I noticed was the large dog, black, its face in mine, sniffing.

Have I mentioned yet that I'm scared of big dogs?

Even Nancy Drew, when confronted with a big dog, could be thrown off her game.

I hoped the dog would go away before biting me.

And then the first words I properly heard were:

"Captain! Get out of her face!"

Captain, who I then assumed to be the dog, removed himself. In his place came the face of a man without a helmet, who I then assumed to be the lead rider.

It was an odd face, sharing many of the features of Buster's beautiful one, only in this case, it was as though God had screwed it up a bit. He looked to be a few years older than Buster, his dark hair grayer, his brown eyes sadder and sterner and sharing none of the more benign mischief Buster's had, his teeth when his full lips separated for him to speak creating an almost savage look about him.

He could have used a shave, too.

I remembered from Nancy Drew that bad people were often unattractive—so maybe Icelanders were purely good?—and always obnoxious. And while I would not say this man was unattractive, he was neither attractive in any sense that would be termed so. Certainly, if he was the one who had called out for me to get out of the way, he was capable of being obnoxious.

I also remembered from Nancy Drew that bad people are also fast and reckless drivers. Did that count for horses, too? Of course, sometimes Nancy drove fast, but that was okay. She always had legal reasons, she was careful about it, and no cop ever wanted to give her a ticket.

To be thinking these things, I thought, maybe I did have a head injury!

Although his words to the dog had been sharp, as he placed his face close to mine, his words were soft, if urgent.

"Are you all right?" he asked, covering my hand with his.

Upside down as I was, I gave the matter some thought.

I was feeling battered, to be sure, and the blood continually rushing to my head wasn't helping any. Feeling foolish wasn't helping any, either.

But other than that?

It didn't feel as though anything was broken. If it was, I would know it, right? Nor did I feel, outside of the free associations to all things Nancy Drew, as though I had sustained a concussion. I'd know that, too, if I had, right? Wouldn't I feel confused if I had a concussion? But then I suddenly realized with confusion that felt so strong it was like its own nth degree version of confusion, something I decided to thenceforth christen "conusion," even if Webster's never agreed with me: If I were confused, how would I know it?

"What's your name?" the lead rider demanded.

I got the feeling that he was overcompensating with the sternness, perhaps embarrassed by the concern he felt.

But then, I thought, what did I know? I, after all, was conused.

"Charlotte Bell," I answered after a moment.

"Huh," he said. "You don't sound too sure of that."

His voice was a deep bass. I liked it, even the harsh parts.

"I am now." I forced a smile. "My name is Charlotte, Charlotte Bell."

"Who's in the White House?" was his next demand.

"Do you want me to tell you who in fact is in the White House right now," I countered, "or are you some kind of spy who wants me to tell you who I *wish* were in the White House right now?"

He threw his head back—it was a nice affectation that he took joy so seriously—and laughed.

But, even as I started to join in, his features clouded and he placed his face close by my own again.

"You little idiot!" he screamed.

If we had been standing face-to-face, I would have undoubtedly taken a step backward at that point, retreating from his huge displeasure. But, as it was, my position kept me from moving, so that I was forced to remain face-to-face, in counter-confrontation mode.

"Excuse me?" I said.

"What did you think you were doing, riding a horse when you clearly have no idea how to ride a horse?"

"That sounds suspiciously like one of those no-win trick

questions—'Are you always this stupid?' or 'Do I look fat?' It also sounds like a rhetorical question," I said, "which leads me to ask, do you expect me to answer you seriously or are you in a mood now to just yell at me some more for what you perceive as my stupidity?"

Previously, he'd been crouched beside me, but now he rose, brushing his knees off.

"You're fine," he said.

"Thank you," I said. "That's the nicest thing you've said to me so far today."

"You're definitely fine," he said, unable to stop a smile. "No one who is not fine could be so comfortably sarcastic."

"Speaking of being fine," I asked, pointing to my foot, still caught in the stirrup. "Do you think you could help me with that?"

"Oh, no," he said, swinging into his saddle and mounting his horse, the horse looking small in comparison. "You got yourself into this, Miss Bell, and now you can get yourself out."

He clicked the heels of his riding books against the pony's flanks, twitched the reins—why couldn't I master that?—and shouted over his shoulder, "Come, Captain!"

The dog and the lead rider's three companions, who'd done absolutely nothing to help me, departed behind him.

"Fine, run away," I shouted after them, knowing they couldn't hear me anyway. "I can handle this all by myself."

Feeling like a fox who had gotten the worst end of the hunt, I had to do a jackknife sit-up, which my abs were in no way conditioned to do, in order to stretch up high enough to reach my own foot in order to free it from the stirrup.

And then the one fine day came to an abrupt ending and it started to rain on me.

Iceland and I were so not getting along together so far.

It felt as though I'd been gone forever, but it was only midafternoon when the van from the pony-excursion place deposited me back at the embassy.

I got the impression they thought I should count it a kindness that they hadn't charged me double for abusing their pony.

Pony? The thing was the Cerberus gluepot from hell!

But when the driver pulled up in front of the embassy, saw where we were, his behavior toward me changed rapidly.

"You should have said that this is what was at this address," he said.

"If you'd told me diplomatic asylum extended to alleged horse abuse," I said, getting out, sorer in all ways by the minute, "I might have."

"I didn't mean that," he said. "I only meant you might have saved me the trip."

What?

But I was of no mind to deal with mysteries or cryptic words just then.

So I tipped him handsomely—even the ugliest of horsewomen can be good tippers—and dragged my sorry ass inside.

Mrs. Fairly greeted me at the door.

Was that part of her job, I wondered, to lie in wait and pounce on me whenever I entered?

Apparently, I was of no mind for anything really, certainly not civility.

Mrs. Fairly was more excited than I'd ever seen her as, with a minimal greeting, I brushed by her and headed for the stairs.

"The master came home a day early!" she exulted.

Just what I need right now, I thought.

"That's great," I said, not even bothering to turn around as I dragged myself upward.

"He didn't seem to be in a very good mood though," she added, "said something about not having such a great afternoon."

That's great, too, I thought.

"Oh, Charlotte," she said soothingly, as though seeing me for the first time, "you look as though you've had a rough afternoon yourself."

"You could say that," I said.

"And maybe also a wee tumble from a wee horse."

"You could say that, too."

"Well, no matter." She brightened. "I did tell you that you could have the entire day off today, so why don't you do what you like for the remainder. The master would prob-ably prefer to have dinner alone with Annette on his first day back, so I'll have a tray sent up to you."

I reached the second floor, resting my hand on the newel post as I turned the corner.

"Sounds good," I said.

"But afterward," she shouted, "I do think you should come down and say hello. I know he's dying to meet you. And wear a dress if you've got one! The first night when the master comes home, dinner is always a formal affair. So even if you're not eating with us…"

Just great.

★ ★ ★

If someone had taken the time to ask me, before entering my room, what I planned to do upon gaining entry there, I would have replied with a one-word answer: *Sleep!*

But, having reached the other side of that door, I found myself suddenly feeling shockingly awake.

Perhaps it was that ride in the brisk air, perhaps it was the fall on my cranium, perhaps it was getting rained upon that had done it, but I felt as though something had been knocked loose in me that had been previously blocking free thought and creativity. And for the first time in a very long time, I felt the impulse to write, write the truth.

I sat down at my desk, barely noticing the discomfort of my still-wet clothes.

While Annette had said she had prevailed upon her father to equip me with the trappings of the writerly life, and while he obviously had attempted to do so to the best of his ability, they had left one small item out. How did they expect me to write a novel, in the twenty-first century, without a computer?

And as plucky as I might have gotten since arriving, I wasn't yet brazen enough that I'd ask them to get me one.

I opened the top drawer of my desk, disheartened, and found a large supply of legal pads and a selection of pens. This must be what they had in mind for providing me with everything I needed to scratch my writing itch.

What was *wrong* with these people? Didn't they know I'd go positively crazy if I couldn't do things like cut and paste, moving large blocks of text around a manuscript? After all, wasn't that how writers wrote these days? Who did they think I was, Tolstoy? The next thing you know, they'd be exchanging my lamp for a candle.

I pretended I was a Zen practitioner, closed my eyes and took ten deep breaths, even though I wasn't completely sure that's what a Zen practitioner would do in such a moment.

When I opened them, I saw that while they'd still been closed, Steinway had jumped up on my desk.

"What are you doing here?" I demanded.

"Meow!"

"And stop looking at me like that!"

But then I realized that the cat had a point: back in the days before indoor plumbing and all the other good stuff, writers hadn't had the advantage of computers that could do nifty little tricks to work on. If they were lucky, they had some kind of writing implement, paper and, yes, a crummy candle. If the electricity still held through the storm we were gearing up to get, a storm I could see brewing right outside my window, threatening to replace the steady rain with something more thunderous, I'd at least have something a damn sight better than a candle to write by.

I took out one of the legal pads, clicked open a pen.

Now, for the big part, what had formerly been the hard part: What was I going to write about?

I was going to write a novel based on my experiences. I was going to tell the story of me and Buster, without naming names, tell of my love and pain and desperation. Based on emotional truth rather than emotional fantasy, it would be a good book, even if neither the critics nor the readers—assuming I ever had any of either—ever agreed with me on that. I realized, finally, that it only mattered what I thought of what I wrote.

If the book ever fell into Buster's hands and he actually read it, would he sue me?

Somehow, I doubted it. After all, to take legal action, he'd have to out himself as being the real guilty party. Somehow, I didn't think he would ever do that. And even if he did sue me, so what? The telling of the tale would be my reformation, my regeneration. In telling the tale, I would take back my own life.

I would heal myself.

Writer, heal thyself.

I put pen to paper, started to write.

People think it must be easy for you, when they see you out here on the wire…

It was dinnertime, the knock coming at the door with Mrs. Fairly carrying a tray, before I stopped.

I heard the dog before I saw anything else.

Having slopped spaghetti sauce all over my damp sweater, I realized that it was a good thing I had delayed putting on my dress. Sliding into my heels, running a comb through my tangle of black curls, I glanced in the full-length mirror only long enough to verify that I was indeed as presentable as I ever was. Whatever the image that looked back at me, it would have to do.

I came down the staircase, holding tight to the railing so as not to trip in my unaccustomed heels. It wouldn't do, I thought, to fall at the master's feet as prelude to our first meeting.

As I said, I heard the dog before I saw anything else.

And then an impatient voice, an oddly familiar bass voice:

"Captain! Stop that infernal barking! One would think you smelled the blood of someone you knew."

Oh no! I thought. It couldn't be. *It couldn't be. How could it possibly be?*

It was.

I had just been about to enter the library, where I was to meet my master for what I thought would be the first time, what I now knew would be the second, when I'd heard that bass voice call out its message to the dog. Realizing that there was only one person in the world who could own that voice, and that I had already met him and had no desire to repeat the awful experience, I turned abruptly on my heel.

And tripped, of course, over the edge of the runner in the long hall.

"Who put that there?" I muttered to myself.

"Is that the new governess I finally hear?" the voice called out, an annoying laugh contained within it.

He did not wait for my answer.

"Well, do not dawdle," he went on. "Delay no further. Annette has been spending this last hour telling me all manner of wonderful things about you."

Meekly—what choice did I have?—I brushed off my dress, entered the room.

And there he was: sitting in a leather armchair beside the great fire.

Captain, upon seeing me, commenced to barking again.

"You!" said the man in the chair, clearly shocked.

"I," I said, rising up to my full lack of height and steeling my courage.

I moved to stand before him, hands clasped behind my back as though to prove I had nothing to hide. What could he do, I had realized, fire me? There was nothing too awful he could do to me that life hadn't already done. I was almost sure of it.

"*You* is right," he said. "You're the woman who scared my dog."

"*I?*"

"Yes, *you*. If you hadn't been such an abominable horse-woman, if you'd had more control—"

"If you and your, your...*compadres* hadn't trampled at my heels, if you hadn't let that horse you call a dog bark at me so—"

"If you hadn't been in the wrong place at the wrong time—"

"Nor you," I countered.

I was reminded yet again of how somewhat unattractive he was.

By now he had risen from his seat and was staring me down, hands on hips, as though with no more than his stern gaze he could destroy me.

But I stood my ground. "Nor you," I said again, just in case he hadn't heard my insult the first time.

Just when I was beginning to think he looked angry enough that he might indeed hit me, an extraordinary thing happened: he laughed.

It was that same laugh I'd heard earlier in the day, a life-time ago it seemed, when he had laughed on the horse trail.

In that moment, I forgot how somewhat unattractive he was.

Surprising myself even more than I surprised him perhaps, I started laughing, too.

"It is a good thing," he said, getting his own laughter

under control, a smile still dancing around his lips, "that we both have good senses of humor. I do not think Annette would like it, were we to go on fighting so in front of her."

"No," a little voice piped up.

I had not seen her there before. He so sucked up all the oxygen in the room, there was no space for anyone else.

"Annette," she said, "would not like that one bit."

She bounced out of her chair, came up to us. I saw now that she had on a pretty, overly girlish frock, just as she had the first time I met her in New York. I assumed her father liked to see her this way.

"You and Papa must become friends," she said to me. "It would not be fair to make me choose between you."

"Oh ho!" her father said, turning a look to me that was half amusement, half accusation. "You've only been here a short time, yet already your importance has grown so much that my daughter thinks any choice between us would be equal?"

Hearing the two of them, father and daughter, speaking in the same room for the first time, I was finally able to see where Annette got her peculiar formality from. Edgar Rawlings was nothing if not formal. I would have thought it a by-product of being an ambassador, whether the job caused the formality in the man or the man had been chosen for the job because he was so formal, but I had already known one ambassador, hadn't I? And Buster Keating had never been like this.

"I'm sure she didn't mean that at all." I blushed. "Children have a tendency to overstate even the simplest of cases."

"Oh no, Miss Bell," he said, sitting down again. "Once a thing has been said, it cannot then be unsaid. My daughter has declared by implication that her feelings for us are equal. We must now deal with the world such as it has been presented to us."

"If you insist," I said, no longer knowing what to say to this strange man.

"Please sit," he said abruptly. "It makes me nervous having you tower over me so."

I hated to give up the advantage, but saw no polite way in which I could refuse.

"If you insist," I said again, tucking my skirt carefully under me as I took a seat beside Annette on the sofa.

"Do you find me attractive?" he asked suddenly.

I wondered if he had somehow read my mind earlier.

"Why do you ask?" I countered. "Is that a requirement for employment here?"

"No requirement." He shook his head. "I was merely curious. You seem so…unsettled by me."

"I don't even know you," I said. "I cannot answer such a question without knowing you."

"Not even objectively?" he said.

"I don't know how to be objective," I said. "It is a trick I have never learned."

"Papa has brought me a present!" Annette cried, no longer able to contain her excitement in the face of all this boring adult talk.

"Papa always brings Annette a present when he comes back after having gone away," Ambassador Rawlings said. "And," he added, looking at her pointedly, "if Annette behaves herself and lets Papa continue his conversation with the new governess, perhaps Annette will get her present from Papa tonight."

"That hardly seems fair," pouted Annette, crossing her arms. "Why should I have to wait?"

"Because waiting for good things builds character," said her father. "Now then," he continued, turning to me, "Annette has been filling my head this last hour with how accomplished you are at a wide variety of things."

It seemed to me that Annette and I had barely talked since I'd been there. What could she have been talking of then?

"I am guessing that," he went on without waiting for an answer, "like the last governess, you play the piano well?"

"The piano?" I almost choked on the words.

He put a hand to his ear, obnoxious man. "Is there an echo in here?"

He indicated the piano in the corner with an abrupt gesture.

"Play," he commanded.

"Play?"

"Yes, Little Sir Echo, play something for us, for our amusement."

That's Little *Ms.* Echo to you, I thought, rising to my feet and striding to the instrument. If they wanted amusement, I could surely provide them with that.

Sitting down, I tilted my head to one side with eyes staring into space affectedly, as though I were waiting for Beethovenish inspiration to come.

Then I tickled the ivories.

Duh, duh, duh. Duhduhduhduhduhduh. Duh, duh, duh. Duhduh—

"Stop!" he cried.

I looked up. "You do not like my song?" I asked.

"Chopsticks?"

"You are familiar with the tune, then?" I said.

"Yes, I…" he sputtered. "Surely you can play something other than *that*…can't you?"

I gave the matter a moment's serious thought, head tilted again.

"I can play the first twenty-five notes of 'Stairway to Heaven.'" I thought some more, counting on my fingers this time. "And I can also play the first sixteen notes of *Für Elise*. I can even repeat them so it sounds like a bit of a song. But when it gets to the part where it changes? That part I don't know how to do at all." I thought one last time. "I'm pretty sure that's it," I said.

He looked at Annette as if someone had to be to blame for this turn of events.

"Don't blame her," I said. "I don't believe for a second that she misinformed you about my musical talents, of which I have, as I've amply displayed, none. I'm sure that she must have merely said I have some sort of talents and you, basing your extrapolation on your experience of previous governesses, leapfrogged to this insane idea that I could play on demand."

I rose from my seat, prepared to take my leave.

"Since it is now obvious that I cannot entertain you in the way in which you desire…"

"Sitsit*sit*." He was impatient as he pointed to the couch. "There is no need to be so prickly with me all the time, Miss Bell… *Sit!*"

Now, *there* was an invitation that would be hard for a girl to resist.

Despite my instinct to bolt and run, I obeyed the instruction.

"Your lack of piano…*finesse* is not really important. The last governess played well enough, but she had the tendency to play the same song. She played it over and over again. I really thought, after a point, that I might go mad with it."

"And what song was that?" I couldn't help but ask.

He rolled his eyes, smiled ruefully.

"Für Elise," he said.

I stifled a smile.

He settled back in his own chair, a lion temporarily appeased.

"Well," he said, "if you can't play the piano, and you most clearly cannot, then what can be these sparkling talents of yours that dear Annette is so keen on?"

"Miss Charlotte is a great writer!" piped up Annette, no longer able to remain out of the conversation.

"A great writer?" He looked at me with mocking interest. "Annette did say something earlier about you being a writer, she was insistent that you should have writerly…*things* in your room, but I assumed she must be talking about something that was no more than a hobby of yours."

"Some would indeed call it just that," I conceded.

"Oh no, Papa!" Annette was truly distraught at this. "Miss Charlotte is going to be a bestselling novelist!"

"A best…?" There was that mocking look again. "Why then have I never heard of you before?"

"Perhaps you don't like novels," I said.

"Oh, I like novels very much," he said. "Tell me—which bestselling novels did you write?"

"Didn't you hear the part where Annette said 'going to write'?" I said. "I haven't written any yet."

"Ah." He gave a smile, more like a smirk or a sneer, that I did not like at all. "You are one of *those* kinds of writers."

"Which kind is that?" I demanded, trying my best to impersonate a woman who could *do* haughty.

"The kind that want to be writers without having written, of course," he said.

How dare he?

"You asswipe," I muttered under my breath.

"What was that, Miss Bell?" He placed his hand behind his ear as though straining to hear me better. "You speak so softly at times."

"I said—" I smiled sweetly through gritted teeth "—You. Are. Wise."

I turned to Annette.

"Somehow," I said, "I don't think your father is impressed."

"Not impressed?" She looked surprised, wounded. Suddenly, she brightened. "Then how about this." She turned to her father, challenging him. "Miss Bell is a star!"

"A *star?*" He was incredulous.

So was I. What was Annette talking about?

"Oh, yes," Annette bubbled. "Mrs. Fairly told me all about it."

Oh, no, I groaned inwardly.

"What exactly did Mrs. Fairly tell you?" he asked.

"She said that, when Miss Charlotte was a little girl, even younger than me, she starred in commercials!"

He turned to me. *"Commercials?"*

I barely nodded.

Please, I prayed, *don't let Annette say any more.*

"What commercials did you make?" he prodded.

"I was the Gubber Snack Foods Kid," I muttered so quietly I could barely hear myself.

"What?" he asked.

"She was the Gubber Snack Foods Kid!" Annette shouted.

"The Gub...? *What?*"

"Gubber Snack Foods," I said tersely. "They make organic snacks. For kids."

"How...*progressive.*" He smirked. Then: "My, you *are* a star."

"She is!" said Annette. "She really is! Miss Bell, tell Papa your famous line."

I felt like a particularly silly bug under his microscope. "Please do," he said.

I studied the floor. "'It's...'" I couldn't get the words out. "'It's...it's...*Gubber*licious,'" I finally said dumbly, leaving off the exclamation point from all those commercials.

"'It's...*Gubber*licious'?" he asked.

I nodded.

He settled back in his chair, smirked again.

"Yes," he said, "a real star. We are lucky to have you, I see."

Perhaps he grew tired of taunting me about one thing, for he moved on to something else.

"Do you know anything at all about the country in which you find yourself, Miss Bell?" he asked.

I shrugged. "It is an island," I said. I shrugged again. "The people here are almost invariably tall. And blonde. They do not seem to be much like me."

"It also has the highest percentage of books per capita than any other country in the world."

"I didn't know that," I conceded.

"Perhaps one day they will have *your* books here."

Don't hold your breath, I wanted to say. But this time, at least, I was wise enough to hold my tongue. Why give him anything at all, since every time I spoke, it only seemed to provide him with more ammunition with which to embarrass me.

Perhaps he took pity on me, or had grown bored with the game, for he turned to the little person beside me.

"Annette," he commanded, "if you look in the hall closet, behind my briefcase, you will find a prettily wrapped present that is solely for your enjoyment. Go get it and bring it back here so that Miss Bell and I might have the pleasure of watching you open it."

He was such a different person with her—still stiff and formal, but with an underlying and unmistakable feeling of love—that it would have been easy, in that moment of watching the two framed together, to forget what a jerk he could be.

But, of course...

While she was gone, we engaged in a staring contest, one I refused to lose. And for the first time, it occurred to me that I was *enjoying* myself. I had led such a solitary existence that, previously, I had rarely had the chance to wrangle with a man's mind. Buster, by virtue of his job, had been a smart man, and his connections should have made him an interesting man, but whatever smarts he had possessed, he had never bothered to use them with me.

But this sparring was something new in my existence. I found that I liked it. I was good at it!

If I had wanted a change from tranquillity, I had certainly found it in the person of Ambassador Edgar Rawlings. And, if I had been Buster Keating's subordinate, I vowed that I would never be this man's and I resolved never to utter the odious phrase "I guess" again.

Annette returned with the present. It was easy to see that it had taken all her meager powers of restraint to keep from opening it as soon as she laid hands on it.

The wrapped box, tall and rectangular, and covered with crinkly pink metallic paper, was almost as tall as she. But, whatever it contained, it must be light, for she only struggled with the awkwardness of its height and not its weight.

"May I open it now, please, Papa?" she asked, eyes all aglitter.

I could tell that Ambassador Rawlings saw her anxiousness and he at last smiled, genuinely, and showed some pity.

"Ohhhh—" he drew out the word, as though still considering "—I suppose."

The wrapping was being torn asunder before the final syllable had even left his mouth.

But then there was the tape on the end of the box to be dealt with.

Ambassador Rawlings watched her struggle with it for an amused few minutes, then finally showed mercy a second time.

"Here," he said, withdrawing a rather lethal-looking knife that opened on a switch from his pocket. "You will harm your pretty little fingers if you keep tearing at it like that."

With an expert series of flicks of the wrist, he sliced the tape from across the ends of the box and with a wide swath cut it straight down the middle.

Annette buried her head in the opening, not too different from a puppy rooting around for a toy. Then, when she could not get whatever was inside out using that method, she tilted the box so it fell at her feet, the noxious Styrofoam popcorn thingies spilling out onto the floor.

She thrust her head inside among the popcorn, at last extracted what she obviously assumed would be her heart's desire.

It was a dancing doll.

I had read about them in books and seen them on TV as a child, but I had never met one like this before.

It was life-size, or as big as Annette's life, at any rate. It was made out of some kind of soft padding, covered in colorful fabric and thread: ragged yellow hair, rouged cheeks and ruby lips, big blue eyes with spider lashes. It wore a ballet costume in pink with matching, slightly heeled dancing shoes on its oversize feet. Across the tops of the doll's feet were large elastic straps; presumably, Annette was supposed to insinuate her own feet beneath those straps and be led around the dance hall of her mind by this creature that was at once exotic and common.

Her father had found for her the perfect dance partner: a partner that would always be there and would never complain if one stepped on the partner's toes.

"Do you like it?" Ambassador Rawlings asked, a trifle anxious for her pleasure.

Anyone could see that she adored it, the sparkle in her eyes said as much, but it was a nice thing in him, I thought, that he should care if she was sufficiently pleased by his present or not.

"It is the greatest present you have brought me yet!" she cried. "It is even better than the nail-polish kit!"

"I'm glad then," he said, and I thought he blushed a bit

as he submitted to her overly enthusiastic kiss. "Now," he said, all seriousness again, "why don't you take your new toy out for a spin here and see how well it works."

Annette didn't have to be asked twice. As if she'd done it a thousand times before, and perhaps she had danced before with princely partners in her juvenile dreams, she propped the doll up in her arms, one arm around its waist, the other holding its hand out to the side, fit her feet into the appropriate spots and commenced to waltz.

For a six-year-old, she was damn good.

We watched her for a moment in silence. Then:

"What do you think they are dancing to?" Ambassador Rawlings asked me, leaning in as though to impart a confidence. "Do you think perhaps they are dancing to…'Chopsticks'?"

I actually did find it funny, but I refused to let him see me smile, certainly not when the joke had been at my expense.

"Oh," I said, "I am quite sure that the musical score that forms the sound track to the life of a six-year-old must by definition be far more sophisticated than any sound track accompanying mine."

"What sound track does score your life, Miss Bell?"

I continued to watch Annette prance around the room as though I could hear her music now. Tapping my hand to the imaginary beat on the arm of the sofa, I did not answer him. I was beginning to think it rude of him to ask me so many personal questions. After all, I had been merely hired to be his daughter's governess. I should not be required to make myself sport, as well.

"Annette loves presents," he said, abruptly changing the

subject. Then I felt his face close to mine again, studying me from the side. "Do *you* like presents, Miss Bell?"

As soon as I heard his words, asking something I had never given much thought to before, it became an acutely painful question for me. It was all I could do not to wince. Just those few words were all it took to send me spiraling back down to my old lowly self.

"I have had little experience of them," I said.

"Little experience?" His surprise was a mixture of things I couldn't quite make out. Shock, perhaps? Contempt?

I thought of my life so far. Buster Keating, the only man I had ever been with, had never thought to give me anything material. As for the nonmaterial thing he had given me, himself, well, it had turned out that that was just a shadow version and not the real man at all. And, before Buster, I never had what anyone else would term a real boyfriend, never went to any prom or was invited to any dances. Even the girlfriends I'd had were not of the gift-giving variety, no exchanges of trendy clothes or makeup or jewelry. The only presents I had ever known then had been the mean little things that Aunt Bea had given me at holiday time and on my birthday…if she even remembered it.

"I suppose," I finally said, "that I am not the kind of woman that people give presents to."

"Not the kind—"

I put my hand to my ear and cupped it, hoping to lighten the moment.

"What?" I said, forcing a smile. "Is it Little Ambassador Echo who has joined us now?"

But he would not be lightened.

"What kind of life have you lived, Miss Bell, that you should know nothing firsthand of presents?"

If I were to answer truthfully, I would have had to have said, "A lonely one."

But I wasn't about to do that.

"Not even on your birthday?" he prompted when I failed to answer.

"I've always hated my birthday," I said honestly, evenly.

"That's awful," he said. "I've never heard anybody say that before. Who hates their own birthday?"

I remained silent, eyes on Annette.

"I think you have been greatly hurt by life, Miss Bell," he spoke softly, "something far worse than falling off a pony. What is it that has happened to you?"

If I wasn't fighting back tears in my eyes, I might have had the objective presence of mind to turn the inquisitorial tables on him. A moment ago, I had thought us equals. But now we were equals no longer. The game was all to him.

If I had any presence of mind left at all, I might have said, "What about you? What in life has damaged you so to cause you to be such a sarcastic and invasive individual?"

But no such self-protection was left to me.

All I could find it in myself to do was to say:

"It has been a very long day, Ambassador Rawlings. I had been told by Mrs. Fairly that I wasn't expected to work today and yet it feels as though I have worked the whole day through. And tomorrow will undoubtedly be a full day with Annette. If it is all the same to you, I should like to retire now."

I did not wait for his answer, nor did I turn back to see his expression as I rose and left.

If he does not like my attitude, I thought, *then let him fire me.*

★ ★ ★

In the middle of the night, I woke to the smell of something burning. Throwing the covers off me, my mind was barely conscious as my feet struck the hardwood floor and I raced out the door, down the hall and toward the smoke.

It was coming from Ambassador Rawlings's room.

I turned the handle on his closed door and was thankful to find it unlocked. If it had been locked, I'm not sure what I would have done. I had no hatchet at my disposal and the house was sturdy, its doors too strong to yield to any assault I might make on the structure.

Entering the room at a rush, I saw it was already filled with smoke, the edges of the blankets just beginning to spark.

"Wake up!" I screamed at the figure, still slumbering beneath the sheets.

When my screams went unanswered, I cast about to find something to stop the sparks from turning into a conflagration. Near a narrow closed door, probably a closet, was a second door, half-open with a night-light on.

It was a small bathroom.

I turned on the overhead light above the sink, looking for something that could transport water.

All I could find was a toothbrush glass.

It would have to do.

I suppose if I could have existed as a being outside my own body, observing my actions, I would have laughed at the picture I made: rushing back and forth from sink to bed with what amounted to not much more than a thimbleful of water, like a contestant playing *Beat the Clock* or some retro game show, tossing my thimblefuls on the smoldering sheets as I repeatedly cried, "Wake up, Ambassador! Wake up!" As I grew more desperate, that cry turned into something along the lines of, "Wake up, *you idiot!* Wake up!"

The drops of water seemed to have at last put out all the sparks, but still the sheets smoked.

Turning to the closed door now, I opened it, hoping to find something I could use to beat out the remainder of the smoke. Isn't that what firefighters did? Or Boy Scouts?

A spare blanket would have worked perfectly, but I didn't see any of those. So I grabbed the first thing my hand touched, yanking whatever it was off the hanger.

I beat at the bottom of the bed until I was satisfied that whatever had been living there would cause no more danger. Then, for good measure, I beat at the bed around Ambassador Rawlings's head, somewhat alarmed that he hadn't wakened yet.

Had the smoke asphyxiated him?

Desperate once more, I rushed back to the bathroom for one last toothbrush glass of water. Returning to the bedroom proper, I hurled my thimbleful at that sleeping head.

That did the trick.

"What the…?"

He reared up, shaking his head like Captain might, coming out of a bath.

"Miss *Bell?*"

I took an involuntary step backward.

"Yes, sir?" I said.

"What in God's name are you *doing?*"

"You were in danger, sir. I was only trying to save you."

"What are you *talking* about?" he demanded.

I suddenly felt myself growing angry. How dare he put me on the defensive, how dare he use that italicized snottiness on me, when all I'd been trying to do was save his stupid life.

I should have let him burn.

"Your sheets were on fire, *you idiot,*" I said, stepping forward.

Now it was his turn to take a step back at my attack, or as much of a step as one can when one is lying down; having been in similar circumstances myself just that afternoon, on the ground after my fall from the horse, I knew what that was like. He pulled his head back a bit, raising his eyebrows at me like I was some kind of new creature, different than the one I'd been before.

It occurred to me that while we were bickering, there could yet be some danger to him. I remembered then that crying laugh I had heard on the previous night, that unexplained locked door next to his.

"Do you think it was the madwoman who did this to you?" I demanded.

His eyebrows rose farther.

"The *madwoman?*" he asked.

"Yes, yes, the madwoman! That person I hear laughing sometimes, that eerie sound in the house."

He looked stunned. And maybe I could see why. Still...

"Okay," I said hurriedly, "I'm having Jane Eyre thoughts, so sue me later, just get out of that bed before it ignites again."

He started to laugh, a little bit at first, but then it got away from him, until it became an uncontrolled and roaring thing.

"The madwoman?" he gasped one last time, visibly struggling to contain his mirth. "There is no *madwoman* here! Here, Charlotte," he addressed me by my given name for the first time as he reached toward the end of the bed, yanking back the damp and sooty sheets. "Here is your madwoman."

His yank revealed a glass ashtray, half filled with butts.

"When I fell asleep," he said, "one of them must not have been completely out. I've always been too lazy about such things—a bad habit, I know."

"Dangerous is more like it," I said severely.

I was almost sorry I had saved him now, seeing as it had been his own stupid fault.

Then I wondered: Why had no one else rushed in here to save him? Even if they had not smelled the smoke, I had certainly screamed loud enough.

When I said as much, he merely shrugged.

"The one, Mrs. Fairly, is too old to be troubled by the odd noise in the night. The other, Annette, is too young to have her sleep troubled by anything."

Well, he was neither too old nor too young. So why had he not wakened sooner himself?

He indicated with a nod of his head a nearly empty brandy snifter on his bedside table.

"Too much of that before retiring, I'm afraid," he said. "It's probably why I was so careless with the cigarette, too."

So it was all his own fault, after all.

"You seem to be safe now," I said, moving to take my leave. "And I'm sure you can find yourself some clean bedding…"

"Stay a minute, Miss Bell." He reverted to how we had been before. And yet his actions belied the distancing of his address, because as he spoke to me, he reached out and grabbed my hand.

His fingers sent a shock through me. It had been months since any man had touched me, other than to formally shake hands.

"I am tired, sir," I resisted halfheartedly, with what little strength was left in me. "It has been an unimaginably long day."

"Then I will not keep you too much longer," he spoke softly. "But I must say, I am surprised."

"How 'surprised,' sir?"

"That you saved me," he said. "You thought I was in danger, you even thought some madwoman—" I could see it was a struggle for him not to start laughing again at that "—was responsible, and yet, rather than running away from danger or depending upon someone else to take the risk, you rushed in and saved me."

His eyes were all wonder, like an infant looking up at the night sky and discovering the moon for the first time.

I was sure it was all an act.

"Oh," I said. *"That."*

"Yes," he said, dark eyes still wondering. "*That.* It's quite a big that. You must care for me, Miss Bell."

I absolutely could not let him go on making sport of me, not like *that*.

I withdrew my hand from his, finally having to yank it to get him to free the last pinkie.

"You must have a strange notion of *care,* Ambassador Rawlings." I laughed with what I hoped sounded like a harsh laugh, moving toward the open door to the hall.

"What does that mean?" he asked.

If he had been standing, I was sure he would have had his hands on his hips, belligerently.

Good, I thought. *Let him return to being that harsh man I first met on the pony path. There was nothing tender about that man. I don't have to like that man.*

"It means," I said over my shoulder, "that in the same circumstances, I would have rushed to save Captain. And I don't even like dogs!"

Then I slammed his door behind me.

Okay, so I caught the bottom of my white nightgown in the door when I slammed it, causing me to have to open the door just wide enough to remove it, thus making my exit something less than smooth, but still...

And thus rang down the curtain, ending the longest day of my life.

chapter 7

One is required by some unnameable law to live each day of one's life, the boring ones as well as the extraordinary ones. But when one is telling another the story or stories of one's life, there is no similar requirement to give a narration that spans the arc between brushing one's teeth in the morning and brushing them again at night.

This is to say that the minute treatment I gave to my first full day in Iceland will not be repeated in kind for the subsequent days. On my second day, there was no rising to a perfect day, no shopping, no sunshine, I didn't discover a previously unseen cat, didn't fall off a horse, didn't make an ass of myself in front of my new employer for the first time without realizing who he was, didn't get scared of a dog, didn't start writing a new novel, didn't spill spaghetti sauce all over myself, didn't officially meet my new employer for the first time and realize that it was he in front of whom I'd made an ass of myself earlier, when I'd fallen off the horse, didn't have a fire break out, didn't save anyone's life, didn't go to bed excited or exhausted.

What I did do on the second day was wake up to Mrs. Fairly searching all around the house for the master's favorite blue blazer. Apparently, he had somehow managed to misplace it from his own closet.

Of course, I knew where it was: it was in the bottom of my own closet now, a sodden and ashy thing, since I'd beat the smoldering sparks on his bed to death with it the night before.

How was I to know it was his favorite blazer?

I was trying to save the stupid man's life!

Well, I certainly wasn't going to hand over the blazer now. Surely he could afford a new one. After all, the stupid man was an ambassador.

What I also did do on the second day was I began my duties with my new charge.

So, really, when you think about it, the only thing the two days had in common was that at either end of each, I did in point of fact brush my teeth.

It has been said that having the care of a small child is something akin to watching paint dry. I do not doubt the boredom of the task for many. I can only say that for me, perhaps because I had never had a child of my own, it was more a delight than a burden to see the changes, the growth, in one who looked to me to help with her interpretation of the world.

And Annette was a good child, none better that I had known, for unlike Stevie and Kim, who had already had something of the skeptic bred into their small lives, whatever unhappy event had rendered Annette the sole property of her papa had failed to similarly make her jaded. She was more like a sun that would never burn out.

Still, though, as enjoyable and fulfilling as her company was for me, as dutiful day piled upon dutiful day, I yet found I had a need for adult company.

And Mrs. Fairly, pleasant as she was to me, just wouldn't do.

Since I had been told repeatedly that I could go out anytime at night once Annette had finished with her supper, my duties for the day discharged, I at last took advantage of this generosity.

I had heard that Broadway at Hotel Island was the largest restaurant and dance hall in Iceland, capable of holding more than one thousand guests at a time. It seemed like a good place for me to go in order to get lost. It offered a great advantage, in that I could be among a large quantity of people, giving the illusion of company, and I might yet remain alone.

As an aside, I had become aware of a change in my own tone of voice, even the tone I thought in, since coming to Iceland, specifically since my first disastrous meeting with Ambassador Rawlings. I was much more formal, more stiff than I had ever been in New York. I suppose it should have puzzled me more, troubled me even, but I guess I've always been something of a chameleon. Too many Southern novels in a row and my vowels always had a tendency to soften. Read too many hard-boiled mysteries and I'd start to swear. I guessed that now, so much in the company of stilted Annette who had got it from her stilted papa, I'd gone a bit European.

Or maybe I was just changing, just becoming possessed by the place.

No, too fanciful.

Enough.

Ever since my arrival in Iceland, I had been trying to figure the place out; more specifically, the people. I, of course, remembered what I had read about Icelanders being the longest-lived people on the planet, but that wasn't the most salient feature about them. Having come into contact with many of them during my daily outings with Annette—through wind and rain, we must always go out, at least once every day—I had noticed that there was something different about them than the people I had come into contact with back home: they were more placid and laid-back. It was almost as though, having to contend with a geology that meant that at any given moment a volcano or geyser might erupt, that geological uncertainty had instilled in them a calm that was the emotional embodiment of laissez-faire.

I had also read somewhere that the vast majority of Icelanders, when polled, admitted to believing in "hill people," or, to put it another way, trolls.

This little bit of whimsy pleased me greatly, leading me to think, however erroneously, that if they could believe in trolls, and some of them obviously put great faith in Nancy Drew by reading her books, then they might also one day be persuaded to believe in the worth of one governess from New York.

One could only hope.

If my intention in going to Broadway at Hotel Island had been to hide in plain sight, I couldn't have made a worse decision. No sooner did I enter the place, and hear the loud music all around me, than I found myself flanked on both sides by blond giantesses, determined that they would become my dear friends.

Their names were Britta and Gina.

And they refused to believe me when I said that I had come there, essentially, to be alone.

"Nobody comes to Broadway to be alone!" laughed Britta.

"You need us!" said Gina.

I asked them if they were sure they were Icelanders.

Almost as soon as the words were out of my mouth, I regretted them. What Would Nancy Drew Do, in similar circumstances, were she to find herself alone in a bar in Iceland?

She'd make a couple of friends, of course. Nancy Drew always had friends.

Wasn't it high time that I, essentially friendless for so long, should at last make some friends?

Not that Britta and Gina gave me much choice in the matter.

No one had ever found me exotic before, except perhaps for Annette—and Buster Keating had seemed to, but I knew now that was just part of his seductive act.

But Britta and Gina certainly found me exotic—was it my dark coloring? My lack of any significant height?—and it soon became apparent that nothing would do but for me to spend the evening at the bar, letting them buy me round after round of these drinks that seemed harmlessly fruity enough but that I fast suspected were strong enough to make a sailor walk funny.

I suspected that because they were making me very drunk.

And, as I got drunk, my tongue got looser.

At first, I had played it safe, letting them do all the talking.

If I asked them what they did for a living, they were happy to oblige me at length:

Something to do with working at the library, but nothing so basic as standing at the circ desk punching out summer-reading lists. I don't know. I think it might have had something to do with translating ancient texts that had already been translated many times before, in the hopes of either deconstructing them or reconstructing their original meaning and intent. Like I say, it was confusing to me.

If I asked them how old they were, they said things like:

"Older than you, to be sure!"—Britta.

"But not so old that we forget that girls just want to have fun!"—Gina, who kind of had a taller version of Cyndi Lauper-thing going on.

If I asked them where they lived:

Britta told me all about living with her parents, three brothers, two dogs and cat, and what each did for a living. Well, not the dogs and the cat.

Gina told me about how she missed living with her parents, two sisters, one dog and three cats, what everyone's main occupation was, including the pets—the dog was a big barker, the cats spent a lot of time sleeping. "Living alone can be too much like living without people," she concluded wistfully.

They made me wonder just what exactly were these ancient texts they were working on and just what exactly awful kinds of things they were doing to them.

Not that I didn't like them, of course. What wasn't to like? For the first time in I couldn't say how long, someone was talking to me who was: 1) not my relative, 2) not my employer, 3) not my charge. And there were two of them! How lucky could a lonely girl get?

I'll tell you one thing: I swear, I did not bring up the topic of men.

"So," said Britta, surveying the bar scene, "what do you think of the men?"

I shrugged noncommittally.

"They're not women," I said.

"Ha!" Gina howled. "That is so good, it should be on a T-shirt! 'Men: they're not women'—ha!"

"You have been...*burned,*" Britta said.

This was when I started feeling the non-fruity part of the fruity drinks kicking in.

"*Burned* is such a strong word," I said. "And so limiting."

"Then what would you say, if you wanted to be more accurate?" Britta led, clearly doing her best to get me to deconstruct myself.

"Objectively?" I asked.

They nodded.

"I would say," I said reflectively, sucking on my straw, "that I had my heart stalked, then it was seduced, then, once the seducer had secured it, it was ripped out of my chest, thrown in the dust and stomped on until there was barely anything beating left." I stopped, gave the matter one more moment's reflective thought, nodded, shrugged. "That's pretty much it, more or less."

They shook their pretty, big heads in sympathy.

"Man," said Britta, "men really aren't women, are they?"

This last made me feel uncomfortable. Even though I had been the originator of the whole "Men: they're not women" thing—destined for a T-shirt near you—I had never been one for the whole "women, yes; men, no" school of thought that filled so much of popular culture, in particular self-help books and daytime talk TV.

What can I say? In the Keating household, the wife had kept a lot of those kinds of books lying around the house; and when Stevie and Kim were in school, there wasn't much else to do, since I wasn't doing any writing, than to watch daytime television.

And what I'd seen, I'd never much liked. How can one gender blame another for all of its problems? It would be like me blaming Britta and Gina because they were blond and I was not.

Okay, so maybe it wouldn't be the same thing at all, but the fruity drinks persuaded me it was close enough, so still.

"I'm sure," I sighed wearily, "that the other side could just as easily get T-shirts printed up that say, 'Women—they're not men'."

"Aha!" Gina snap-pointed at me. "Then you admit there is something that can be called 'the other side'?"

"Who do you work for, really, Oprah?"

"The real question is," said Gina, "who do *you* work for? As yet, all you have done is get us to talk about ourselves."

"That's not exactly true," said Britta. "She did tell us about her heart being ripped out and stomped on."

"Yes," said Gina, "but then she went ahead and defended the other side."

"Whoa!" I put up my hands. "Who is this 'she' you keep talking about? Am I even sitting here?"

They had the grace to look positively mortified at least.

"Sorry," said Britta, looking into her drink and taking a sip. "Too many of these, perhaps."

"We get carried away with curiosity sometimes," Gina admitted. "It is a real treat for us to meet someone who is so...*foreign.*"

That was rich. Still...

"It is only natural," said Britta, "that we would then want to learn everything we possibly can about you."

Okay, maybe it was all kind of weird. But what person, unless the person has the personality of a turtle, doesn't relish having other people take an interest in the circumstances of their life and thoughts? I admit it: I was flattered. Here were these two gorgeous blond women, who surely had better things to do with their time—didn't they?—and all they wanted to do was hear about me. If I were a man, I would have been in heaven.

And so I caved. I, who had never really confided anything to anybody, caved to telling my story to interested ears.

I told them about my upbringing.

"You have overcome adversity," said Britta.

"A less strong woman would not have become so strong," said Gina.

I told them about my early job on TV.

"*You* were the Gubber Snack Foods Kid?" said Britta.

"*You?*" echoed Gina.

A less strong woman might have taken offense at their surprise.

But a smart one would have been incredulous that they'd even seen the commercials.

"How...?" I wondered.

"American TV gets exported everywhere eventually," said Britta.

"And don't you remember," said Gina, "you did a guest

spot on that show about the boarding school, *The Fats of Life?*"

"The Facts of Life," I automatically corrected.

"You played yourself as the Gubber Snack Foods Kid, at six years old," said Gina, "falling in love with George Clooney's character."

"My tastes have changed since then," I said.

"You said your famous line from your commercials," said Britta.

And both at once, they said, "'It's *Gubber*licious!'"

"Of course, we never saw the actual commercials," said Gina.

"And we've never eaten Gubber Snack Foods, either," said Britta. "They never made it here. Are they as good as they sound?"

"They suck," I said.

"Ah," said Gina, looking embarrassed for me, "capitalism at work. Well, I at least did like the way George Clooney gently let you down when he had to explain that he was looking for a girlfriend closer to his age."

"Yeah," said Britta. "That man can really wear a tool belt."

What do you say to that?

I went on.

I told them about Ambassador Buster Keating's house and everything that happened to me there.

"You have had your heart broken," Britta sniffed.

"You have had your heart ripped out and stomped in the mud," Gina sniffed so hard she had to blow her nose.

Just then, a trio of men who'd been seated at the end of the bar made their way over to us. They were a weird combination of bluff arrogance and high-school awkwardness, like they thought we should be grateful for their attentions but were insecure that we might not be.

"Buy you fine ladies a drink?" offered the tallest of the three. They were all tall, of course, but he was the tallest.

Gina whirled on him.

"What is *wrong* with you?" she demanded.

"I, um, thought you might be thirsty," he stuttered.

"God," said Britta. "Can't you see there's an emotional crisis going on? We're bonding here!"

"Shoo," said Gina, as though he were the family cat.

Was she the one who lived with her family or was that Britta? I looked into my drink for inspiration, found none, shrugged, took a sip. I could no longer remember.

"Scat!" Gina said more vehemently, when her "shoo!" failed to elicit the desired response.

"I *hate* that," said Gina.

"What?" I asked.

"Every time you go to a bar, some guy thinks you're going to a bar to meet a guy."

Suddenly, the idea of meeting a guy sounded appealing.

"Hey!" I called after the retreating trio. But they'd already moved on to other girls.

"You have had your heart crushed." Britta covered my hand with hers.

She was right, I realized glumly. I was a pathetic loser.

"The last thing you need," said Gina, covering my other hand, "is to get into another situation where you are subordinate to some dominating...*man.*"

She was right, too.

"Then what do I need?" I sighed morosely.

Gina's eyes lit up like two bright blue moons. "You need to become a devo!"

"A *what?*" I snatched my hands back.

"A devo!" she went on excitedly. "You know, like one of those women, Cher or Madonna but definitely not Britney Spears, who get the world to lie at their feet while they insist on getting perfect lighting and an endless supply of tiny pitted olives, imported from some country no one has ever heard of."

"Oh," I said, the dawn breaking, "you mean a diva."

"Yes! Yes!" she said. "One of those!"

"I'm afraid it would never work," I sighed again.

"Whyever not?" she asked.

"I'm just not diva material. Even if I were a character in a Nancy Drew book, I'd never be Nancy. I'd be the maid. Or the family dog. Did they even have a dog?"

Gina no longer cared about dogs.

"*You* are a fan of Nancy Drew, too?" she asked, at which point Britta opened her handbag and exultantly extracted a copy of #41, *The Clue of the Whistling Bagpipes.*

"What is it with you people, you Icelanders, and Nancy Drew?" I asked.

They looked hurt, stunned.

"Why," said Britta, "she is the greatest heroine of all time."

"So plucky," said Gina, "so sure of herself."

"And she has great hair," said Britta.

"You must admire her, too," said Gina, recovering from her hurt. "After all, you brought her up, so she must be important to you."

I explained how, in the wake of my bust-up with Buster, I'd read all the Nancy Drew books before coming to Iceland.

"...hoping to mend your broken heart," Britta finished up for me. "So, how long are you planning on vacationing here?"

I couldn't believe we had been talking for so long, had covered so much ground, that I knew what they did for a living and yet they had still to learn what I was doing in their country.

"I'm not on vacation," I said.

"You're not?" Gina looked wounded again. "But I thought you were here to mend what had become of your brokenheartedness."

"That, too," I said, "but I'm also working."

"Doing what?" asked Britta.

I explained about the governess job I had.

"Oh my goodness!" said Gina. "*You* work for Ambassador Rawlings?"

I might have been surprised at their recognizing his name so readily. Back in the United States, people never knew who any ambassadors were unless there was some kind of sex scandal. But then I remembered where I was: under-populated Iceland, where a chauffeur could call up his cousin the president to do lunch.

"Why?" I asked, referring to Gina's apparent surprise that I worked for who I worked for. "Is that shocking somehow?"

"Why," said Britta, "he is the sexiest man alive!"

What?

"What?" I shouted. "No, he's not."

"Oh, but he is," said Gina. "He is so...all man, plus he is such an American."

"No, he's not," I said again. I thought of his formal speech patterns that had seemed so European to me, so stilted when compared to the casualness of most Americans. "He sounds more like...*you* than me."

"Oh, but he is so arrogant," said Britta. "You know, that's really sexy in a man."

"What's he like to work for?" Gina asked eagerly.

I told them a bit about the household and how in most of my dealings with him, he was so, well, arrogant.

"See? See?" Gina said. "He is just as I imagined he would be."

"You are the luckiest of women among women," sighed Britta.

"But, oh no!" Obviously, something else had occurred to Gina, only this time it wasn't anything good.

"What's wrong?" I asked.

"I just realized," she said, clearly horrified, "you have gone from the fire right into the frying pan."

I didn't feel like it was my place to correct her metaphor, certainly not when I needed to react by saying *"What?"* again.

"You have gone from working for one ambassador to working for another," she said. "Your history is repeating itself!"

That same thought had occurred, just as uneasily, to me, as well.

"Aren't you scared?" Britta asked.

"Of what?" I countered.

"Why, of making the same mistakes twice, of course," said Britta.

"Fool you once, and he's a cruel bastard," said Gina. "Fool you twice—" she wagged her finger at me "—and you're a big fat idiot."

Ouch!

"Well," I defended myself, "that's not going to happen this time."

"How can you be so sure of yourself?" demanded Gina.

"Of course she can be sure of herself," Britta surprised me by defending me. But then she ruined it by adding, "She's an American."

"Oh, right," said Gina. "You're probably arrogant, just like Ambassador Rawlings."

"No," I defended myself, since there was no one left to defend me, "I'm not. It's just that things are different now."

"How are they different?" Gina asked.

I explained how I was older, wiser.

"Right," scoffed Gina, calling the bartender for another round, "like that ever helped anybody."

"Plus," I said, "I'm much more focused on my work now. I'm not as easily distracted as I was before. Not to mention that, unlike you two, I don't find Edgar Rawlings to be at all attractive."

"Oh?" said Gina. "So it's Edgar now, is it?"

"Methinks you doth protest way too much," said Britta. "Everyone finds Ambassador Rawlings attractive."

"Well, I'm not one of that everyone," I insisted.

Hey, wait a minute. What had happened here? A while back, they had been my champions, ready to stand between me and the cruel "other side," that other side consisting of men who might hurt me. Now it was as though I had to defend my every word, as though I had to fight to win back their support.

"Look," I said patiently, "part of the problem with my previous posting, with Buster, was that I felt like a subordinate."

"Well?" said Gina. "He was the ambassador, you were the nanny. So, weren't you?"

"Yes," I said, "but what I mean is that, not only was I in a subordinate position in terms of the whole employer/employee thing, but I also *felt* like one..."

"What are you saying?" said Gina. "That he forced you, that he made you do it?"

"Not physically, no," I said. This was getting all twisted. "I'm talking about emotional feelings of subordination. It's why it's considered to be unethical for lawyers to date their secretaries or for politicians to pursue interns. The person in the subordinate position feels almost compelled to comply. It's like a form of brainwashing with the deck stacked unequally."

"That sounds like something I would say," Gina observed.

"Then you were never really in love with this...*Buster?*" Britta queried.

"Of course I was in love with him," I sighed. "But maybe, just maybe, if I hadn't perceived him as being my superior in every way, I wouldn't have been."

"Ah," she said. "It is sort of beginning to make sense now."

"And that unfortunate piece of my history will never repeat itself," I said. "I'm positive of that."

"But really," Gina said pityingly, "how can you be so sure of that?"

"Because I don't even feel like a subordinate this time," I said.

"No," Britta said, as though I was deluding myself, "of course you don't, dear."

"I *don't!*" I said, growing exasperated. "How can I feel like his subordinate, when *I* saved *his* life?"

"What?" they both said.

And suddenly, as I told them about the whole thing—the waking in the night to the smell of smoke, the fire, the running back and forth with the tiny toothbrush glass, the ruined blue blazer and all the banter in between—I saw myself being elevated in their eyes again.

"You are a heroine!" said Gina.

"You are just like Nancy Drew!" said Britta.

"Well, not exactly," said Gina. "Nancy Drew would have admitted right away to destroying his favorite blue blazer."

"She would have found a way to return it as new," said Britta. "And, failing that, she would have replaced it. Or, perhaps, she would have even hand-sewn him a new one."

"Oh," I said, "what does Nancy Drew know?"

"Everything," they said vehemently. "So bite your tongue if you can't show respect."

God, they took this stuff seriously. So okay, maybe I did, too.

"Anyway," I said, "there I was thinking the incident might have something to do with the madwoman, but it all turned out to have been caused by a stupid cigarette that he—"

"Wait a second," said Gina. "Time out, hold those ponies and back up. What madwoman?"

I explained about the eerie sound I thought I'd heard coming from behind that other locked door.

"But I've concluded," I said, "that is, I've come to realize, that I just have an overactive imagination. For a while there, I was having Jane Eyre thoughts, like I was trying to be Nancy Drew playing Jane Eyre, but then I realized that there isn't any explanation for that fire other than the obvious—Ambassador Rawlings left a cigarette in the ashtray that wasn't completely out, then he fell asleep like an idiot, and it smoldered until it became a fire. End of story."

"Then how do you explain the eerie laugh?" demanded Gina.

"Well," I said, "you guys do have a lot of wind around here."

"A wind and an eerie laugh are not the same thing," Britta scoffed. "If they were, we would be driven crazy living here."

"Maybe it is Ambassador Rawlings's wife!" suggested Gina with glee.

"Does he even have a wife?" I asked.

"Nobody knows!" said Britta. "He never talks about it publicly."

"You can't dismiss this, Charlotte," Gina said.

"I can't? Wait a minute. What can't I dismiss?"

"The mystery of the eerie laugh," said Britta.

"The mystery of Ambassador Rawlings's wife," said Gina.

They raised their glasses in toast.

How many of these had we all had? I wondered.

"You have mysteries to solve!" they said.

chapter 8

I awoke the next morning with a hangover worthy of Lucky Jim and two crumpled pieces of paper on my desk: Gina's and Britta's phone numbers. I vaguely remembered them insisting on the exchange of numbers at the end of the previous evening, extracting promises to "Keep in touch-tone!"

There was also a dim recollection of their appointing me head of the mission to solve the mysteries of the Rawlings household. But in the dim light of a new day—there was less light here now each day and more cold as we moved into Iceland's autumn, making Manhattan's own flirtation with that same season seem like Hawaii—this seemed like fanciful nonsense. After all, it wasn't as though that eerie laugh I'd heard was some kind of regular thing; it had been only an occasional thing and it had indeed been a while since I'd heard it at all. And, as for the absentee Mrs. Rawlings, any queries I'd made about her in the past had been met with either stony silence or weird verbal sidestepping. What was I supposed to do, grill Annette?

I certainly wasn't going to exploit my relationship with the child.

And so, the days piled up, with me enjoying my time with Annette, with no other mother anywhere on the scene for her. Although Mrs. Fairly could be said to be a motherly figure, she was more of an age to be the child's grandmother. Honestly, I sometimes fantasized that I *was* her mother. I knew, of course, that this wasn't true, would never be true, but I did feel so close to her, and she to me, even more so than had been the case with the Keating children. Perhaps because there was only one of her, we were able to form a single bond? Whatever the case, it made me wonder if I would ever get a second chance at pregnancy, if I would ever have my own child. Somehow, I believed I would not.

That thought made me sad. But what could I do? You get dealt certain hands in life, I believed, and I was playing mine.

As for the rest of the household, with the exception of the occasional coffee break with Lars Aquavit, who proved to be a funny man with dynamic stories to tell, I had few dealings with them. Mrs. Fairly was always cordial to me, of course, but so long as I was doing my job well with Annette we had little to discuss, save for her updates on when the master might be in residence, what might be required of me when he was.

Usually what was required was my presence.

This seemed a little...*excessive* to me, since hadn't Mrs. Fairly told me, at the very beginning, that once dinner was over he would usually want Annette to himself?

But it was his signature, or at least his signature copied

by someone else, on the payments I received. So if he wanted me to sit idly by, on the few nights he was in residence every couple of weeks, as he teasingly invited Annette to bring him up to date on what she'd been learning in the meantime, what grounds did I have for complaint?

Still, it impressed me as...*odd*. Why couldn't the two of them perform this ritual by themselves? Sometimes, it seemed to me that he wanted me there as a witness.

"See?" he seemed to be saying. "Look at me. I am a good father. You can't fault me for this."

I think the thing I minded most about those little sessions were always the last few minutes. Ambassador Rawlings would send Annette upstairs to brush her teeth and change into her nightgown—"See? I'm a good father! I tuck my child in!"—leaving me alone with him. Then, for the first time, he would speak to me directly, in that invasive way he had, and the questions were always personal.

"Are you happy here, Miss Bell?" he would ask.

"I enjoy Annette," I would answer each time.

"Are you happy?" he would insist.

Why did he always ask that? As though happy, even if once attained, could ever be a permanent thing.

"I like my work," I would say. "I have nothing to complain about."

"And is that the best one can hope for in life?"

I thought about that one for a longer period. "At times," I finally said.

"What are your dreams?" he asked. "Surely, you must have them."

"Not at the moment," I said. "May I be excused?"

"You say that as though I am keeping you here."

"Well, aren't you?"

He ignored that.

"You may not be happy yet," he said, "but I would certainly say that you are happier now than you were when I first met you."

I realized he was right: since I'd been in his household, I had become steadily happier. I even enjoyed our sparring and the challenges with which he presented me, even as they made me uncomfortable. Well, I certainly wasn't going to tell him *that*.

"Well, of course I'm happier now," I said.

"See?" he crowed his triumph.

"But that's only because, when I first met you, I had my head on a rock and my foot in a stirrup."

"You never give me anything, do you?"

"Am I supposed to?" I said. "Now, then, may I be excused?"

Not waiting for an answer, I'd disappear up to my bedroom, there to work on my novel.

And so it went.

But I'd be lying if I said that I wasn't flattered by his attentions, touched by his concern for my well-being. I was very flattered. Indeed, I would have been hurt if I felt them to be removed. But I also knew it was foolish of me to dwell too much on such things. After all, he was who he was. For my part, I knew my station: I was only the governess.

There was to be a house party.

"Ambassador Rawlings is having a few friends and associates come to stay for a while," Mrs. Fairly informed me.

"Here?" I was shocked. Sometimes, it seemed as though there was barely enough room to contain all of us here, let alone however many additional people he now wanted to add to the mix.

"Don't be ridiculous," she said. "Of course they will not all stay here. Where would we put them?"

Where, indeed.

"Oh, no," she answered herself. "Having them here wouldn't do at all. I'm sure they will be more comfortable in one of the finer hotels. It will only be for dinner and for entertainments that they will come here. And I'm sure they will want to go on lots of outings."

"Can you tell me," I asked, "who is to make up the party?"

"Oh, it's usually just embassy types," she said, "plus some of the people the master meets in his travels. But it is fun for a change, having the house fill up like that. The house gets all topsy-turvy. Annette just loves that."

A letter had come from my father.

At least once every few months, ever since I was little, these letters would come, but I had not received any since my arrival in Iceland. As I perched on my bed, Steinway beside me, I slid open the envelope, expecting the usual innocuous message: updates on how his work was going, vague and nonintrusive questions about my life.

Dearest Charlotte,
The new dig here is going splendidly. We've unearthed all sorts
of things we never expected to find and I have a new assis-
tant who's been a godsend. It is, of course, very hot here. Well,
you know: Africa!

I could picture the rueful grin as he wrote that, but I did not know, of course, never having been, never having been asked.

I'm sure it must be quite different from where you are: Iceland! I am still not sure what possessed you to go there and was rather surprised when Beatrice told me that that was where you had taken yourself off to. Another nannying job with another ambassador: are you sure that is wise?

No, I wasn't always sure that it was wise, but I was an adult now and made my own decisions. If I wanted to be unwise in those decisions, it was hardly his place any longer, particularly since he had made himself absent for most of my life, to rudely point that out.

I would like to come visit you there. There is something I'd like to share with you, but I prefer to do it in person. Do you think it might be possible for me to come at Christmastime? I'd be bringing a guest...

A guest?

Please let me know as soon as possible so that I can make the appropriate travel arrangements. You know, even in this day and age, going from Africa to Iceland is quite an ordeal!
Love,
Dad

I picked up Steinway, who purred, looked him in the eyes.

"Do you think at least my own father could be depended upon to remember I'm Jewish?" I asked.

"Meow!"

"Yes, I know all that. But don't you think it would have been more appropriate for him to suggest we spend Hanukkah together instead?"

"Meow!"

"You're right. I am being insensitive. Of course you'd give all the catnip in the world to see either of your parents again. But where will I put him? He can't stay here."

"Meow!"

"A hotel. Of course. Why didn't I think of that?"

"Meow!"

"Hey! That's not nice!"

"Meow!"

"Right. I guess I'm just a little touchy these days. Now, what do you make of all this stuff about him wanting to bring a guest?"

"Meow!"

"You're right again, of course. I do expect too much from you at times. You are, after all, only the cat."

"Meow!"

"Hey! Don't go away mad!"

But he was already out of my arms and out the door.

"Why does everyone always have to be so sensitive?" I muttered to myself.

Then I got out some stationery and wrote Dad back. Of course I'd love to see him—*at Hanukkah*—but of course he and his guest would need to stay at a hotel. My master—cross that out—*my boss* couldn't be expected to put up my family, but there were some lovely hotels in Reykjavik and I would include that information. I looked forward to seeing him again—it had been so long!

I was tempted to sign it *By Order of the Cat,* since Steinway had been the one to provide me with most of my wit and wisdom here, but I figured my father wouldn't get it and, anyway, the cat had been given far too much credit already.

Meow!

★ ★ ★

The house bustled with activity.

Oh, it wasn't as if there were any new faces around, except for extra staff put on for the express purpose of making sure that Ambassador Rawlings's guests, none of whom we saw, were not denied any comfort, but the place still bustled. Silverware was polished, formal china I'd never seen before suddenly appeared, the crystal globes on the chandelier over the dining-room table were washed repeatedly until their sparkle was almost scary.

And still the guests did not come.

"Why do they stay away?" Annette pouted, unable to concentrate on her lessons. She stared out the window at the view beyond, like a grizzled sea captain's wife impatiently awaiting his return.

"I'm sure they'll come here eventually," I tried to placate her. "Mrs. Fairly says they're just busy doing…other things right now."

That was indeed what Mrs. Fairly kept saying.

"The party is going to lunch!" she would say.

"The party is going to see a play tonight!"

"The party is going horseback riding!"

The first two sounded okay enough to me—I liked to eat, I liked theater—but as far as I was concerned, they could keep the last.

But still Annette moped.

"Oh," she sighed wistfully, "once they come, life will be so grand."

She sounded like someone much older, the kind of woman who says, "Oh, when I just lose these ten pounds, life will be perfect."

The only time we saw the master in those first few days his guests were here was when he came home to change his clothes, which was fairly often. Well, a person did need to wear different things for lunch, for riding, for nights filled with art. But he had hardly a word for anyone as he bounded through the house, unless it was to shout orders to Mrs. Fairly about some forthcoming need of his guests.

"Where's the tie to my tux?" he would call out.

"My riding boots need shining!"

"Where's my favorite blue blazer? I *still* can't find it!"

Well, I knew where *that* was. But I certainly wasn't going to tell him.

God, it was amazing to me, how the entire household was expected to spin according to the whims of one very demanding male. It seemed to me that the only time a household should ever revolve around one person's whims would be if that one person were me.

Well, that wasn't going to ever happen.

"Miss Bell," he asked pointedly, "have *you* seen my favorite blue blazer?"

He'd already asked everybody else, including Captain and Steinway. They all called him that now. Mrs. Fairly had told me that, before my arrival, they'd merely called him "Cat."

I didn't even bother looking up from my copy of the *International Herald Tribune*.

"What's Paraguay up to now?" I muttered, pretending to be absorbed in Paraguay's affairs.

"I *asked*," he said, "have you—"

"And I heard you," I said, still not looking up, "but I'm

your daughter's governess, not your valet. How should I know where your blue blazer is? Do you think I'm hiding it in the bottom of my closet?"

I don't know what I would have said if, given the mood he was in, he'd demanded, "Well, are you?" But, thankfully, he didn't do that. Rather, he just turned sharply on his heel and left the room to go hound Mrs. Fairly again, saying something about good help being hard to find.

"Not if you don't expect them to do jobs you never hired them for in the first place!" I yelled after him.

Then, the day Annette had been so waiting for finally arrived.

"They're going to be *here* tonight!" Mrs. Fairly crowed.

God, she sounded like a schoolgirl who'd just learned that some minor rock star had answered her plea to take her to the junior-high dance and while he couldn't do that, he'd stopped by her house and pinned a corsage on her, singing a special rendition of one of his minor hits just for her before jetting off to Gstaad.

"That's great," I said, trying to force enthusiasm into my voice. "I'll just eat dinner early with Annette and disappear afterward. I haven't seen Britta and Gina in a long time. Perhaps I'll—"

"Oh, no!" she interrupted me, clearly horrified. "That won't do at all."

"Not do?"

"No. The master has left explicit instructions—while he doesn't expect you and Annette to join them for dinner—he doesn't think Annette would like sitting still for such a long period of time—he most definitely expects you to

bring her downstairs to meet his guests and for the entertainments afterward."

"But why do *I* need to bring her down?" I couldn't stop
from whining. "Surely she can walk downstairs by herself.
I've seen her do it before. She's a very capable little girl."

"Who cares about the *why?*" For once, she was out of patience with me. "He pays our wages. If he wants you to
bring her downstairs, then you will. Maybe he's worried
she'll be bored without you there. Or maybe he's worried
she'd be too much underfoot without you there. It doesn't
matter why. Just do it."

I moved to leave.

"And be sure to wear your best dress!" she shouted after
me. Suddenly, it seemed as though everyone was always
shouting at everyone else as they were about to leave rooms.

I turned back.

"My best dress?"

"Yes. The party will be very formal and just because
you're not to be sitting with them at dinner, it doesn't mean
that you should wear one of those sweater outfits you're forever wearing."

Best dress?

The words mocked me as, that evening, preparing to go
down, I stared dismally at my wardrobe. I only had one dress:
the one I'd bought at the mall and worn downstairs the first
night I met Edgar Rawlings. I supposed I'd thought it nice
enough when I bought it, but it certainly wouldn't qualify
as a winner of "best" anything, unless I was going to a con-
vention of grammar-school teachers, not when I was sure
that all the other guests would be resplendent in all kinds

of finery. I sighed, supposing further that I could have asked Mrs. Fairly that afternoon to watch Annette for an hour—it wasn't like we were getting any schoolwork done anyway—so that I could go out and buy something more impressive. I had hardly spent any of my wages since coming here and could certainly afford it. But, I supposed finally, taking the now-detested garment from the hanger, a perverse part of my personality must have felt Edgar Rawlings and his guests should be forced to take me as I was. I was merely the governess. There was no point in trying to dress myself as a silk purse.

God, I thought, surveying the effect in the full-length mirror. *What had I been thinking when I bought this thing? I looked like old photos of Marie Osmond.* Sigh. Another fashion faux pas.

Annette clearly had no similar doubts about her own fashion sense, I saw clearly when we met at the top of the long flight of stairs. Earlier, she'd told me quite insistently that she didn't want any help getting ready for "the big evening," as she called it.

"I know exactly what I want to wear!" she'd said. "I do not need your help tonight!"

How quickly they grow up.

Looking at her now, I had to say that what she had achieved amounted more to a well-intentioned effort than a resounding success. Funny, the longer I knew Annette, the more I felt we were somehow kindred spirits despite her dainty ways.

She had on a party dress in purple—of course—with frilly sleeves and hem. The bows placed at intervals along her pigtails, which she'd done herself and which were not quite, um, tight, were velvet in orange and teal and black, the latter of which I assumed to be a stab at precocious sophistication. Her frilled white socks with black patent-leather shoes were okay enough, but she'd done her own nails, I presumed using some of the polish that her father had once upon a time given her. The color chosen was more like what you might expect on a Paris hooker, being a shade close to pomegranate, and she'd been something less than accurate in her enthusiastic application of it, getting more on her skin than on her tiny nails.

"You look...*very* pretty, Miss Bell," she said.

Well, at least her manners were good.

"Thank you." I gave a slight curtsy.

"But what about me?" Her lip almost quivered. "How do *I* look?"

We were two of a kind. I was one step away from saying something jokey about how awful we looked, how out of place we would be in our two-of-a-kindness, which was true.

But then I saw how important this was to her. What else was there for me to do? I took her hand.

"There won't be another woman there tonight—" I smiled "—who looks even remotely like you. You are an original, Annette."

She liked that.

The music coming from downstairs was classical.

Great, I thought. *This will be one stuffy evening.*

I thought about how all those smart people would receive us. I had to admit that I was curious about Ambassador Rawlings's guests. I wanted to see, I just didn't necessarily want to be seen.

"Let's just sit here for a while," I suggested, pulling Annette down on the top step beside me, "and prepare for our entrance."

Wouldn't it be better to just sit down on the top step and listen to everyone else having a good time?

I was about to suggest this when Annette, who'd been impatiently tapping her pretty little foot to something Beethoveny beside me, snatched her hand away and, rising, bolted down the stairs.

"Annette!" I called, racing down after her.

Never mind my earlier thoughts of us being two of a kind. Where I wanted to remain a wallflower for as long as possible, she wanted to be the centerpiece in the vase.

"Annette!" I screamed a little quieter, not wanting to be overheard sounding like a fishwife over the sounds of the increasingly loud music as I raced behind her down the hallway to the library, where all the activity was.

I entered just on her heels.

I entered just in time to run smack-dab into a waiter, entering from the opposite direction and bearing a tray of what once must have been half-filled glasses of red wine.

Half-filled, before the wine got all over my white dress, the glasses smashing against the library's solid wood floor, the rugs having been rolled up, the furniture pushed back to allow room for dancing.

Everything except for the music—dancing, conversation—came to a crashing halt at our loud entrance. Even the tall blond woman who had obviously been dancing in the ambassador's arms, her scarlet silk evening gown making a strong fashion statement against his tux, stopped talking.

But only for a moment. Then:

"I see what you meant about your daughter's governess being…not the usual governess," she said in an icy Icelandic accent. "Can't she do a better job at keeping the little girl controlled?"

I drew back at the offense to me, at the offense to Annette—Annette was a very good child, if a bit exuberant at times—all the while pushing back that unexpected twinge I felt at seeing her in the ambassador's arms.

I steeled myself for his reproach. He would undoubtedly tell me to watch over Annette better. He would undoubtedly tell me to change my soiled dress, which I refused to look down at, sure that I must look like the victim of a drive-by shooting, although I could feel the stickiness of the wine seeping through against my skin.

But he surprised me.

"What a delightful entrance!" he roared with laughter. "I was beginning to worry we might get drunk if we all drank much more. But now you, Miss Bell, have managed to expertly and inventively save us from ourselves."

The icy blonde did not look pleased at his pleasure.

"Edgar," she pouted, "you promised me a dance and we still haven't completed this one."

"Oh?" He looked unaccountably surprised to see her, still there in his arms. Then he smiled. "Of course, my dear."

I grabbed Annette's hand, trying not to meet the eyes of any of those assembled, and gently tugged her toward one of the sofas that had been pushed up against the walls.

"Come," I whispered.

"But I want to meet everybody!" she resisted.

I tugged harder. "Come," I said again. "You must wait until your father is ready to introduce you." Then, looking back at the happily dancing couple, muttering under my breath, I added, "If he ever even notices us again."

Once we were seated on the velvet sofa, Annette stopped squirming. I supposed that now, since she could observe everybody herself, it wasn't half so frustrating as when she could not. For myself, as I looked round at all the men in their tuxes and the perfectly coiffed ladies in their couture dresses, I tried to remain as unobtrusive as possible, wishing I could disappear, counting off the seconds in my head in the hopes that this monotonous activity would bring me closer to the time when we could politely leave or the ambassador deemed it time for Annette to go off to bed.

Back when I had lived in Buster Keating's household, I had longed for the day when I would be invited to an embassy party, imagining that when that day came it would be because I was attending as his wife; or, at the very least, openly as his companion. Well, now I was finally at an embassy party and all I wanted to do was leave it.

But not Annette.

"Do you know who any of these people are, Miss Bell?" she asked, bouncing on the seat beside me, eyes all aglow.

"How should I?" I asked with more terseness than I was accustomed to using when dealing with her. "Do you?" I countered.

"No, but I wish I did." She scanned the room. "Well, except for that man over there." She pointed.

Automatically, gently, I pressed her pointing finger downward.

"Not polite," I said. Then curiosity got the better of me. "Which man?"

"That one over there," she tried to whisper, this time pointing with her chin, but with her exuberant way of speaking, it came out more like a mini-shout. This was okay since general conversation had long since resumed and we were relatively far from the main action. "The one who is not dressed like anybody else."

I saw who she meant. He was standing a little apart from the rest and looked to be in his early forties, medium height, medium build, brown hair, brown eyes, dressed in a cheap suit that made him look like a fed on a pension. Why hadn't I noticed him before? I wondered. Then I realized that his sore-thumbness hadn't been apparent because he was so innocuous, he simply blended into the background, like a waiter who'd forgotten his uniform or something.

Then Annette looked from the man to me.

"He looks like he could be your date," she decided.

"Gee, thanks," I said.

The man in question must have had X-ray hearing, or been bored senseless, because I suddenly saw that he was making a beeline for us.

Oh no! I thought. *I'm not going to actually have to talk to somebody, am I?*

"What are you two fine ladies doing over here all by your lonesomes?" he asked, surprising me with his American accent.

How painful—he wanted to make awkward small talk with us!

"Miss Bell will not let me generally mingle, Mr. Miller," Annette sniffed. "And I would so like to mingle."

"I've heard a lot about the indomitable Miss Bell." The man smiled.

"You have?"

"Yes, Edgar has spoken of you, if not often—" he paused "—then energetically."

"He has? What has he said?"

He suddenly appeared reticent. "Only that Annette is thriving under your care." He paused again, as though trying to think. "Oh, and that you saved his life."

"He told you *that?*"

"Well—" he smiled ruefully "—he did say that he could have burned to death because you used a toothbrush glass instead of something more substantial, but he was damn grateful."

I looked sharply at Annette, concerned that she might be upset at first learning of the danger her father had been in and concerned she'd pick up bad words from this crass man that I'd later somehow get blamed for, but I saw that I might not have bothered. He, in all his boring lack of finery, was of no interest to her; her eyes were glued on all the peacocks and hens in the room.

"I'm Robert Miller," he said, offering his hand.

"Mr. Miller," I asked, "tell me, how do you know the ambassador?"

"Why, you could say he works for me," he said.

"Really?" I was surprised. "I didn't think ambassadors worked for anybody, unless of course the president. You must be joking."

"If you like," he said indulgently. "But ambassadors do generally work for the people, so I guess you could say he works for me. Come to that, he works for you, too."

Now, *there* was a thought I'd never had before. I liked that thought.

"Mr. Miller always knows who everybody is," Annette suddenly interrupted. "Tell us who everybody is, please."

But as he went through the list of people before us, it was of far more interest to Annette than it was to me. I found myself, curiously, only interested in learning the identity of one person there.

"Bebe Iversdottir," he said of the Icelandic beauty who was now seated at the piano, her red skirts spread about her on the bench as she prepared to play for the ambassador.

Bestowing a possessive look upon him, she lowered her fingers to the keys, proceeding to whip off some impressive classical piece with the same ease with which I put on my socks. She smiled that possessive smile throughout and I felt a sharp pain inside when I saw him smiling back at her. Apparently, he did not mind being possessed.

"Who is she?" I finally asked.

"The daughter of a dignitary," said Robert Miller. "They make quite a lovely couple, don't they?"

I wondered that Annette did not seem to mind seeing her father with this woman. And then I wondered at my own reaction. Surely I could never compete with a woman like that. Bebe Iversdottir was everything I wasn't. Cool. Self-assured. Poised. Beautiful.

It made my heart hurt to look at them.

Oh, well, I told myself. *It's probably indigestion.*

I saw that Annette was so enraptured by what she was looking at, she was no longer paying attention to what must seem to her our boring adult conversation.

As Bebe's fingers moved into a round of Broadway show

tunes, perhaps in tribute to her American host, I turned to Robert.

"Should they really be doing this so…openly?" I asked.

"Doing what?" he asked.

"This public display of obvious affection," I said.

"Are you jealous, Miss Bell?"

"No, of course not," I lied to him, lied to myself.

Now that the moment was here, and I could ask someone about the ambassador's wife, I couldn't bring myself to do it.

"I guess I just think a man in his position should be more careful," I finally said. "Plus, I don't think it would do him any harm to consider how this might be affecting Annette."

Robert looked down at the charge at my side: she was clapping her hands in time to some song from Bob Fosse's *All that Jazz* and laughing with glee.

"Isn't Miss Iversdottir the most amazingly beautiful creature you've ever seen?" she asked.

"Don't look now," Robert leaned down to whisper, "but I don't think Annette is traumatized by this."

"Well," I said, "maybe that's because small children don't always know what they're seeing when they look at something."

"And you're sure you do?" he countered.

I shrugged. "I see an ambassador behaving indiscreetly with one of his guests," I said.

"I see a man who often works far too hard having just a little bit of fun for once in his life," he said.

"Then we'll have to just agree to disagree."

"You look like you could use a bit of fun for a change too, Miss Bell," he said. "How about a dance?"

"Oh, no," I started to protest, already picturing the decidedly *un*fashionable statement we would make: he in his cheap fed suit, me in my Sunday Bloody Sunday dress.

He wouldn't be deterred, though.

"Come on—" he tugged a little harder "—Edgar won't mind."

I was about to protest that, as well—what was it to me whether Edgar minded what I did or not?—but he already had one hand at the base of my spine, taking my hand in his other. And before I could think to say anything else, my feet remembered all sorts of moves they hadn't been encouraged to use in a long time.

"You can really dance, Miss Bell!" His surprise was evident.

"She really can," I heard the familiar ironic voice say behind me.

I turned in Robert's arms to find Ambassador Rawlings standing there. Then he reached over and tapped Robert Miller on the shoulder.

"May I cut in?" he asked.

"Well…" The other man looked reluctant to give me up. "I suppose the etiquette of this sort of thing dictates that I say yes, doesn't it?"

"It does."

"Well, I suppose I could always ask her again later." Robert started to hand me over.

"Hey," I said, "don't I get any say in the matter?"

Ambassador Rawlings placed his hand at the small of my back, where Robert's hand had been a moment before, and looked down at me.

"No," he said, "you don't."

As we began to move, I tried to ignore how good it felt to have his hand there, how different the feelings were in me than when I'd danced with the other man. Shouldn't an employee, particularly a governess, feel awkward about dancing with her boss?

Suddenly, I felt so awkward, had talked myself into it really, that I stepped on his toe.

"Ouch!" he couldn't help saying.

"Sorry," I said.

"It's all right," he said. "Just try to leave the other intact so I can at least hop around."

"Sorry," I said again, wishing myself elsewhere.

"What happened?" he asked with surprising gentleness. "A minute ago, you were practically dancing like Julie Andrews."

"I must have gotten distracted," I said.

We danced for a moment in silence and I managed to get my rhythm back.

"There!" he said finally. "You're doing it again. Wherever did you learn to dance so well?"

I explained how when I was younger, my aunt insisted on lessons.

"She said I was such a klutz, I might learn some grace that way."

"You certainly are graceful," he observed.

"Only when I dance," I said, ruefully looking down at the stain on my dress. "The rest of the time, I'm still me."

The music stopped so abruptly that we were still moving for a moment afterward, until stopping abruptly ourselves. It was as though we, the ambassador and I, had been an old-fashioned record spinning on a turntable and someone had decided they didn't like the tune, picking up the needle and dragging it across the vinyl.

We were just disengaging when Bebe Iversdottir came up beside us.

She smiled sweetly at the ambassador, but there was a lot of ice there.

"I did not play so that you could dance with another woman," she said, still smiling all the while as though she was just teasing, when it was clear to me at least that she wasn't.

"I'm sorry, my dear," he said, taking the hand she held out. "I didn't mean to make you feel neglected."

Odd, he was holding her hand but he was still looking at me.

"It's okay," I said awkwardly, since no one had said anything that should have elicited that response from me. "I should be taking Annette upstairs soon anyway."

"Yes," agreed Bebe. "That sounds like an excellent idea."

I was halfway back to Annette when I heard her say to him, "I'm sure Annette's governess is adequate, if a bit shoddy in appearance, but wouldn't your daughter be better off going to boarding school? Myself, I went to a fine place in Switzerland from an early age. If you'd like, I can recommend…"

I didn't stay to hear any more from her, to hear an answer from him.

"Come on, Annette," I said. "It's time both of us went to bed."

"But I was hoping to meet Miss Bebe personally! I am sure she would like me very much!"

"I'm sure that's true," I said, not believing it for a second. What kind of cold woman would suggest sending a little girl to live somewhere that was several hours by plane away from her father? I knew what it was like to be separated, at such a young age, from my father, to feel alone in a world without parents. No matter what else might be right, the wrongness of that had skewed my entire childhood.

"But," I told Annette, "it looks like your father and…Miss Bebe are dancing again, so perhaps it's best you meet her another time."

As I looked back at the happy couple, I tried to tell myself it didn't bother me at all.

Upstairs, it seemed to take forever to get Annette settled in for the night. She kept coming up with excuses—she needed to brush her teeth a second time, she needed a glass of water, she needed to pee—to delay having me turn out the light. But I saw it for what it was: she wanted to relive what she saw as the grandeur and romance of the evening and I was the only person available with whom to do so.

"Have you ever seen such beautiful people?" she bubbled.

"They were an attractive crowd," I admitted, pulling the blankets up over her.

"And Miss Bebe was the most attractive of all!" she said.

I tucked the blanket up under her chin, thought about what she'd said.

"I suppose that's true," I said.

"I wonder what kind of mother she would make," Annette asked dreamily.

A positively horrid one, I wanted to say. *She'd make the Evil Stepmother look like Snow White.*

Out loud, I said, "Who can ever guess what kind of mother a woman would make? Sometimes, people surprise you."

"Papa really enjoyed dancing with you," she said out of the blue.

I was caught off guard.

"Do you really think so?" I couldn't stop myself from asking.

"Oh, yes. You would have seen his face if you had not had your own turned down almost the whole time. He was smiling bigger than I'd ever seen him smile before."

That made me feel unaccountably happy, a feeling I quickly shoved aside.

"Oh," I said, "he was probably overcompensating, trying not to let the pain show of me stepping on his feet. I'm sure he was happier dancing with Miss Bebe."

"It's hard to say," she said, taking the matter quite seriously. "He did seem to smile a lot with her, too."

"Well," I said, kissing her on the forehead, "if you don't go to sleep soon, you'll be too tired to do any smiling yourself tomorrow."

"Good night, Miss Bell," she said, at last giving in to a yawn as she rolled over onto her side, tucked her little hands under the pillow. "Even if you are not as glamorous as Miss Bebe, I love you all the same."

She was so sweet, so dear to me. I hated to think I might not one day be with her, hated to think of Ambassador Rawlings succumbing to Bebe's suggestion to send her away.

"I love you, too," I said softly, turning out the light. "Sweet dreams."

Safe at last in my own room, I removed my dress and tossed it in the trash basket; those wine stains would never come out. Then I prepared for bed, brushed my teeth, put on my white gown.

But once I was beneath the sheets, sleep wouldn't come. I kept replaying the events of the evening, a different version than Annette's, the good and the bad. And if that weren't enough, the sound of loud music and increasingly boisterous merrymaking from down below would have kept me awake. Perhaps Annette could sleep through anything, including a fire, but I couldn't. Honestly, didn't these selfish people downstairs think of anyone but themselves?

I punched my pillow, tossed, turned. After counting enough sheep to fill both Australia and Argentina, I at last slept.

But my sleep was fitful.

First I dreamed that I was back with Buster Keating, but then he was replaced by Ambassador Rawlings. No sooner did I find myself in his arms than I was replaced in my own dream by Bebe Iversdottir, who was no longer wearing her red dress, but rather had on a long white Victorian wedding gown. I stood by Annette in the dream, throwing rice—the one thing that told my relieved unconscious mind that it was a dream, since I'd never throw rice in real life because of what it does to birds and all. I held Annette's hand as we waved the happy couple off, tears streaming down my face, not of joy, but of sadness.

I woke abruptly to the feel of wet tears streaming down my cheeks and a gentle tapping at my door. That tapping, growing more insistent, was the only sound in the now-quiet house.

"Yes?" I called, wiping at the tears.

The handle turned and then Ambassador Rawlings was in the room.

I saw that the tie of his tux had been undone, the shirt collar opened. His hair was disheveled and a scent of alcohol entered the room with him. I suppose that for the first time since I knew him, I could see that he was a bit drunk.

"As I came up the stairs," he said, "I thought I heard someone crying."

"Perhaps it was the madwoman," I suggested, trying to make a joke of it.

"No—" he shook his head in earnest "—I could have sworn it was coming from in here."

"Then you were mistaken," I said, hoping the room was dark enough that he wouldn't see any remnant tears on my cheeks.

"Oh," he said, sitting on the edge of my bed as though I were Annette and he were, well, me, "then I am relieved."

"Relieved, sir?"

"Of course. Do you imagine that I wish you unhappy, Charlotte?"

I figured he must be very drunk to call me Charlotte again.

"No, of course not," I said. "But I also wouldn't imagine you give my happiness any thought one way or another." It didn't matter that he asked me about it every week; I hadn't believed his queries about my happiness were sincere.

"Then you must think me a very hard man."

"Hard?" I echoed him again. "Not at all. I merely think you're my employer."

"Meaning?"

"Why should my happiness matter to you in the slightest, so long as I do my job well enough?"

"I see," he said, and then he just sat there for a moment.

His proximity was making me uncomfortable.

"Is there anything else, sir?" I asked

Now it was his turn to echo me. "Anything else?" he asked.

"Yes," I said. "Anything else. Now that you know that whatever sound you heard was not me crying, is there anything else?"

"No," he said, rising slowly and heading for the door, "I suppose not." Then he turned. "Did you enjoy yourself this evening?"

"I liked seeing Annette so happy," I answered truthfully. I always liked seeing Annette happy.

"Yes, of course," he said, "as do I. But did you enjoy dancing...with me?"

I couldn't lie.

"Yes," I said quietly.

"Thank you," he said. "Good night, Miss Bell."

"Ambassador?"

"Yes?"

"You're not really going to send Annette away to boarding school, are you?"

"I'm certainly not going to do it tonight," he said.

"Nor tomorrow?"

"Nor tomorrow, either. Sweet dreams, Miss Bell."

"Good night, sir."

No sooner had he closed the door than I heard that eerie

laugh, that awful sound I hadn't heard in a long time. To me, it sounded as though someone was objecting to the closeness we had shared for a moment there.

chapter 9

Normally, if you get disturbed in mid-dream and want to return to it, it's impossible to do so. No matter how you try to retrieve the wonder, it evades you, your subconscious mocking you as if to say, *You want it so badly? Well, ha! I won't give it to you!* But have a screaming nightmare, as I'd had many over the years—the usual one where I'm too late to take an important final exam or the more troubling one in which my own father has a gun and is trying to kill me—and each time you try to raise yourself to consciousness in order to escape the horror, just as soon as you close your eyes again the same awful images come rushing back.

And so it had been the night before after Ambassador Rawlings had left me. No sooner did I close my eyes than the dreadful picture came back of Bebe Iversdottir as his grinning bride.

Abandoning sleep at dawn, I rejected the images. There had been real closeness between him and me the evening before, had there not? I refused to let myself imagine what this might mean, refused to let myself dwell on what my own feelings might be, but a hopeful feeling awoke in me coincident with my rising, even as that hope was at war with a vague uneasiness that my haunted dreams of the night before must surely function as an ill omen.

Feeling more upbeat than I had in a long time, I hummed as I prepared for the day, taking more time than usual with my dress. When I at last went down to breakfast, it was with the optimistic expectation that I would see him there. After the late night he'd had, surely he would be taking it at a slower pace this morning. How would he speak to me? I wondered. Would I be able to see evidence of the affection I'd felt between us?

But when I got to the table, there was only Mrs. Fairly and Annette, dining on pancakes and juice, and Lars Aquavit, finishing a last cup of coffee.

"Where's Ambassador Rawlings?" I couldn't stop myself from asking.

"What's it to you?" Mrs. Fairly asked with unusual tartness.

But then I noticed the bags under her eyes. Despite that she was usually a sound sleeper, and like Annette could sleep through a fire, the noise from downstairs on the previous evening must have kept her awake.

"I was only curious," I said, "that's all."

"Gone already," Lars Aquavit said, taking another sip of his coffee. "I drove him and Miss Iversdottir to the airport earlier. They wanted to catch a plane to the Westman Islands."

"The Westman Islands?" I echoed dumbly.

"Yes," he said. "Miss Iversdottir said she wanted to do some rock-climbing there and the ambassador was only too happy to accompany her."

How...outdoorsy of her, I thought. I hoped that, with the hangovers they must surely have, they didn't fall to their deaths. Or at least I hoped one of them wouldn't.

"Does that not sound romantic and adventurous?" Annette enthused.

I admitted that it did, thinking all the while that no one would ever catch me climbing rocks. I hate heights. Have I mentioned that already?

"They'll be back this evening?" I asked.

"Oh, no," Mrs. Fairly spoke the words as though I were being incredibly silly. "They won't be back for at least a few days."

"I see," I said. "Annette, as soon as you finish your breakfast, we really should get down to work. What with all of the silly fuss and bother here the last few days, there's been precious little time to get anything serious accomplished."

"Aren't you going to eat anything?" Lars Aquavit asked.

"I'm not hungry this morning," I said.

Despite what I'd said to Annette about the need to get serious, I found myself unable to concentrate once we had her workbooks arranged on the table before us. Honestly, who cared if the letter S was made the way it was supposed to be or if it was a little backward? I could still read what she was trying to write: Bebe Iversdottir Rawlings.

"Why don't you get out your art things," I suggested.

"But you don't usually let me paint until I have finished my lessons," she objected.

"What," I said, feeling unaccountably testy, "you're suddenly a stickler for rules? You'd rather work on your letters than draw a picture of, oh, I don't know, a cow?"

"I'll take the cow, please." She smiled.

"That's what I thought."

Once I had her squared away, enough black and white acrylics squeezed onto the palette, plus a dab of pink for the nose, her smock on, I excused myself to make a phone call.

I needed to talk to somebody, so I decided to call Gina.

"What a grand surprise!" she said, answering her work phone.

"Can you talk?" I asked. "You won't get in trouble with anybody there?"

"Trouble?" My question clearly puzzled her. "Oh, no. I was just retranslating a book by Czeslaw Milosz. In English, you would call it *The Captive Mind.* You know, it really is amazing, how much more you understand of totalitarianism when you translate this kind of thing repeatedly."

"I'll bet," I said, not really sure what I was agreeing with. "But I thought you worked on ancient texts?"

"Yes, but every now and then we get to play around a bit."

"Well, it still sounds like pretty serious work. I suppose you must be anxious to get back to it."

"A bit," she confessed. "I was just getting to the exciting part."

I was sure it would be a mistake for me to ask, so I didn't.

"That's okay," I said. "I just wanted to talk about some silly stuff that's been going on over here in the ambassador's house."

"Ooh!" she shouted. Then, in a hushed whisper that still somehow shouted her enthusiasm, "Political gossip!"

"Well, I don't know how political it is. And, anyway, I know you have to get back to—"

"Why don't you come to dinner tonight," she suggested.

"But won't I be intruding on your family?" I asked.

"What family?" she said. Then, "Oh. You must be thinking of Britta. She's the one who still lives at home. I'm the one who lives by herself with a dog and three cats."

"Of course," I said, as if I'd known all along. "But wait a second—I thought they still lived with your family."

"They took pity and gave the pets to me, but not the sisters. So, you see," she said, "you'd be doing me a favor. This way, I won't have to dine alone. Well, except for the dog and three cats."

I recalled her saying, on the first night we'd met, that living alone could be too much like living without people.

"Glad I can be of service, then," I said.

Lars Aquavit offered to drive me, but I'd told him I wanted to walk. The address Gina had given me didn't look too far away on the map.

But as I trudged through the cold night, hostess gift of a bottle of wine in hand, I regretted my impulsiveness. Who was I trying to be, outdoorsy Bebe Iversdottir?

"Fucking cold Iceland," I muttered to myself as I trudged. "Can't somebody do something about this?"

"Your face is so red!" Gina observed, opening the door for me.

"That's because it's freezing cold outside!" I said, not wanting to remove my head scarf, not ever.

"It is?" she asked.

"Oh…never mind."

Sullenly, I relinquished the scarf. She was never going to understand. We were at a cultural divide.

Gina was thrilled when she saw the wine.

"Wonderful!" she said. "We can bind some more!"

"Do you mean bond?"

As she went to open the bottle and get glasses, I took in my surroundings. They were charming, if a little sterile. The living room was painted a green that I instantly free-associated with hospital rooms, and my hand rose involuntarily to my absent tonsils. But that was made up for by the sweetness of the selection of items in the vitrine: tiny glass animals making up their own three-tiered menagerie. Who would have guessed Gina could be so wistfully girlish? On the walls, there were several photographs, all in matching teak frames. I looked at them more closely: everyone in the pictures was blond, not a dark head in sight. I realized they were all members of Gina's family; not looking just generally like Icelanders, they looked specifically like her. As she reentered the room, I was studying a particular one in which she looked to be about half the age she was now, with two much older women beside her.

"Your aunts?" I asked.

"My sisters," she laughed, handing me a glass. "Lina is ten years older than me and Nina is twelve years older. My parents always said I was a delayed reaction. What about you, do you have sisters?"

I explained how I'd grown up in a household with my three younger cousins and how I'd never felt like siblings with them.

"Well, you might not be missing much," she said.

"But I thought you missed them," I said.

"Oh, I do, but the fighting used to make me crazy."

"Fighting?"

"Oh, yes. They used to fight like crazy. And not just verbal, but physical, too."

"They hit you?"

"Oh, never. I was too small. But they were always hitting each other and kicking, still do sometimes. Why, I remember one time, when Lina was breast-feeding her first baby—" she indicated a picture of one of the older girls with a tiny Icelander in her arms "—Nina said something to really piss her off."

"So what happened?"

She giggled. "Lina pulled out her other breast and sprayed Nina with milk."

"She didn't!" I wasn't sure if I was amused or horrified.

"Oh, yes…" She giggled some more. "Then she sprayed all the clothes in Nina's wardrobe—the family still laughs about it!"

"I'll bet," I said.

"Women," she said, at last controlling herself. "Put too many of them under one roof, and all hell breaks loose."

As she spoke, for the first time I saw the three gray kittens curled up as a single mass on the beige sofa. They were girl kittens. I could tell from the way they were licking each other's genitals as the rather large dog looked on. I didn't even want to think about it.

"I think I see what you mean," I said.

She brought out appetizers and then dinner—something vaguely fishy that I longed to decline, but knew etiquette dictated I must eat—and we talked about safe subjects, like deconstructing translations of ancient texts.

I tried to pretend that I didn't mind the fact that the fish still had its head attached to its body, and I'm fairly certain I failed miserably, but at least Gina didn't seem to notice. She was too busy getting a buzz off the wine and digging into her own fish head.

"So," she said, her face taking on an expression of sheer pleasure as she put the first bite of flaky white flesh into her mouth. "You wanted to discuss the new doings in Ambassador Rawlings's house? You have some good gossip for me?"

I filled her in on everything since the last time I'd seen her: the house party, the advent of Bebe Iversdottir, the dance, the talk, the dream, the nightmare. And how Ambassador Rawlings had now gone off with Bebe to the Westman Islands.

Gina dropped her fork in the fish's belly.

"But wait a second," she said, eyes wide, "what about his wife?"

"That's what I'm wondering, too," I said. "If there's a Mrs. Rawlings, and he's a public figure, how can he just go off with this other woman? Doesn't he care what people think?"

She looked at me closely, then her eyes widened.

"Oh my God!" she said. "Charlotte!"

"What?" I asked, concerned.

"You are in love with him."

"What?" I shouted so loud, my uneaten fish jumped on the plate. Hey, wasn't that thing supposed to be dead?

"You're out of your tiny Icelandic mind!" I screamed.

"Perhaps," she laughed, "but not over this. Why else would you be so concerned with Ambassador Rawlings's private affairs if you weren't in love with him?"

"I can think of a lot of reasons."

"Oh?" She crossed her arms. "And they are?"

"I'm concerned about Annette. I'm worried how she'll take it."

"From everything you tell me about Annette," she spoke reasonably, "she is a remarkably well-adjusted and happy child."

"Okay, then I'm worried about his reputation," I said.

"His reputation doesn't appear to be suffering," she said. "Did you see other people at the party running to get away from him?"

I admitted that I had not.

"Fine," I finally said. "It's because I'm an American. We take a prurient interest in these kinds of things."

"Now, *that* I believe," she said.

"See?"

"But I don't believe for a second that it's the reason you are so obsessed with his private affairs."

"'His private affairs,'" I echoed. "You keep using that phrase. Could you stop saying that?"

"See?" Her "see" was a lot more triumphant than mine had been just a few short seconds ago. "None of this would bother you if you were not yourself in love with him."

"How about we go back to saying this is because I'm worried about Annette?" I suggested.

"You can view it your way, if you want to—" she smiled knowingly "—but please allow me to view it mine."

"But you don't understand," I spoke with some urgency. "If somehow it turns out that Ambassador Rawlings can marry Bebe Iversdottir, it will be the worst thing in the world for Annette."

"How so?" she asked.

"Because that ice princess wants to send Annette away to Switzerland to boarding school!"

"Oh no!"

"Then you agree that would be awful?"

"Absolutely! No child should be separated from her parents at such a young age." Then she stopped herself, looked at me more closely. "That's what happened to you, was it not?"

"It was," I said.

"And you hated it?"

"Still hate it whenever I think about it."

"Then you must do whatever it takes to stop this."

"But how?" I practically whined. "What am I supposed to do? Sure, he told me he wouldn't send Annette away, yet, but who knows what Bebe might get him to do later? I can't just tell Ambassador Rawlings what to do. He'd never listen to me—I'm only the governess!"

"Of course that's true, but you're getting ahead of yourself. The first thing you need to do," she counseled, "is find out if there is in fact a Mrs. Rawlings and what the status of their relationship is. If there's still a Mrs. Rawlings somewhere then it's entirely possible that whatever Bebe Iversdottir's nefarious plans concerning Annette are, they will fail."

"How do you figure?"

"If they are not divorced, maybe it's because he doesn't want to be."

Ouch! That hurt almost as much as thinking of him with Bebe.

"If they are," Gina went on, "then perhaps the threat of a new woman moving in would be enough incentive for Mrs. Rawlings to take on a larger role in Annette's life, preventing her from becoming a boarding-school orphan."

"I think I see what you mean," I said.

"The important thing," Gina said, "is to gather as much information as you can, so you know what you're up against. Once you do that, you'll be able to stand on a leg."

"Thanks for the help."

"Honestly," she said, looking stunned, "I cannot believe you have forgotten all about Nancy Drew! What do you think she would do in your situation?" She didn't wait for me to answer. "She would gather and assemble all the *facts*," she said. "Nancy wouldn't sit on her thumbs, twiddling them while Rome burned. She wouldn't let her imagination race helter-skelter all over the place."

Actually, I seemed to recall Nancy having quite a big imagination. It was what enabled her to take seemingly innocuous events, like a truck rushing by a little too quickly, and extrapolate it into, "Gadzooks! There must be a den of art thieves around here!" Of course, she was always right.

When I pointed this out to Gina, she had a ready answer for this too.

"Yes," she said, "Nancy does have quite an imagination, but it always takes her places. And once that imagination starts to take off, she immediately starts looking for facts and clues. That is what you must do, too."

I could see that she was right.

Then she looked at me with real sorrow in her eyes.

"I'm so sorry, Charlotte," she said. "You would undoubtedly be better off if you had not fallen in love with him."

"I'm not—"

"As you Americans are so fond of saying, bullshit."

"Hey!"

"Oh, that's right, I forgot—" she winked "—this is all about Annette."

The bracing walk back to the embassy should have killed any residual wine buzz, but we'd drunk so much after dinner, arguing all the while—"You are *so* in love with him!" "I am *not* in love with him!"—that I still felt pretty intoxicated as I let myself in the door. We'd argued so strenuously, it occurred to me ruefully that it was a good thing Gina wasn't one of her lactating sisters.

If the bracing walk didn't kill the wine buzz, the wine buzz should have made me drowsy enough to go right to sleep, but this proved not to be the case. My mind was so unquiet as I moved through the quiet household that I knew I'd have to do something first to tire myself out.

Then I had a brilliant idea. Gina's advice came back to me and I realized there was no time like the present.

Hey, kids? Want to put on a little drunken detection show?

Feeling like the queen of stealth—"Hee, hee," I couldn't help giggling to myself—I removed my boots, tossed my wet outdoor things in the general direction of the coatrack.

I missed.

Oh, well. Who said I needed great aim to find information? I'd only need great aim if I ever needed to hit somebody with something.

Where to start? Where to start?

Imagining myself to be like Steinway, I tiptoed toward the back of the first floor. Ambassador Rawlings's office seemed like the logical place. Turning the doorknob gently, I was surprised to hear the door squeak.

Shouldn't an embassy be better oiled than this?

I giggled again, then shushed myself sharply, "Shh!" It was like I was two separate people, conflicted by what I was doing. Take it too lightly, take it too seriously, take it too…

Only after I'd carefully shut the door did I realize how dark it was in here. It was a room I'd rarely entered before, having no business there—"And what business do you have here now, hmm?"—and I stumbled over a chair on my way to where I remembered the desk was.

"Ouch!" I rubbed my shin.

"Be quiet!" I cautioned myself again.

"Okay," I said. "But you don't have to be so grouchy about it."

Achieving the desk, I played my hands around the edges until I felt the outline of a lamp on the far corner. I pulled the cord and the area immediately surrounding the desk was bathed in a romantic illumination.

"Gee," I said, "if only I had someone to make out with in here, this could be fun."

When I got to the far side of the desk and looked up, I noticed for the first time the switch on the wall beside the seam of the door I'd just entered. Damn! If I'd thought of that earlier, I could have saved myself from barking my shin.

Nancy Drew would never have missed that, I thought.

I started going over the items on the top of the ambassador's desk, trying to be careful to leave things just as I'd found them. Not sure exactly what I was looking for, I was sure I would know it when I found it.

There was a part of me that was uncomfortable with what I was doing. Wasn't it wrong for me to be snooping around in here like this? But then I figured that so long as I confined my investigation to what was already on the desk, it was okay. I mean, if someone keeps something out in plain sight, isn't it fair game? Feeling more virtuous by the minute, I resolved not to go through any of the drawers, which really would qualify as snooping.

Besides, the drawers were locked and I had no idea where the key was kept. Perhaps it was under Ambassador Rawlings's pillow? I giggled to myself. After all, Nancy Drew always said that if you needed to keep something safe, you should sleep with it under your pillow. She also always said that if you were trapped in a closet, you should look for something to use as a lever.

I picked up the stapler and contemplated it as an evidentiary device.

When is a stapler really just a stapler? I pondered.

Gee, it felt kind of spooky, being in here all by myself while the rest of the house slept on around me.

And then spooky started to feel like lonely.

I addressed the stapler, "Alas, poor Stapler, I knew him well. He was an office tool of infinite jest—"

What would Nancy Drew look for? I wondered.

She'd look for correspondence, I decided.

There were certainly a lot of papers on the desk. Didn't this guy ever get anything done in here?

All of the correspondence looked official. Well, I supposed that figured. It was his office. But as I looked at the return addresses, I saw a surprising number of pieces were from the CIA.

That was odd.

But how annoying! All of the letters were unopened.

These must just be new items from the day's post that had arrived after he and Miss Bebe had taken off. I didn't know what to do. If I were Nancy Drew, I was sure I'd know how to steam these babies right open so that I could take a peek inside. But if I knew nothing else, I knew that no matter how intrepid I ever became, I'd never be enough of a sly boots that I could steam open a letter and reseal it without getting caught. Why, I never even bought clothes that weren't wash-and-wear, because I sucked with an iron!

Besides, I yawned, placing the letters back, this wasn't getting me anywhere. What I needed to find was some personal correspondence, something that would help me get a handle on the ambassador's personal life.

But, wait a second: there wasn't any personal correspondence here! Wasn't that kind of odd? I mean, even I got the occasional letter from my father, and Mrs. Fairly got letters from Ireland all the time.

I yawned a second time, replacing everything, including my new best friend, Mr. Stapler, exactly as I'd found it, switching the light off on the way out.

I made my way upstairs in the dark, thinking about turning in. But when I got to the top of the stairs, I caught my second wind.

I hadn't found anything out yet! What kind of detective was I?

Back to tiptoeing, I stealthed my way to that secret door, the room from which I was sure that strange laughter always came. As I turned the knob, I could have sworn I heard a slight whirring sound coming from inside. But, as always, the door was still locked.

Damn! Where was a hairpin or credit card when a girl needed one?

Then I had a sudden inspiration.

No, I wasn't going to break into the room. That would constitute criminal behavior, right?

But Ambassador Rawlings's room was right next door and Ambassador Rawlings was busily away in the Westman Islands. So, how hard would it be to turn the knob on his unlocked door, like so? How hard would it be to sneak around, no matter how incriminating that sounded, hoping to find evidence of the kinds of personal effects I hadn't found below?

Was there a picture of Mrs. Rawlings anywhere in here? Were there some papers, perhaps, evidence of a divorce in progress or better yet a divorce decree?

I didn't hear the light pad of feet until whoever possessed those feet was nearly right there in the room with me. Without a second thought, I threw myself to the ground and rolled under the bed.

"Papa?"

I heard Annette's voice sounding tired, confused.

Oh, no! This was the worst thing that could happen.

Okay, well, maybe it would be worse if Mrs. Fairly found me like this or, worse still, if it were the ambassador. Maybe if I just stayed quiet, she'd go away.

"Did you decide to come home early?" she asked.

Oh, shit! This was awful! I couldn't leave her to think that maybe her father was here but was ignoring her. She'd feel unloved.

Feeling like the Grinch getting caught by Cindy Lou Who, I rolled out from my hiding place.

Annette's eyes widened.

"Miss Bell?"

"Hi," I said, and gave a little awkward wave.

"What are you doing in my father's room in the middle of the night?"

"I came to steal the Christmas tree?" I gave an awkward laugh.

"What?"

"I heard a noise in the night," I said, which wasn't technically a lie since there had been a noise in the night, only it had been made by me, "and I came to investigate."

"But why were you under Papa's bed?"

"I lost an earring and was looking for it."

"But you don't have earrings."

"That's because I lost it."

I couldn't believe I was lying to this sweet child! But I was doing what I was doing in order to help her in the long run, right?

"Yes," said Annette in a very precise way. "But you have no earrings on at all. If you lost one, wouldn't you still have the other?"

"Oh," I laughed nervously. "It's an American custom— just one earring at a time."

"Do you forget I'm American, too?" She was confused. "And I don't remember any such custom…"

It took some more fancy footwork on my part, and anyone could see how good I was at that, before I finally convinced her to go back to bed.

I had found nothing. If there was a Mrs. Rawlings, if there ever had been a Mrs. Rawlings in the world, I'd found no evidence of her.

If I really were Nancy Drew, some kind of amazing epiphany would have occurred to me before drifting off to sleep, something that would explain either the truth about Mrs. Rawlings or the truth about that locked room.

But no such epiphanies were in sight.

Annette had decided to tell me the story of her mother.

I wasn't sure if I should take as truth such a serious story told by such a small child, but then, why should she lie to me?

It was the next morning, the second day that the master was gone, and the house had finally settled down to its normal routines. As I sat down to the usual big breakfast spread, I marveled not for the first time at how much food there always was.

Back when I'd been doing my Nancy Drew marathon of reading, I'd been flat out amazed at how much food that girl could put away. On one memorable occasion, Hannah had served Nancy and her father an appetizer of orange and grapefruit slices in sorbet glasses, followed by a dinner of spring lamb, rice and mushrooms, fresh peas and chocolate angel cake with vanilla ice cream. Reading that, I'd felt like shouting, "Hel-*lo*! Don't you ever have to worry about your waistline at all?" I'd wondered if Nancy might not just have a *lit*-tle bulimia problem on her hands. But then I realized that back then such things weren't the issue they are now. Besides, she was just a character in a book. The dietary laws that applied to the rest of us didn't apply to her. She could carb-out until the cows came home and still maintain that same slim silhouette.

I guess I should say it wasn't so much that I was eating more as for the first time in my life I wasn't worrying about it. Since I'd been here, I'd been so occupied with things out-side of myself that I'd forgotten to be obsessive about eat-ing and I'd also forgotten all about using food as either a comfort or an instrument of self-destruction. As a result, I tended to eat whatever I wanted to, whenever I was hun-gry, but stopped eating before I felt full. As a result of *that,* I'd slowly gained back the ten pounds I'd lost during my post-Buster devastation—I knew, not because I'd stepped on any scales like I used to do every morning, but because my clothes fit me differently and I no longer looked gaunt in the mirror. I realized I'd never win any bikini contests—Bebe Iversdottir was the one who would win those, the only part of getting slightly bigger that still bothered me—but I was comfortable with my reflected image. Maybe this was the way I was supposed to look.

I enjoyed some fresh fruit, toast and eggs, passed on Lars Aquavit's usual offer to join him in coffee—wouldn't he ever learn?

But first…

"Don't you think it's time you two went to church?" Mrs. Fairly prompted.

Oh, right. Church.

"You do remember that was supposed to be part of your job, don't you?" she said.

"Of course," I said, "but it's not my fault that every week-end something else has seemed to come up. If you're not having me take Annette on bracing hikes, then it's the am-bassador coming home unannounced and not caring if we go or not—"

"I'm not blaming you," Mrs. Fairly cut me off. "But it's Sunday and you both have a free morning. *It's time.*"

And so I found myself a short time later walking with Annette up the steep Skolavoroustigur, thinking I'd much rather be ducking into one of the art galleries than going to the massive Hallgrimskirja, which looked more like a spaceship about to take off than anything else, even if it was made out of stone.

"You look very nice," Annette told me as we entered, perhaps sensing I needed reassurance.

"Thank you," I said.

"That parka you have on entirely covers the wine stains on your dress," she added.

"Gee, thanks," I said.

Now even little children were aware of my fashion short-comings. But what else could I do? I was sure religious services here would be more formal than back home, I wanted to show proper respect, and this was still the only dress I had, having retrieved it from the trash the morning after the night I threw it away.

The church was already nearly full as we took our seats, and I saw Gina and Britta, seated closer to the front, turn and wave excitedly.

I could almost hear their minds thinking: *There is our weird American friend! And she has the handsome ambassador's adorable daughter with her! I wonder if she's made any progress in solving the mystery of his wife yet?*

As a matter of fact, it felt as though *everyone* was paying undue attention to us. Well, I guess that, with our dark coloring, we did stand out; kind of like two blueberries in a five-hundred-piece jigsaw puzzle where everything else was totally white.

"What kind of church is this again?" I whispered, trying not to notice the stares.

Mrs. Fairly had told me she'd brought Annette at least once herself before my arrival, so I figured she knew more about it than I did.

Annette shrugged now. "Lutheran?"

The preacher entered and started talking in a language I could not understand at all.

"Icelandic is a very difficult language to learn," Annette whispered.

"Do you understand it at all?" I asked.

"Not a word."

"So why are we here again?" I asked.

"Because Papa wants us to be," she said.

Oh. Right.

"How tall do you think that organ is?" I asked, indicating the magnificent instrument with my chin.

"About fifty feet," she guessed.

"And how many pipes do you think it has?"

"More than five thousand, looks like."

"And how long to we have to stay here again?"

"Until the very end."

"Even though we don't understand a word?"

"Exactly." She smiled.

As we exited an hour later, the preacher thanked us for coming. Over his shoulder, I saw stairs winding upwards toward the bell tower and it occurred to me what a steep flight that must be and how I'd hate to be at the top of that church.

Back at the embassy, I at last got down to work with Annette, even if it was Sunday. Besides, the work I had in mind was the kind that would seem more fun to her than anything else.

A teacher's book I'd purchased had suggested having kids make scrapbooks of their own life story. It would be a great way to work on memory, precision cutting with scissors and forming letters, all at the same time.

Annette was delighted with the idea of the project—"A book all about me!"—in the narcissistic way I'd anticipated. Children, I'd often found, can be great narcissists. Of course, adults can, too; we just camouflage it better. We keep journals or write memoirs. If we're lucky, some publisher buys those memoirs. If we're even luckier yet, we're former presidents and someone advances us ten million dollars for our navel-gazing.

As I said, Annette was delighted…in the beginning.

She went straight to her father's bedroom and started rooting around for old photograph albums and ticket stubs. It must be nice, I thought, to feel so free to look around to your heart's content. But then I grew worried that Ambassador Rawlings might mind her going through his things in this way.

"Mind?" She didn't understand. "Why should Papa mind? He lets me come and go as I please in here. He never minds anything I do."

It was true, I realized. I had yet to see him ever be upset with anything she did. Well, why should he? She was an extraordinarily wonderful child, well mannered and precociously sympathetic to the feelings of others…even if she had brought up the shadowy wine stain on my dress earlier. Any parent would be proud to have her.

Carrying an album that was almost as big as she was, she led the way back to her own room to start working.

But when she started to remove some of the pictures that had carefully been placed in there by some unseen loving hand, preparatory to replacing them in the new book she was going to create, I felt a fresh objection. Maybe this hadn't been such a good idea in the first place.

"Won't your father mind us disrupting things this way?" I said.

"Mind?" she echoed again.

"Yes," I said. "Don't you think he'd prefer we kept the memories intact in this album?"

"No," she laughed, "he won't mind. When he sees we have created a new book about *me,* he'll be thrilled!"

I found myself laughing with her.

"I'm sure you're right," I said. "What could be better than that?"

She started on the album in earnest, moving from back to front, explaining things to me all the while.

"Here is Papa and I at my last birthday," she said. "It was before we met you. There was a clown *and* a huge cake."

"I see that," I said as she removed the picture from the album, taking great care to glue it onto the colored construction paper she was using for her scrapbook.

"The clown was behaving a little strange," Annette said, "so Papa had Mr. Miller ask him to leave, but the cake was good."

I ignored the non sequitur part of her statement. Of course the cake was good.

"Strange?" I asked. "How so?"

She shrugged, as though such minor details never bothered her.

"I don't know," she said. "They never said. But Mr. Miller took care of it."

"Mr. Miller was at your birthday party?" I asked.

"Yes. Look, here is a picture of Papa trying to teach me to ski. I wanted to learn, but he was worried. Finally, he agreed, but I wasn't any good. Perhaps when I'm older."

"But isn't that odd, him being at your party?"

"Not really." She shrugged again. "Mr. Miller is always somehow around. He comes, he goes. But he always comes back."

"Really?"

"He's been at every birthday that I can remember. And whenever we go on vacation, he always shows up." She shrugged. "He is nice enough. He is the only man Papa sees regularly. I suppose they are best friends."

I recalled Robert Miller saying he was Ambassador Rawlings's boss. Would they really be best friends, too?

Annette spent the next half hour on her project, happily moving backward through the book. I was surprised at how many pictures there were of her and her father. Considering how busy he always was here, it was amazing to see how much time he'd made over the years for his little girl, and Annette was clearly thrilled to be given this opportunity to wax nostalgic over her short past.

"This is when Papa took me for a pony ride," she would say. "Doesn't he look handsome on his horse?"

I allowed that he did, unable to prevent myself from calling to mind the first time I'd met him and the equine connection between us. At the time, I'd thought him to be unattractive, but I realized now, looking at the picture of him, that my feelings had changed. It was surely a sign of something, although I refused to admit to myself that it was what Gina said, that I was in love with him.

"Oh, and these!" she said, holding up a narrow strip of four black-and-white photos of her and her father, faces pressed close together, mugging for the camera. "We had these taken in a booth at the mall!"

She had a lot of happy memories with her father. Suddenly, I envied her that.

Of particular interest to her were the pictures from her birthday parties. In addition to the clown one, as we moved backward through the album, she showed me pictures of herself at age five, at a circus party; at four, at a karate party ("I wanted to keep taking it, but Papa said it was too dangerous"); at a gymnastics party at three; at a family party at home at age two.

The album ended there.

Or, I suppose I should say more properly, the album began there, with no pictures coming before age two.

"Where are the rest?" I asked. "Another album?"

"No," said Annette, looking puzzled herself. "This is the only one I've ever found."

"That's too bad," I said, thinking it was odd. Most parents tended to take a gazillion pictures the first years of a child's life, a half of a gazillion pictures the following year, and increasingly less each passing year after that. Even Aunt Bea, who I never considered to be the most natural of parents, had behaved so with her children. The Keatings certainly had, as well.

"I always thought so, too," said Annette, her expression swiftly moving from puzzled to sad.

It was so strange to see her looking like this. Ever since

I'd known her, she'd always been so sunny. Even the times of day when most small children acted up had never affected Annette. "The witching hour" was what 4:00 p.m. had been referred to in the Keating household, the time of day when you couldn't make a phone call without there being screaming interruptions, and if you wanted to start dinner preparations, you could only do so with little people attached to your thighs. It took this moment of seeing Annette looking so starkly woebegone to recognize what a remarkably happy child she normally was.

Impulsively, I took her in my arms.

"What is it?" I asked, smelling the fresh-soap scent of her sweet head against my shoulder. "What's wrong?"

And it was then that I got one of the answers I'd been looking for.

Just when I'd been despairing that I was never going to learn the truth about Annette's mother, she told me herself.

"All those pictures of me and Papa," she said in a half sob.

"What's wrong?" I asked again. "Don't you like them? I think they're perfectly marvelous pictures. He clearly loves you so much."

"I know that," she said in a voice that was eerily reminiscent of her father's, the kind of voice that said I was an idiot for missing the forest for the trees. "But where is Mama?"

"Where is Mama?" I asked quietly. I'd felt so close to the information for so long and yet it had always eluded me. I sensed I needed to be extra careful now.

Annette took a deep breath for such a little girl, as though bracing herself.

"She is dead," she said at last.

Of all the things I'd imagined—that her parents were divorced, in the process of getting a divorce, that her mother had abandoned her, that her mother was a madwoman locked away in the secret room who made herself known by cackling maniacally every time I came close to a moment of happiness with her husband—I'd never imagined this.

"Yes," Annette explained. She was tearful at first, but then grew stronger as she went on. "Mama died when I was born."

"What?" I asked dumbly.

It was like hearing my own life story, except in my story, after that awful beginning, my father had left and I'd wound up having an awful middle story, too. In Annette's lucky case, her father had stayed.

Thinking of him in this way only served to strengthen my feelings for him.

"I really do not mind that so much," Annette said bravely. "I mean, of course I mind that Mama is dead. But since I never knew her, really, how much can I mind her not being here?"

She made sense, more sense than I usually made of the same topic.

"What I *mind*," she went on, "is not having any mama at all. When I look at all these pictures—" she indicated the albums, her father's and the one she'd just made "—I am of course happy that Papa is with me in the pictures. I only wish there were a mama, any mama, in the pictures with us, as well."

That was when she told me her secret wish.

"When you first came to us," she said, "I used to dream at night that somehow you and Papa would fall in love and then we would become a family."

I said nothing.

"That was silly, wasn't it?" she said with precocious wistfulness.

"It's never silly to dream," I said, taking her in my arms and hugging her close.

"Anyway—"she took in another big breath "—after I gave up on that silly fantasy, and I saw Miss Bebe for the first time, I began thinking… Wouldn't it be great if Papa married her?"

Wouldn't it be great if Papa married her?

I couldn't get those words out of my head. They taunted my every second.

Would it be great if Edgar Rawlings married Bebe Iversdottir?

Annette would finally have a mother then, a beautiful blond mother who would undoubtedly be an asset to her husband's diplomatic career. After all, hadn't Robert Miller said she was the daughter of a dignitary?

But I didn't like Bebe Iversdottir. To me, there had seemed to be something…evil about her.

Then I told myself that was my imagination going into overdrive. But Nancy Drew also had an overactive imagination, I'd remarked on more than one occasion. Every time something happened that would impress most normal human beings as being not such a much, like a car driving by too quickly, Nancy would conclude something outrageous like, "I'll bet that driver is a jewel thief!" Of course, she was always right.

But what had Bebe done, really, to arouse my suspicions?

Sure, there was that whole thing with her suggesting Ambassador Rawlings send Annette away to boarding school. But was that really so awful? Maybe she'd been at boarding school herself. Maybe she was suggesting it, not because she was so selfish that she wanted the ambassador all to herself, but because she was really selfless and wanted what she thought was in the best interests of the child. It was possible.

Okay, so maybe it didn't seem likely, but it was possible.

And if she was really not evil, if she was really just some nice, blond, beautiful woman who happened to be in love with the ambassador, then what did that make me?

I saw what it made me.

It made me jealous.

Worse, it made me in love with him.

For the first time, I saw that Gina was right in what she'd suspected and I saw the extent of her insight: somehow, without realizing it, or at least without admitting it to myself, I'd fallen in love with Edgar Rawlings, deeper than I'd ever been with anybody.

What had my subconscious mind been thinking?

I knew what it had been thinking. It had been thinking that I could do over the past, exchange the mistakes I'd made with Buster for a success story with Edgar Rawlings.

I saw the futility of it.

Why in the world would he ever pick someone like me, whose sole claim to fame in life was as the Gubber Snack Foods Kid, over someone like Bebe Iversdottir?

The answer was simple: he wouldn't.

Whatever I'd been dreaming of, a world in which I became Mrs. Ambassador, suddenly beautiful and dancing my life away in the arms of a man who loved me, a world in which, petty as it might sound, I would be on an equal footing with Buster and Alissa Keating, only I would be on an even better footing, since my love would be real and true while theirs would only ever be false and false—whatever that foolish dream was, it was just that and would only ever be that: a foolish dream.

It was enough to make me cry.

But I couldn't cry. I needed to remain calm, do my job, I needed to be Annette's competent governess, the woman who would turn her over to her new mother when the time came.

I decided to drown my sorrows by learning how to drive.

I know that might not be the solution most people would choose. But I was responsible, to a certain extent, for a young child, so it wasn't as if drinking in the afternoon was an option.

Besides, Lars Aquavit had been after me for a long time to teach me.

"How is it possible for a person not to drive?" He would laugh at me often.

"Well," I'd say, "it's not like it's every person's calling, in the way that it's yours. I suppose I could just as easily say to you, 'How can you not be a governess?'"

"Because I am the driver," he would say quite reasonably.

"Well, there you go," I'd say.

On that day, however, I said something different.

"Today's your lucky day, Lars," I informed him.

His eyebrows rose.

"I'm going to finally let you teach me to drive," I said.

"God bless the trolls," he said. "Let's go."

I wish I could say it went well.

The way I'd figured it, if I could just be competent at this one thing that most adults in the world were reasonably competent at, it would restore my sense of confidence.

But such was not to be.

In the Nancy Drew stories, the young sleuth/girl detective had been a great driver, zipping around in her convertible. Of course, in the Nancy Drew stories, the cars of other drivers often functioned as weapons. One time, someone even hit Nancy's frisky terrier, Togo! (Of course he was okay.) And even sleuthing around Amish country, Nancy's horse and buggy were run off the road by another horse and buggy! Still, despite averaging one near-death close call for each of the fifty-six stories, she never once hesitated to get behind the wheel or pick up the reins again. She was just unstoppable.

Now here was I, who had never had any appellation attached to my name, unless it was that of the Gubber Snack Foods Kid, hoping to become equally competent behind the wheel, so that, should it ever become necessary, I'd be able to give all the bad guys a run for their money.

Of course, Nancy and her friends always gave cute yet important-sounding names to anything they did that smacked of mystery or danger. Need to get an owl out of a friend's house? Dub the mission Operation Owl!

Maybe, I thought, if I could find something cute yet important sounding to call my learning to drive, my mission would be a similar success.

"Ready for Operation Cruise Control?" I said with forced cheer, placing my hands on the wheel in the ten and two positions I'd seen other drivers adopt; well, the careful ones.

"*What?*" For the first time since I'd known him, Lars Aquavit looked at me with scorn; well, except for every time he teased me about being the only adult in the world who couldn't drive.

"Ready to teach me to drive?" I amended meekly, already starting to feel dejected about the whole thing.

I tried to listen carefully as he patiently explained the controls of the car to me: brake, clutch, gas; first through fifth gears.

Somewhere around clutch and second gear, I felt my brain shut down. I'd always had a mental block where geography was concerned, just couldn't figure out where in the world anything was, and I'd long suspected that my aversion to driving was because I knew I'd have a similar block there and that even if I could learn how to drive, I'd never be able to find anything anyway.

Still, how hard could it be? Sixteen-year-olds all over the United States learned how to drive every day. On farms, five-year-olds were probably learning to drive tractors. So, really, how hard could it be?

And it wasn't like I was going to need to know gears above first, certainly not right away. The main thing Lars Aquavit was going to teach me to do on the first day, I was sure of it, was how to go forward and how to reverse. Even an idiot could do that.

"Okay," he instructed, "slowly reverse the automobile out of the driveway."

I adjusted the gears and hit the gas.

There was just one problem. I had somehow got the Drive and Reverse parts of the stick confused, so we surged forward instead.

All right, *two* problems: I hit the gas really hard.

"Brake!" Lars Aquavit yelled. "Hit the brake!"

But my mind froze and I was unable to do anything but stare straight ahead, hands still at ten and two, as we hit the corner of the embassy. Lars Aquavit was quick. Seeing me freeze, he immediately reached downward and, with his fist, punched the brake.

But not quick enough to prevent me from crumpling the front end of the car and putting a healthy dent in the structure of the building.

"Reverse!" he yelled. "Put it in Reverse! Not the D! The R! Look for the P with a tail on it!"

This time, with his explicit abecedarian instructions, I had no problem finding the appropriate gear. The problem was that I still had what I would come to learn was known as a "lead foot" and I'd used that lead foot so strenuously while reversing that I literally flew us backward into an enormous bank of snow and dirt.

"Stop," he groaned. "Please stop. You are awful at this."

"Oh, God!"

"Please turn off the car, Charlotte," he begged, fist once again on the brake.

Even *I* knew that driving, even learning to drive, wasn't supposed to go like this.

Meekly, I obeyed.

Lars Aquavit took his fist off the brake, wiped a relieved hand across his brow. He was always so cool. I'd never seen him rattled like this before. He slowly pushed open the door, walked around to the back of the car. I got out my side, walked around to the back, as well.

The back of the car really was buried.

"Give me the keys," he instructed.

I handed them over.

"At least," he said, "if I can get the car out of that bank, I can see how bad the rear damage is."

"Damage?" I echoed. "I'd think an embassy car would be specially reinforced."

"It is," he said, "but that's against assassin's bullets. It's not reinforced against *you.*"

Ouch!

But try as he might, no matter how hard he hit the gas, even harder than I'd hit it when I'd hit the side of the embassy, he couldn't get it out of the snowbank.

He climbed out of the car, ran his hand through his hair.

"There's probably snow and debris caught in the tailpipe," he said. "There's probably so much…*shit* in there."

I'd never heard him swear before!

"What are we going to do?" I asked.

"*We?*" he asked. "*You're* going to go find me a shovel and then *I'm* going to spend the rest of the day shoveling all the snow away. Hopefully, if I relieve the outward pressure, I'll be able to finally move the car, filled tailpipe or no filled tailpipe, and take it for repairs."

"I always thought my learning to drive was a bad idea," I said.

"Ha!" he laughed bitterly, surveying the work ahead of him. "Well, I guess you thought right."

At dinner, I was so subdued, even Annette commented upon it.

Young children are supposed to be almost completely self-absorbed and yet, as with so many other things, she belied that stereotype.

"Why so blue, Miss Bell?" she asked, a worried frown furrowing her pretty little brow. "You have barely eaten anything. Usually, you eat like Captain!"

Nothing like having one's appetite compared to that of a very large dog to cheer a girl's spirits.

"Thanks for your concern," I said. "I'm fine, really. I guess I just lost my appetite a bit after the incident with the, um, car."

"Don't give it a second thought," said Lars Aquavit, who had regained his cheerful equilibrium since that afternoon. "As soon as we get the car back from the shop, we can resume lessons."

"You can't be serious," I said.

"I couldn't be more serious," he said. "I refuse to have you be my first failure as a driving instructor."

I suppose it should have cheered me, that Lars Aquavit refused to give up on me after what I'd put him through, but it did not.

Pleading a slight headache—"Perhaps you injured yourself more than you thought!" Annette said, "Perhaps we should call the doctor!"—I assured them that I was otherwise fine and just needed an early night.

I had not put in much time on my writing lately. Now I pulled out the short stack of sheets, looked to see where I'd left off. It was at the point where I was about to tell Buster I was pregnant, after which he would show his true colors. I started to write the scene, got halfway through it before realizing my heart wasn't in it.

Somehow, now, those events felt very far away, as though they'd happened to someone else. In the past, when I'd sat down to write my story, the pain had been fresh all over again. And, in a way, that had been cleansing. But now there was a new pain that eclipsed the past.

All day long, since working with Annette on making the scrapbook, as I moved through my day, I'd pushed the memory of her words aside: that she wanted a new mother to fill up the vacant space in the family-album pictures of herself and her father, and that she hoped that new mother would be Bebe. As I put aside the book I no longer felt like working on, as I dressed for bed, I let the feelings of sadness and loss fill me; I no longer tried to fight it.

If I were Nancy Drew, I thought, placing my head on the pillow, I'd be a lot more resilient. Nancy never gave up. No matter what outlandish thing happened, she bounced back, as if she had springs in her. One time, after the ceiling literally fell on her head, and after sweeping up the debris, she'd been filled with good cheer once again. Well, that was no surprise, since she came from such good and sturdy stock. Her father, Carson Drew, was a hero, too, after all.

Maybe if my father had been more like Carson Drew, he'd never have left me with Aunt Bea in the first place. Maybe if my father had been more like Carson Drew, I'd have been more like Nancy. It seemed to me that there were times when a person should just give in to their feelings, let the tears flow. But I didn't feel resilient like Nancy Drew.

I tried to stop, tried to fall asleep, but it was no use. All I could remember was the dream I'd previously had, where first I was with Ambassador Rawlings and then my place was taken by Bebe Iversdottir as his bride.

I had to move, had to get out of the bed. But I didn't want to go downstairs. Even though it was the middle of the night now, I didn't want to run the risk that someone else in the house might wake and run into me in my present condition. Even Steinway was nowhere in sight to offer comfort.

Sliding into my slippers, I crossed to the chair in front of my writing desk, where I'd been sitting earlier. Positioning it so that it was under the trapdoor I hadn't used since the day Mrs. Fairly showed it to me, I climbed on top, pulled the door down and ascended the stairs. At least the air would feel fresh up there.

It was freezing!

But who really cared?

I could have gone back down and got a coat to warm me or at least a hat to protect my head from getting wet by the light snow that was falling, but it would have required more energy for self-preservation than I had at the moment.

As I looked out at the night sights of the city, unseeing, tears blurring my vision, I remembered how even while hanging on for dear life on a steep roof, Nancy took the time to balance against a chimney, taking in the view of the surrounding countryside: the picturesque panorama, the lazy river sparkling in the sunlight, the white daisies sprinkling their way across the green fields.

Wiping my nose on my sleeve, I was glad no one could see me. I could be as brash and intrepid as I was capable of being, I could be clearheaded enough to sit up here and, while miserable, count the stars in the sky or muse about what wonderful things might be going on in the tidy houses below me; it wasn't going to change a thing. I would still have my heart broken.

I couldn't even drive a car.

I heard the tread of slow steps on the pull-down stairs before I heard the voice.

Who was it? I wondered, rubbing at the tears in my eyes. Mrs. Fairly, wanting who knew what in the middle of the night? Annette, needing comfort after a nightmare?

"Miss Bell?"

Oh no! That familiar deep voice was the last voice I'd expected to hear!

And then he was there in the rectangle made by the open trapdoor. How handsome he looked to me. How just out of reach, no closer to me in spirit than the stars I'd been unable to care about a moment before.

"When I called earlier in the day," he said, sounding breathless, as though he'd been running for hours, "Mrs. Fairly told me you'd been in an accident with the car."

"I'm so sorry," I said. "You can take the repairs out of my pay." I stopped, thinking of all the damage I'd done. It was a lot of damage. "For however many weeks is necessary," I added.

I'd probably never see another cent of pay.

"I don't care about the stupid car!" he said.

"You don't?" I was surprised.

"No," he said. "I care about you."

"You do?" Now I was really surprised.

"Yes," he said. "I came rushing home because I was worried, took the first available flight, caught a cab from the airport, since, well, the car is in the shop."

He smiled ruefully at that last statement.

"But didn't Mrs. Fairly tell you I was fine?" I asked.

"Of course she did," he said. "But I was still worried. Mrs. Fairly always tells me that things are fine when I'm on the road, no matter what has happened. She has this bad habit of not wanting to concern me with things. Sometimes I think she thinks I'm incapable of doing my job properly, if I have too many things on my plate."

Now it was my turn to smile ruefully. I had often had the same instinct about Mrs. Fairly's thought processes, only in relation to myself. Since coming to learn the truth of Annette's mother, I had concluded that the only reason Mrs. Fairly had kept it from me was that she believed if I knew it, I would be too distracted with sympathy for Annette to ever discipline her properly. Not that needing to discipline Annette was ever an issue.

"Well, sir," I said, "now that you are here, you can see for yourself that things really are fine."

"But they are not fine, Miss Bell!"

"How can you say that?"

"I come rushing home, I run up to your room in the middle of the night, naturally expecting to find you sleeping safely in your bed. Instead, I find your bed empty, the trapdoor to the roof gaping open. And, as I start to come up here, I hear you."

He reached out then with one finger, gently traced the path of one dried tear down my cheek.

"You were crying," he said softly, "weren't you?"

It seemed ridiculous to lie, when the evidence was right at his fingertips.

Dumbly, I nodded.

"And that last time," he said gently, hand beneath my chin now, making me look at him, "after the party, when I came to visit you. You were crying that night, too, weren't you?"

Again I nodded.

"Why, Charlotte? Why were you so sad? Why are you so sad?"

The words came out of me in an unbidden rush.

"Because you are to be married!" I said. "And when you are married, it will change everything!"

"Yes—" he smiled in the dark, carefully drawing out the word as though it might contain more than one syllable "—I hope to be married one day, hopefully in the not-too-distant future. But how will that change everything?"

I could not let him see my real thoughts.

"Because Annette will be sent to boarding school!" I said, unable to stifle a sob from escaping me, not even thinking of him now but thinking of the real pain, the other pain, that being separated from Annette would cause me.

"I hadn't thought that far ahead," he said. "I had only thought of the marriage. Of course, I would have to give the matter grave consideration, if that is what my bride wishes."

"Of course that is what your bride wishes!"

"It is?"

He seemed surprised.

"Yes!" I said. I couldn't seem to help myself from making every statement I uttered an exclamation. I was exclaiming all over the place. And now my anger had replaced sadness. "Of course it is! I heard her say it with my own ears! You were there, too—*you* heard her say it!"

"Charlotte, if I may be so bold as to ask, just what in the world are you talking about?"

"Bebe Iversdottir, *your bride,*" I spat the words out, "wants to send Annette away!"

"What?" he said. "Bebe is not—"

But I no longer could hear him. The words were tumbling out of my mouth, as though my brain, my heart, were pushing them out into the air.

"The two of you are to be married and Annette will finally have the mother she has always wanted, but then you will send Annette away because that is what Bebe wants you to do and then I will never see Annette again!" I shouted. "And I will never see you again," I added, almost in a whisper.

At last, I had stopped exclaiming.

He grabbed my hands, surprising me.

"You're freezing," he said. "Come inside."

"No," I said obstinately.

"Then let me give you my jacket," he said, moving to remove it.

"No," I insisted. "Then you will be cold."

"Then let me get you *a* jacket. Will you at least let me get you a jacket, Charlotte?"

I reverted to type. "I guess," I allowed.

He descended the stairs. The night was so silent, so few cars left out now, I heard his every step downward, heard him open my wardrobe door. A moment later, he was back up again, a dark blue jacket draped over his arm.

"Funny," he said, "I found this crumpled in the bottom of your closet."

He held it up. I knew what it was, of course: his favorite blue blazer, the one I'd used to beat out the sparks around his bed. It was still scorched in spots.

"How do you think it got there?" he asked, an amused smile on his face. "And in such condition?"

He held it out for me and I slid my arms into the too-long

sleeves. I was sure I looked ridiculous, but I had finally started to feel the cold and the jacket was at least some protection.

"I always knew I should have just let you burn," I said, recovering some of my spirit. "If you're going to whine about the ruin of a measly jacket—"

"Do you hear me whining, Charlotte? I'm not whining."

"Okay, complaining then. If you're going to—"

"I'm not complaining, either. I think you look rather nice in my jacket, burn marks and all. I think you should keep it."

"Thank you," I said sarcastically. "You are far too generous."

"Where were we," he asked, "before I went downstairs to get you a jacket, a jacket you have accepted with precious little gratitude?"

"I—"

"That's quite all right. I understand it's hard for you to accept gifts. I seem to recall you telling me you had not much experience of them. Hopefully, in time and with practice, not to mention incredible patience on the part of the giver, you will learn to accept them more cheerfully."

"Ha!" I said, surprising myself. "It's not what I'd call much of a present," I said. "A used jacket, the wrong size, burnt, that no one would ever want to wear again."

"You're welcome," he said cheerfully.

"Thanks," I said through gritted teeth.

"Now, then, you still haven't told me—where were we?"

"I. Don't. Remember."

"And. I. Don't. Believe. You."

"Whatever," I said, feeling reckless now.

"That's okay," he said, "because I do remember."

Oh.

"You had just finished informing me that I was going to marry Miss Iversdottir, that I was going to send Annette away, that you were never going to see Annette again if that happened, that you were never going to see me again."

"I suppose I might have said something like that," I admitted.

"Would that be so awful?" he asked.

"I would miss Annette greatly," I said.

"Would it be so awful never seeing me again?"

"Yes." I admitted that, too.

"Why?"

I wouldn't tell him that. I told myself he couldn't make me.

"Say it, Charlotte."

"Because I love you."

There. It was finally out there in the world. There was no taking it back now.

I braced myself to hear him laugh at me.

"That's very good to hear, Charlotte," he said.

"What?"

"I've asked myself over and over, when did I first fall in love with you? Was it when you woke me amidst the near flames by throwing toothbrush glassfuls of water at me? Was it that very first day when you fell off the horse? I have no answer for it. Sometimes, it seems like it must have been from the moment I first heard your name. Surely, when Mrs. Fairly told me you'd been in an accident involving the car, I knew I was in love with you then."

"In love?" I asked. "Are you crazy?"

"Perhaps…" He shrugged. "But you're the real crazy

one, if you think for a second I would ever choose that insipid Bebe Iversdottir over you."

"Ambassador—"

"Edgar." He stopped me. "Don't you think it's time you called me Edgar?"

"Edgar." It took great deliberation for me to make myself say it. "You told me you were to be married."

"Yes," he said.

"To Bebe Iversdottir."

"No." He shook his head. "To you."

I closed the space between us, hesitantly raised my fingers to his lips. It was like touching a dream.

Then I kissed him, like I'd never kissed anyone in my life.

And, wonder of wonders, he kissed me back.

After an eternity, he was the one to break the spell.

"Don't you think we should go inside where it's warmer?" he suggested.

"I'm not cold," I said, going on tiptoe to kiss him again. I was that hungry for him.

"Well, I am," he laughed. "Come on, Charlotte," he invited. "Come inside."

Feeling the need to be obedient for once—and, it really was freezing outside—I followed him back down the stairs, hopped off the chair, watched as he sealed up the trapdoor.

Now I felt awkward, in a way I hadn't when I was still outside.

"Come back, Charlotte," he said, his voice almost a whisper. "Don't run away from me now."

A part of me, a big part, the part that was ruled by both instinct and common sense, said that running away would be the wisest thing I could do.

But I couldn't bring myself to do it.

"Okay," I said, moving closer to him, "*Edgar*. If you insist on being crazy, then I guess I'll be crazy, too."

I kissed him again, hard, like I'd never get another chance.

He seemed taken aback by the strength of that kiss. Was he surprised? Had he been expecting some kind of meek I'll-follow-your-lead subservience in keeping with our positions in the household?

Whatever Edgar Rawlings had been expecting from Charlotte Bell, the nanny, I'd wager my wages I wasn't it. But, having waited so long to be with someone I truly *chose* to be with—for now it did not seem as if I had ever really chosen Buster, but rather, had somehow been entrapped by him into a slow fall from life's grace—I didn't want to waste any more time. Why waste time, when it was so obvious that he wanted what I wanted, too?

"You're...aggressive," he observed as I pulled off my jacket, formerly his jacket, and pulled off the jacket he was wearing.

"Is that bad?" I asked, creatively using my teeth to remove his tie. It was an Oxford rep tie, red and navy stripes on the diagonal. It probably hadn't been designed for such a removal. Oh, well. If he was going to have to replace his favorite blue blazer, he might as well replace the tie at the same time.

The way I figured it, in this instantaneous rush of confidence I was feeling, if he didn't want me the way I was, the way I wanted to be, then he didn't properly want me at all.

"Not at all," he said, tilting his head backward, the better to let me kiss his neck. "I rather like it."

Off went his shirt.

His chest was rather hairy; I should have expected that from the dark hair on his head, the generous amount of hair I'd glimpsed on his lower arms whenever his sleeve had ridden up. His chest was broad, his stomach well muscled; I should have expected this from his riding ability.

But I hadn't expected it. Never once allowing myself to believe that this moment would ever come, I had never expected anything.

Open went his belt.

Odd, you would think that this geisha-like activity of undressing another person would feel servile, but it didn't. It felt powerful. It felt like for the first time, in being with a man, I was in control of the situation.

He stayed my hand as my fingers found the top of his pants.

"Do you think," he asked, pushing back the hair from my neck and lowering his head to place his lips on that spot, "I might have a turn?"

"Oh, all *right*," I conceded with ill grace. "If you insist."

Oh…*oh!* That was nice…

It was nice to feel so thoroughly taken care of and it was nice when he slipped my white nightgown over my head. It was nice right up until…

"What's this?" he asked.

He was looking at my panties. They were the ones that my mother, if I'd had a mother, would have warned me never to wear in case I suddenly had to have my clothes cut away by an emergency-rescue worker.

I blushed. "I wasn't expecting company."

They were my comfort panties, the ones I wore if I was expecting my period or if I was feeling fat and depressed.

"Hey," I said, feeling bolder, "if I'd known you were coming, I'd have worn the ones with a cake."

"It doesn't matter," he said, laughing. "They're some-how...you."

"Oh, thanks," I said.

"And they're charming," he said. "Really."

He really was crazy.

But that was okay. It was more than okay. It was perfect.

I continued what I'd started earlier, removing his pants. The way I figured it, the quicker I got us both out of our clothes, the quicker I could kick my panties under the bed and then hopefully the hideous things could be forgotten.

I pulled his shorts down, silk boxers, black with a tiny gold heraldic pattern on them, for those who keep track of these kinds of things. What was inside the shorts proved to be, well, impressive.

"Do you need a separate diplomatic passport for that thing?" I joked nervously.

Then, not waiting for a reply, in my haste to get us both unclothed as quickly as possible, I started to yank down my own wretched panties.

"What's the rush?" he asked, stopping my hands. "Is there another fire?"

I blushed again at the reference.

Then I watched as he slowly, using great care, slid my panties down over my hips and down my legs, gently lift-ing each foot in turn to help me step out of them. I stood stunned as he folded them, once again with great care, as if perhaps they were Agent Provocateur, rather than Sears' finest.

"You don't have to..." I started to say as his tongue found

the inside of my knee, trailing a path upward to the cleft between my legs.

But then I stopped myself.

Why stop him, when his tongue was doing that…and that?

As he licked, teased, kissed, sucked on the swollen nub between my legs, his hands reached upward, making contact with my hardened nipples.

I was tempted to make a joke—it was so much easier to make jokes than to say something real—like perhaps asking him if he'd needed to show such dexterity when seeking approval from the Senate Foreign Relations Committee.

But I became so caught up in the wonder of sensation, the wonder and surprise, that I forgot all about being the kind of person who habitually uses the defense mechanism of humor as a brick and a barrier between herself and the rest of the world.

His mouth was already on the places on my breasts where his hands had been a moment before, his mouth was on my neck again, it was on my mouth, the taste of myself on his tongue.

"Okay, Bosco," I said, unable to bear the seriousness of it all a moment longer.

"Bosco?"

"Yes, Bosco," I said, placing my hands hard against his chest, turning him around so that his back was to the bed and pushing him down on it. "Now it's your turn."

"I hope you're not expecting me to object?" he asked as I reversed the order in which he had done things, starting by kissing his mouth, then his neck, snaking my tongue down his body. "Because if you're expecting me to object," he said hard on the heels of a gasp, "then I don't think I'll be able to accommodate you."

"I don't expect anything," I said. And in that moment, I didn't. "Honest."

He sat up, reached toward me and touched the side of my face.

Everything after that was pure heaven.

We fell asleep in each other's arms afterward, but he awoke an hour later, looked at the clock, jumped out of bed, hunted around for his shorts, pulled them on and found his pants.

"Not another fire?" I asked, half-asleep.

"I just don't want Annette to wake early and find me here. You understand, don't you?"

"Of course," I said, coming more fully awake. And I did. I didn't want Annette upset by anything, either.

Now he was searching for his shirt, his tie. He turned back to me, knelt beside the bed, still speaking in a rush.

"But everything I said last night, on the roof, I meant it. You'll marry me, Charlotte?"

I hadn't been planning on holding him to *that*. But:

"Of course," I said simply.

"That's good," he said. "That's really good. But we can't tell anyone yet, okay?"

"What?"

"It'll be our little secret." He kissed my hands. "For Annette. Don't you think it would be a bit too abrupt for her if, one day you're her governess and the next day you're her mother-to-be?"

"Well, when you put it like that, it does sound—"

"Promise me, Charlotte, promise me you'll wait. We'll just let everything go on as normal around here until the time is right to tell everybody."

"I promise," I said.

"That's wonderful," he said, kissing my hand one last time. "You're wonderful." Then he rose, grabbed his jacket.

His hand was on the door when he turned.

"I love you, Charlotte," he said. "I swear to God I do."

I believed him.

Whatever else, he was telling the truth about that.

"I love—"

But he was already gone.

It wasn't until a full five minutes after he left, as I lay there staring up at the ceiling reliving the last few hours, that I heard the sound I hadn't heard in a long time: that eerie laughing noise.

It must have just been the wind.

chapter 10

I had not planned on falling in love with him.

But what are plans?

They say that man plans and God laughs, but sometimes I think it must be God just laughing at Charlotte's plans.

Life continued as normal, or rather, what was the new normal for me. My days were still filled, as they had been for months now, with Annette: her schooling, her playing, taking her to church sometimes on Sundays, even if neither of us could ever understand the services.

Only now there was a new feeling to it.

Before, I had loved her, most definitely that, but I had dealt with her from the stance of a governess, albeit a loving one, armed with the sad knowledge that even if Bebe Iversdottir did not part us with boarding school in the short term, something else would in the long. But now I saw into a future for us, one in which I might be allotted the luxury of time granted to a mother. It colored my feelings for her, made everything brighter, permitted me to take a deeper joy in her.

The one difference in my days was the driving lessons. Lars Aquavit was still intent that I should learn. The car had been repaired and returned, but I had yet to make it successfully out of the driveway. I tried to tell him that some people are just not cut out for driving, that some of us are not cut out for a lot of things: horseback riding, really anything that involved coordination with any kind of vehicle, geography. But he took it as an affront to his skills as a teacher that I would not, could not learn, and renewed his efforts. While doing so, he did however remark on the recent changes in me.

"You are…different now, Charlotte."

See?

"How do you mean?" I asked, my mind half on what he was saying, the other half occupied with the gears. First? Fourth? What did they all mean and why did there have to be so many? I was sure if the damn car were an automatic, I'd have at least a fighting chance.

"When you first arrived here," he said, "you did not seem… It's just that you have a new, I don't know exactly, maybe it's a joy about you. Before you seemed so very sad, so lost. And now you seem found. Yes, that's it."

"Maybe it's because I'm getting so confident at dri—"

"Don't grind the gears like that!"

Even Mrs. Fairly commented on the apparent change in me.

"When I first hired you, you seemed like such a meek little thing," she said, "like a bruised flower."

"And now?" I prompted, wondering why she would ever have wanted to hire a bruised flower in the first place.

"And now you're positively blooming, Charlotte!"

"You mean like a peony?"

"Well, no, perhaps not anything as showy as all that."

Rats.

"I think you might be more like bachelor's buttons," she added thoughtfully.

O-*kay*.

Even *Steinway* commented!

"Meow!"

"I *know!*" I crowed in the privacy of my own room. "I can't believe it, either!"

"Meow!"

"Who would have ever dreamed that *he* would love *me?*" I danced the cat around the room.

"Meow!"

"Oops, sorry." I was embarrassed. "I forgot how you hate to waltz."

I set the cat gently down on the bed, lay down beside him, whereupon he nuzzled my nose with his.

"I love you," I said.

"Meow!"

"Yes, I do know," I said as he purred. "Love is grand, isn't it?"

Of course, Gina and Britta wanted to know all the details of what was going on with me.

"You have a *man!*" Britta said when we went out drinking.

"It's *him!*" Gina added. "Isn't it?"

But I wasn't saying. I wasn't telling any of them what was going on, wasn't telling anyone what the catalyst had been for the changes in me. After all, I'd been sworn to secrecy, hadn't I? And I'd given my word, right?

Naturally, I wanted to be able to tell them, I wanted to be able to tell everybody, shout it to the world. I wanted to say that the difference in my days had to do with the difference in my nights.

At night, every night when he was at home, Edgar visited me in my room.

We made love. God, did we make love! I thought that maybe I should be thinking about a different form of birth control, what with how enthusiastically we both pursued this new endeavor of ours, but he didn't seem to mind the condoms and neither did I, so we continued as we'd begun.

And we talked. God, did we talk. A part of me cautioned myself that this was all too eerily similar to what had happened to me with Buster.

But then the newer, braver side of myself busted all those negative thoughts by pointing out the differences, the big one being that this time, there was no wife on the scene.

This time, I was going to get to have my cake and eat it, too. This time, there would be no heartache waiting for me at the end.

It was just a matter of being patient enough and biding my time.

This time, everything was going to end differently than last time.

I was sure of it.

And then my father came to visit.

He called from the airport.

"I know it's only November," he said, "and that I said I

wouldn't be here until Christmas, but I just couldn't wait to see you."

That was odd, since I couldn't remember a time in my life when he couldn't wait to see me, but he sounded so eager and Edgar was out of the house for the day, so I asked Mrs. Fairly if it would be okay if he came by for lunch.

"Of course," she said brightly. "I'd love to meet him."

It had been a while, over a year, since I'd last seen him, but he hadn't changed much. He was still incredibly tall, lanky, his straight blond hair just beginning to dull to gray, his skin a deep tan now that would probably never leave him, not even if he one day decided to leave Africa behind for good.

He didn't look at all like me, never had. My curly black hair, my shortness—I'd gotten both from my mother.

It was awkward seeing him, just as it always was. He was a stranger, a recurring stranger in my life who just happened to be my father.

"It's so wonderful to see you, Charlotte!" he said with a parental enthusiasm I was wholly unused to.

"It's great to see you, too, Dad," I stumbled on the words, not really knowing if I meant them.

It was too strange seeing him in Edgar's house.

He took my hands.

"Let me look at you," he said. "You look so different. I guess it's to be expected, though," he said wistfully, letting my arms drop. "You're not exactly my little girl anymore, are you?"

I wish I ever was.

Lunch was a bit fancier than usual. Mrs. Fairly, perhaps wanting to impress my father—although why she should care to impress the governess's father, unless it was with the fact that they weren't unduly abusing his daughter in a household that boasted at its head someone referred to as "the master"—had instructed Cook to eschew the usual sandwich fare, the result being a chilled salmon served in the dining room with real china and silverware.

"I hate salmon," Annette pouted prettily.

"Why?" my father asked with real solicitude, the kind I would have loved if only he'd bestowed it upon me when I was her age.

"Because it is so pink," she said.

"But you love pink!" I laughed.

"Yes," she said, wrinkling her nose, "but not on fish."

Lars Aquavit laughed. "So close your eyes," he suggested, "and pretend it's cake."

She squinched up her eyes and took a bite after only missing her mouth once with the fork. Then she chewed as we all watched.

"I guess it's not so bad," she finally said, "but it could use some frosting."

The meal passed with my father regaling Mrs. Fairly and Lars Aquavit with tales of Africa. I wouldn't have expected the latter to be so interested in a place so drastically different from his island home, particularly since he never mentioned any other country at all unless it was to mildly disparage Americans, and the former had never shown any interest in anything that didn't directly concern the running of the household. After all, just because they were in the employ of an ambassador, it wouldn't necessarily follow that they'd be curious about the rest of the world.

Even Annette got in on the act.

"What kind of dolls do they have there?" she asked with total seriousness.

"Actually," he said, "Africa is a very big continent with lots of countries in it, so there are different dolls depending on where you go. Which kind of dolls do you like best?"

It took her only a half moment of deep thought.

"The kind that dances," she said definitively.

"Oh, I'm sure I could find you one of those. Tell you what, when I go back home—" of course he thought of it as his home "—I'll find one to send here to you."

I couldn't stifle a flare of resentment. All my life, all he'd sent me or brought me, when he sent or brought me anything at all, had been the kind of artifacts that only served to give me nightmares: big scary wooden sculptures with bared teeth and spears in their hands, looking like they couldn't decide whether to kill me first or just eat me alive.

When dessert came, it was cake, which made Annette truly happy. I'd had the pleasure of seeing her eat cake many times before. She liked to pick the frosting off a little bit at a time with her fingertips, licking them like five lollipops. None of us ever tried to dissuade her from what many would term unladylike table manners in this regard, because as her proud papa pointed out, "I'm sure that when she's sixteen and on a date, she won't still be eating like that."

To which I'd queried, "You'll let her date when she's sixteen?"

He did seem like he'd be a very strict father.

"Did I say sixteen?" he'd laughed. "I meant thirty."

But on this day, I wasn't destined to see Annette eat cake at all, because Mrs. Fairly had a different plan.

"You haven't seen your father in so long," Mrs. Fairly pointed out. "And here we've been monopolizing all his time. I think it best we leave the two of you alone so you can chat a bit."

Did I want to be alone with him?

No.

But apparently I was to be permitted no choice in the matter, as Mrs. Fairly rose, indicating that Lars Aquavit and Annette should grab their cake plates and join her for their dessert in the kitchen.

What to say, what to say...

Him: "My trip was—"

Me: "I hope your trip was—"

We both laughed, still awkward, a false tinny sound that rankled. Why couldn't he talk as naturally to me as he talked to Annette and the others? Why couldn't I talk to him as naturally as I talked to...?

Okay, there really was no right way to end that, since there was no one I talked naturally to, not ever, not really. Edgar came closest, but as close as we'd come, I still felt that shadow of a wall between us. Maybe there was one reticent part of myself that was holding back until he'd made some sort of public commitment.

"It really is great to see you," my father said, taking a deep breath for courage as though what he was about to do, placing his hand over mine, needed great courage.

"You said that before," I said.

"And you're so different," he added.

"I'm pretty sure you said that, too," I pointed out.

"Well, you can't blame your old dad for marveling at you, can you?" he asked.

He wasn't old at all, had never seemed old, but yes, I found that I could and did blame him for a lot.

He must have read some of the resentment in my eyes, because he shied back a bit. Then:

"There was someone I wanted you to meet," he said, "someone I brought with me on this trip."

I'll admit my curiosity was piqued.

"But," he went on, "I thought it best I come here alone this first time and now I'm glad I did. This is quite a place you're living in." His eyes took in the grandness of the dining room. "But are you really sure this is the place for you?"

It was a tough question to answer, particularly since I wasn't sure what he meant by that. I wanted to tell him about Edgar, tell him that now this was the most right place for me, but I couldn't do that.

So instead I asked, "What do you mean?"

"Oh, you know."

If I'd known, I wouldn't have asked.

"It's just that," he said, "doing this kind of work was all right when you were younger, but don't you think it's time you found something you could commit your future to? And isn't it awful in a way, working in such a subservient position?"

I wanted to tell him that from where I was sitting, this was all his fault. If he'd imbued me with any sense of self-worth, if he'd ever been *around* long enough to imbue me with any sense of self-worth, I wouldn't have spent my adult working life thinking that the only thing I was fit for was serving someone else.

But then the thought occurred to me, for the first time, that it wasn't all his fault. Oh, sure, he could have been a

better father. I mean, he *really* could have been a better father. He could have been like, say, Carson Drew.

But none of that mattered anymore. I was an adult now.
At least I was supposed to be. And whatever decisions I had
made that had brought me here, I'd made them myself.
They were my choices. They would be my consequences.

I sought to change the subject.

"So, who's this person—" I was interrupted by the entrance of Mrs. Fairly, all abustle.

"The master came home early!" she announced.

My father's eyebrows shot up. "The master?" he mouthed
to me silently.

I started to rise.

"I'd better get back to work," I said.

"Oh no!" she said. "He seemed thrilled your father came
for a visit, but he didn't want to disturb you." She turned to
my father. "He's invited you back for dinner this evening."

"Well—" my father hesitated "—I do have a traveling
companion with me and we were planning on—"

"Oh no!" she said again. "I mean, oh yes! Feel free to
bring your companion with you. I'm sure the ambassador
won't mind. Why, it'll be like a second house party!"

As if the first one had been so much fun. I thought of the
wine stains on my white dress, thought about my jealousy
over seeing Edgar for the first time with Bebe Iversdottir.

"The more the merrier!" Mrs. Fairly called over her
shoulder as she exited the room.

Who knew she could be so trite?

My father rose.

"I'd better get going," he said, "if I'm to wake up in time
for tonight."

Maybe, I thought, he was more like Nancy Drew than Carson Drew. After all, Nancy always took naps when there was a big night ahead. Of course, she was always hiding in closets and checking luggage for false bottoms, too.

"The older I get," my father said, "the more jet lag affects me."

Then he bent over, like he might want to kiss me good-bye, but then stopped. Perhaps he sensed what I felt inside, that I was still distant from him.

"I guess I'll see you tonight," he said.

"Bye, Dad."

I watched him leave, a sight I'd seen all too often in my life. No matter that a moment ago I'd all but forgiven him in my own mind, at least for his parental shortcomings; some bitterness was still there.

Idly, I picked at my uneaten cake with the fork. Then I put the fork down and, with my fingers, started picking at the icing, coating the tips of each of my five fingers before commencing to lick the pink frosting off. Annette's way of eating, I decided, had a lot of merit to it.

I was sucking on my middle finger, the thumb and forefinger clean now, the ring finger and pinkie still bearing their tiny mountains of goo, when Edgar walked in.

How embarrassing!

But what I found embarrassing, he found charming.

"Perhaps," he said, "it is you who should be paying Annette for all she has taught you."

"Hey," I said, feeling daring as I offered out the pinkie, "don't knock it until you've tried it."

He surprised me by bending his head and licking the proffered finger.

"A bit sweet for my taste," he reflected, "but I like what's underneath it."

It felt thrilling, daring, to be flirting in public like this. Well, okay, maybe it wasn't technically public, since no one else was in the room except us, but it felt public. It was certainly the most openly physical he'd been with me outside of my bedroom.

I'd once asked him, late at night, my head on his shoulder, why it was always my bedroom, never his. I didn't really care, but was just idly curious.

He'd replied, "Because who knows what would happen in my room? Your madwoman might set me on fire again."

He still laughed at me about that and I let him. I didn't mind.

Now he pulled one of the high-backed chairs up beside me, looking a bit furtive, like we were two spies on a joint mission.

"I saw your father leave," he whispered.

"Did you introduce yourself?" I whispered back.

"No," he whispered, "I figured that could wait for this evening."

"Why are we whispering?" I whispered.

"Because I don't want Mrs. Fairly to hear us. I told her I was sending you out on a mission—" see? I'd been right! There was a mission! "—and that she was to keep Annette amused this afternoon."

"What's the mission?" I asked.

"You're supposed to meet me up in your bedroom," he said, "where I'm going to make love to you so thoroughly, you'll be helpless to ask any more questions."

Oh!

"How will we avoid detection?" I asked.

"They're all the way back in the kitchen right now," he said. "Annette has persuaded Mrs. Fairly that she should receive a second slice of cake since she only ate the frosting from the first, will only eat the frosting from the second, and so, one plus one in this case makes only one. If we dash upstairs now—dashing quietly, of course—no one will hear us. Of course," he added, "when we get to your room, you'll need to be a little quieter than usual, none of that shouting you're prone to."

I reddened a bit. I was a bit of a shouter.

"Well, if you didn't always—" I began defensively.

"It's okay," he said, licking that last frosting-covered finger, my ring finger, "I like your, um, *loudness.*"

"I'm not—"

"Come on," he said, pulling me to my feet, "I'll race you. But remember—it has to be a quiet race."

As I raced him as quietly as possible up the stairs, I felt as though I were living a surreal dream. He'd never been this playful before and it was wonderful.

I lay in his arms an hour later, feeling at peace. Every itch had been scratched with a luxurious slowness in excruciating silence.

"Are you happy right now, Charlotte?" he asked, playing with my hair.

"Mmm," I purred, sounding like Steinway, who was asleep at our feet, no doubt having sweet dreams of chasing a catchable mouse. It seemed to me that everyone's dreams must be sweet at that moment.

"But you could be happier, couldn't you?" he said.

I lifted my head, looked at him.

"What?" I asked.

"I have a surprise for you," he said, getting up. He crossed to the wardrobe, gloriously naked, opened the door. From inside he pulled out a hanger with a dress on it I'd never seen before. I certainly hadn't put it there.

It was dark red and very pretty, with simple lines. I pictured myself wearing it. The dress would fit me closely, the hem falling above the knee, the sleeves long against the cold that had a tendency to invade the rooms here even when all the windows and doors were closed, the neckline plunging down in a deep V. I could look good in a dress like that.

"I remembered you ruining your other dress the night of the party and thought you might like a new one, in case you had a special occasion."

Then he reached down into the bottom of the wardrobe and came out with a pair of shoes, high-heeled black satin strappy things.

"For dancing," he said.

"I'm going dancing?" I asked.

"Well, no," he admitted, "perhaps not tonight, unless of course you want to dance here. Originally, I'd planned on taking you out tonight. But now, with your father unexpectedly visiting, I think we might as well do it here."

"Do it?" I asked. "Do what?"

He draped the dress over the back of the chair in front of the desk, placed the shoes gently on the floor. Then he picked up his jacket, from where it had been hastily discarded on the floor earlier, and reached into the inside pocket.

When his hand was visible again, I saw there was a small box in it. A jeweler's box.

"I'd thought to ask you to marry me over dinner out tonight," he said with a smile, "but now, with your father here, I thought it best I ask his permission first."

Oh!

Whatever doubts I'd ever had were now gone. If he was willing to do this, then there was nothing sham about his love for me. This was nothing like what had happened with Buster.

I reached a hand out for the box.

He held it out of reach.

"I think I'd best save this for tonight," he said, "and do it properly. Will you say yes when I ask you, Charlotte?"

"Yes," I said simply, "I'll say yes."

I floated through the remainder of the day on angel's wings and when it was time to dress for dinner, I felt as though there were an invisible fairy there in the room with me, helping me with the complicated straps on the shoes, slipping the dress over my head, doing up the zipper, making sure every hair was in place. I looked at myself in the mirror. While it was still true that no one was ever going to ask me to model anything, unless it was my pretty dancer's feet, I felt beautiful.

I don't remember my feet touching the stairs once as I sailed down to the dining room and dinner, although they must have. When I walked into the room, breathless, late for once in my life because I'd actually taken some care with my unruly hair and bothered to put on a bit of makeup, my father was already there, his back to me as he enjoyed a drink at the sideboard with Edgar. They were laughing, having obviously made fast friends.

They turned at the sound of my high heels striking the wood floor and I saw my father had a suit on, a rare thing. I also saw for the first time the woman at his side.

His traveling companion.

She was tall, as tall as he was even without heels, with dark black skin, and wore a yellow dress, her hair braided in a complicated design on her head.

She looked to be about…my age.

"Charlotte," my father said, looking awkward, "I'd like you to meet Sweet Maningue."

"Sweet?" I said dumbly.

"It's a nickname," she said in a richly accented voice.

She put her hand out and as I took it, I saw the diamond ring on her finger. It was large, square, sparkling like a huge crystal.

"Are you two going to…?" I started.

"Yes," my father said, putting his arm around her. "This is what we came here to tell you."

Needless to say, hearing this news knocked my own news out of the water.

The ensuing dinner passed in a haze. It was a good thing Edgar had given instructions that this was to be an adults-only dinner because it would surely have made me feel guilty had Annette been there and me so incapable of being attentive.

It felt like another woman listened as my father explained that Sweet was a graduate student from Nairobi who'd been sent to him to do an internship.

"We certainly didn't plan on this," he said, covering her hand with his, "and we did wait until the internship was over before acting on our feelings."

I tried to picture future family holidays: my father with his bride who would be my age, me with my husband who was my father's age. Sweet and I could talk about pop music while our menfolk could trade Viagra stories.

"Tell me you can be happy for us, Charlotte," he said. "It's important to us."

"It's important to both of us," Sweet added.

It was weird. It actually seemed to matter to them, to both of them, what I thought. I couldn't remember a time in my life when my father had openly cared what I thought about anything.

Didn't everyone deserve a shot at happiness? And didn't he, being one of those everyone, deserve the same shot?

It was as though he read my mind.

"After your mother," he addressed me, "I didn't think I'd ever find a woman I could be happy with again. Hell, it took me twenty years."

I neglected to point out that twenty years ago, his future bride had probably been about three.

So, okay. So maybe family gatherings would be a little weird in a Greek tragedy sort of way. But we'd find a way to handle it.

"Yeah," I said, realizing the truth as I spoke it, "you do deserve happiness." I raised my glass. "Cheers."

Sweet smiled wide as she stretched across the table to kiss me on the cheek.

"Hey," I said, "just don't expect me to call you Mom."

Edgar clapped his hands together in a "that's settled" sort of way, smiling brightly as he placed a hand inside his jacket.

I knew what he was reaching for.

"No!" I screamed.

Dad's and Sweet's heads zipped my way.

"What?" they asked.

"Sorry," I said. "I just didn't want anything to spoil your big moment. If anyone else has anything important to say, they should probably save it for after dessert."

My father looked at me closely.

"You're kind of an odd girl, aren't you?" he said.

I rolled my eyes, gave an embarrassed smile.

"Yeah," I admitted.

"Yeah," Edgar said softly, using rare slang. But I could see from his smile that he meant it lovingly, that he was proud I was willing to let someone else go first with happiness.

After dinner and dessert—two desserts in one day; my life really *was* getting good!—we retired for drinks in the library. If my father thought it was odd that a busy ambassador should take the time to entertain the visitors of his daughter's governess he didn't let on. Perhaps it was that he was finally starting to see me in a more worthy light and thought I deserved such fine treatment. Or perhaps it was that he was so in love with Sweet, he couldn't see anything else clearly.

As well as Edgar had treated me over the last several weeks in the privacy of my bedroom, I myself was not used to being treated with such a public display of his regard for me. True, he had not touched me in their presence, nor had he said anything to indicate that he held me with more than a fond regard, but drinks in the library had not exactly been the norm in my stay there thus far.

And drinking had not much been the norm in my previous life, the few times I'd imbibed with Gina and Britta notwithstanding, so the combination of the two glasses of wine over dinner plus the after-dinner sweet drink Edgar served were enough to go to my head.

Edgar was asking my father and Sweet about the specifics of their wedding plans. Funny, I hadn't thought to ask that myself—what kind of ceremony would they have? And where?—but they were obviously pleased now at Edgar's asking.

Sweet positively glittered as she said, "We will get married near the dig where we first met, of course."

Of course.

She turned to me.

"And we will want you there, Charlotte, of course."

Of course.

I took a sip of my drink, thought about flying to Africa. Iceland was so cold, Africa would be so hot. Couldn't I ever go anywhere where the temperature was temperate?

But it would be special, I realized. My father, the version of my father I was used to, could so easily have gotten married without me present and sent a postcard afterward. It was nice he wanted my approval, nice they both wanted me there.

"Well," I said, "of course I'd love to." I looked over at Edgar. "But only if I can get the time off from work."

Edgar laughed. "Now, what kind of man would I be if I didn't allow you time to attend your father's wedding?"

I pictured Sweet on her wedding day. What kind of dress would she wear? Whatever she wore, I realized, she would be stunning.

But, wait a second: What kind of dress would I wear for *my* wedding? And when exactly would we be getting married? Edgar hadn't said yet. Would it be before them? After them?

Suddenly, I had an overwhelming urge to hear Edgar make the announcement at last. After all, I'd waited—what?—at least an hour and a half since my father and Sweet made their announcement. Surely it was my turn for happiness now.

And it seemed that Edgar was eager for happiness now too, if the way his hand kept unconsciously reaching for the jeweler's box in his jacket's inside pocket was any indication. It was as though, ever since I'd screamed "No!" at him over dinner, when he'd reached for it the first time, he'd been waiting for me to give an indication that I was changing that no to yes, so he could formally, publicly ask me, and then I could really say yes.

Feeling as if I was about to give the most important head nod of my life, I met his eyes, eyed his jacket pocket meaningfully, met his eyes again, and started to nod.

Which was right when Mrs. Fairly ushered a breathless Robert Miller into the room. My eyes were glued on Edgar as he watched Robert enter. There was a wary look in his eyes, but he continued with his motion, slipping his hand inside the jacket.

"Edgar!" Robert Miller said commandingly.

It was a voice that wouldn't be ignored and I turned to look at him.

He was still the same man I'd met the night of the house party. He even had what looked to be the same suit on, making him look like an underpaid federal employee, making him look out of place here. Didn't he own another suit?

"Robert," Edgar said evenly. "I'll be with you in a moment. I was just about to—"

"No!" Robert cried, that one-word utterance sounding

somehow different than mine had earlier. Mine had been of the "no, not now, but definitely later" variety. His sounded more like the "no, not at all, not ever" variety. But how could he know what was about to happen? And, even if he did, why would he want to stop it?

My father and Sweet looked on, confused, as Robert Miller quickly strode across the room, placing his hand firmly on Edgar's reaching hand, stopping him, stopping the beautiful moment I'd been so sure was going to happen right then from happening.

"I insist," said Robert through gritted teeth. "You and I need to talk. Now."

"But surely," Edgar said, "it can wait until after—"

"No," Robert cut him off. "It can't."

If anyone had ever asked me before that moment if it were possible for Edgar Rawlings to be subservient to anyone, I would have said, no, that such a thing was impossible. But I saw now, as Edgar allowed himself to be led from the room with a "Won't be but a few minutes and then we can continue" thrown over his shoulder, that I had been wrong.

What other things had I been wrong about?

I stood there, after Edgar and Robert left the room, wondering what was going on. I turned to my father for help, but there was no help there.

"Charlotte, what's going on?" he asked, concerned.

Nope, no help there.

Sweet moved toward me, put a comforting hand on my arm. Odd, but since I'd met her, despite that she was obviously the same age as me, she'd seemed more mature. Maybe it was because she was marrying my father.

And then, as I stood there, dying with curiosity to know what the two men were talking about, the familiar saving refrain came to me: What Would Nancy Drew Do?

If I knew one thing in this world, it was that Nancy Drew wouldn't just stand around here, balefully, waiting for whatever blow fate was about to deliver. She'd go after the mystery, find out what the hell was going on.

I shook off Sweet's hand, not unkindly, and left the room. Walking on the toes of my shoes so as not to make too much sound on the floor, I made my way slowly down the corridor to Edgar's office. When I got there, I paused, flattening myself against the wall in order to eavesdrop.

In most quarters, eavesdropping was considered to be a despicable, sneaky thing to do. But Nancy Drew eavesdropped all the time and everyone thought the world of her. And, really, how else was a girl to learn what she needed to know?

I could only hear a mumble, but from the deepness of that mumble, I knew it to be Edgar talking. How I wished I could hear the words!

But then the other voice in the duet came in and that voice was angry, stern. I could hear it clearly.

"You can't do this, Edgar," Robert Miller said, sounding somehow sad despite the sternness. "Bebe thinks you were going to ask her to marry you. If you don't do it now, there'll be an international incident."

I felt my heart catch. I'd been given to understand that he and Bebe had not been that close after all. Why should she think he was going to marry her?

I waited breathlessly, waited to hear Edgar say that he wouldn't marry Bebe, that he loved me.

But those words didn't come, because, once again, when he spoke it was all mumble to me.

Then there was Robert Miller again, the now-hateful Robert Miller:

"It doesn't matter," he said, "none of that. I'm sorry Miss Bell has to be hurt right now. But surely you can see it has to be that way?"

Surely *not,* I thought. Surely, Edgar will tell him so.

Silence, long silence. And then, finally, Edgar's voice, loud and clear.

"All right—" he bit off the words, each one a nail "—all right, Robert. We'll do it your way."

I didn't stay to hear any more. What was the point?

I raced back down the corridor, the heels of my dancing shoes, the shoes I'd thought to one day dance with Edgar in, maybe even tonight, tattooing a mocking trail of laughter behind me as I flew.

I heard the door of the office fling open behind me, heard Edgar desperately scream, "Charlotte!" But I didn't stop.

I don't know what my father and Sweet thought when they saw me race by the library, would never know, didn't care.

I hit the front door hard, fumbling with the handle, unable to open it through the tears blinding me. But then I had it opened, finally, just as Edgar caught up to me from behind, put his hands on my shoulders, turning me toward him.

"Charlotte, I can—"

"Don't. You. Dare." I said it in a tone of voice that brooked no argument, even from him. And then using both my hands forcefully, I pushed him away.

Then I was out the door, slamming it behind me.

Having given no thought to what I was going to do, where I was going to go, I raced in the night down the driveway, my dancing shoes hitting the ice at a skid, sliding me along until I at last lost my balance, falling hard.

"Crap!" I shouted, railing at the night sky. "Why does there have to be so much fucking ice in Iceland?"

Then I laughed, laughed at the silliness that was me.

And then I cried, cried at what an idiot I'd been, thinking I could come to this foreign place and my life would be different, thinking things would be different with Edgar than they'd been with Buster, thinking my story would somehow turn out to be a happy one.

There was going to be no happy ending for me. I saw that now. But I also saw that I couldn't just leave right then and there. Outside of practical considerations, like the fact that all I had with me were the clothes on my back and it was the middle of the night and my passport and things were back inside the house, there was the matter of Annette. I could not, would not leave her as I had done the Keating children. It was my duty, my responsibility to stay with her until the future was settled. I couldn't let her wake in the morning and find me not there, never to be seen or heard from again.

So I would go back inside the house, that house I now hated, I would find some flimsy excuse to explain away my bizarre behavior to my father and Sweet. I would bide my time just up until, and not a moment longer, I could make my escape, my conscience clear.

chapter 11

The next day dawned as dreary as a day could dawn.

The night before, after doing what I'd promised myself I would do—make an excuse to my father and Sweet that they would somehow buy—I'd come up here to my bedroom. I was in the process of putting on my nightgown, having taken off the red dress, tearing the sleeve in my haste to get it off me, when the knock came at the door.

I recognized that knock.

I flung open the door, saw Edgar there, looking sadder than I'd ever seen him. For a moment, my heart went out to him instinctively, but then, angry with myself more than with anyone else, I pushed that tender feeling away.

"What?" I demanded. "What do you want from me?"

He moved to touch me, but I pulled out of reach.

"Please, Charlotte, listen. I can—"

"No," I said. "I don't want to listen. *You* listen. I'll stay in this house, under your roof, but only until things are settled for Annette. You instruct Mrs. Fairly to find another governess for her. And, as soon she can find one, I'm out of here."

"Please, Charlotte, I need you."

That was a joke!

I thought about the woman he was going to marry now, the woman who was not me.

"Get out!" I said, no longer able to contain my feelings, not caring who heard me. At least I knew that Annette, the only one I was concerned for now, was a sound sleeper. I picked up the red dress, threw it at him. "Get out! I mean it! I don't want you talking to me, I don't want to talk to you. I'll stay until the situation is settled for Annette. And not one day longer."

Then I threw the shoes, too.

Now that it was daytime, or what passed for daytime in Iceland that time of year, I was as miserable as a human being could be. Whatever strength from anger I'd felt the night before was gone now. In its wake, only devastation.

And nausea.

I attributed the nausea to a combination of things: the drinking I'd done the night before, coupled with the excess of anxiety over all that had gone on afterward.

Last night, while in the daze of trying to explain to Dad and Sweet my bizarre behavior, he'd told me that, mission accomplished in telling me about their plans to wed, they were returning to Africa today. We'd said our goodbyes. This was good, I saw, because I wouldn't have been able to bear witnessing their happiness just now. Right now, the happiness of others hurt too much. By the time their wedding rolled around, whenever that might be, I would be able to function like a proper human being, I would be able to smile and really mean it, but not now, not today.

I would have liked to pull the sheets back up over my head, declared the day over before it had even begun. But like mothers everywhere, you don't get the luxury of indulging your own sickness when you have a small child in your care; there are someone else's needs to attend to first. I may not have been Annette's mother, would never be, but she was still my responsibility until circumstances finally changed for good.

So I dragged myself out of bed, brushed my teeth because that's what people do even if a part of me no longer cared about living, put on clothes without taking any notice what they were and went down to breakfast.

"Isn't it the most wonderful news imaginable?" Mrs. Fairly said upon my entering.

I looked at her quizzically.

"Papa is to marry Miss Bebe!" said Annette. "I will finally have a mother!"

So he had told them already.

Then Annette saddened a bit.

"Of course," she said solemnly, "it is not so nice as if you were to be my mother, but I know now that was just a silly dream of mine."

Mine, too, I thought, my heart breaking.

But then, as quickly as she had turned cloudy, she became sunny again. Well, Annette always was a resilient child.

"But I will have a mama!" she said.

"Yes," I said, practically choking on the word as I touched her head lightly.

I wondered where he was, prayed I wouldn't have to endure seeing him that morning.

It was as though Mrs. Fairly read my mind.

"The master left early this morning for America. He was called back on some urgent business but should be back in two days. I only knew about the engagement to Miss Iversdottir from a note he left me."

What had he done—called that... *blond* woman the night before on the phone, after leaving me in tears, and asked her right then?

It hurt too much to think about it.

"Annette," I said, "when you're finished with breakfast, meet me in your room and we'll get down to work."

"Aren't you going to eat anything?" Mrs. Fairly asked, concerned, as I moved to leave the room.

"No," I said. "I have no appetite today."

My work with Annette proceeded badly that morning.

I wanted her to work on her math—it was about time we each mastered that subject or at least tried to become less awful at it—but all she wanted to do was look over the scrapbook we'd started making for her weeks before.

She kept pointing to individual pictures of herself with her father.

"Here is where Miss Bebe's face will be soon," she said, pointing at a photo of the two of them enjoying birthday cake. "And she will be here, too," she said, pointing to the strip of small black-and-white pictures that had been taken at one of those mall booths.

Yes, I thought, *she will be in all those places and I will be...gone.*

It was too hard for me, thinking about the day that was

sure to come even sooner than I'd previously thought, when I'd be separated from Annette for life.

"You know," I said, trying to distract her, "we don't necessarily have to work on math this morning. We could work on reading or science. We could do an experiment!"

But even that didn't distract her.

"Okay," I said, trying one last resort, "we could just color all day!"

Nor that, either. All she wanted to do was look at her family pictures and dream about the day, soon, when her family would grow bigger.

And all I could do was sit by, helplessly, and watch her. Maybe I couldn't have stood to see the happiness of my father and Sweet that day, but I couldn't stand to get in the way of her happiness, either.

The morning passed.

Lunch came and went, with me still unable to eat due to the nausea of anxiety.

"If you don't eat," said Mrs. Fairly, "how will you work?"

"If you don't eat," said Lars Aquavit, "how will you drive?"

"I'll be fine," I lied, wondering if I would ever be fine again.

Afternoon started and Annette was still obsessing over the scrapbook. In order to protect myself from the pain of observing this activity, I gave my mind over to wondering what I was going to do with my future, now that it was obvious my services here would no longer be required.

Annette was busy enough in a self-contained way that I thought it okay to leave her to her own devices for a while. She hardly noticed my passing.

I went to my room, took out the manuscript I'd been

working on, the roman à clef about Buster. Reading through the pages, I thought that some of it was good, but a large part wasn't; mostly, it was just the bitter tale of a foolish girl. My feelings for Buster had stopped completely, at last, like a broken clock that could not be started again. What a different world it would be if one could enter an affair with the same wisdom one has after going out from it.

I'd thought for so long that I wanted to write, that perhaps my salvation lay there, but I saw now that this was untrue. Whatever I was going to do in life, it wasn't going to be that.

I took the uncompleted manuscript down to the library where a fire was always lit midday and fed the whole lot in at one go. It made a bright flare.

Let someone else tell the stories, I thought. I had already told mine.

Late afternoon was usually the time of day Lars Aquavit reserved for teaching me to drive, or attempting to. Even though Annette was too old now for naps, after a full day's schoolwork she usually needed some downtime and Lars claimed that worked best for him.

"I am exactly between meals," he liked to say, "so there is no risk of losing my lunch, and even if I do lose my appetite, there are enough hours left before dinner that I can regain it in time."

Usually, he made me laugh when he said this, but not today.

And now, not only did I feel nauseous, but I was also feeling light-headed, as well, perhaps from having skipped two meals.

"I don't think I should be driving today," I told him.

"But how can you learn," he said, "if you don't practice?"

I was tempted to point out that if my driving talents were any indication, I hadn't been learning anything at all. Then there was the matter of my no longer really needing to drive at all, with me leaving here soon. Once I was back in Manhattan, I could spend the rest of my life on public transportation whenever I needed to go anywhere.

"I'm just tired today," I finally said. "Maybe tomorrow. Tomorrow I'll learn how to drive."

Having neatly gotten out of taking yet another driving lesson I suppose I could have sought out Annette and played away her downtime with her. But I really was exhausted and decided instead on a nap.

By the time I woke up, Annette had disappeared.

I looked for her everywhere, having seen by the clock it was time, past time, to get her ready for dinner.

But she was nowhere to be found.

How would Nancy Drew go about finding a missing child?

I hunted down Mrs. Fairly, the woman who usually knew everything.

"Oh," she said, laughing, "you were sleeping, so of course you don't know. Miss Iversdottir stopped by. She said she wanted to take Annette for the evening, something about doing something 'spiritual' together."

"And you let her take her?" I demanded.

"Why wouldn't I?" She was surprised. "Miss Iversdottir said she'd spoken about it with Ambassador Rawlings last night when he phoned to ask her to marry him and that he must have forgotten to tell me about it. And, of course, Annette was thrilled at the idea of just the two of them doing something together, just her and her future mama. So why wouldn't I let them go?"

There was no logical answer I could give. Maybe it was just that I had hoped to keep Annette with me, if only for a little while longer.

"Now, then," Mrs. Fairly said brightly. "About dinner. You haven't had anything to eat all—"

"I think I'll go back to bed," I cut her off. Since there was no one here who needed me any longer, there really was no reason left for me *not* to declare the day over and done. "I'm still not hungry and I'm still exhausted. Must be a bug coming on."

I really must have been exhausted, because it was the middle of the night when I finally came awake.

What had awakened me?

That sound, that wretched eerie sound that I'd occasionally been bothered by in this house, the one that sounded like laughter.

"That's *it!*" I finally cracked, speaking the words into the silence of my room. Ever since I'd come here, from time to time I'd been plagued with that annoying noise. Well, no more. I'd be leaving here soon. What was to stop me from breaking into that locked room and seeing just what the hell was going on? It was what Nancy Drew would do. She certainly wouldn't just lie here, staring at the ceiling while a madwoman cackled down the hall. I'd been subservient here for way too long, even if at times I tried to tell myself I wasn't. Coming to this house had screwed up my life and now it was trying to screw up my sleep. Enough was enough.

I cast about for something to break into the room with,

knowing that Nancy Drew would never try something so foolish as throwing herself at a solid door. I finally settled for a credit card I hadn't needed to use once since coming here—good thing, I saw, since it had expired—and a needle from the traveler's sewing kit I traveled with, but also never used.

An expired Amex credit card, not even gold, and a sewing needle. Well, I certainly felt armed.

This time, I felt no need for tiptoeing as I had during the course of my amateur investigations. With Annette out of the house, and Edgar out of the country, there was only Mrs. Fairly, who could sleep through anything. The need for discretion had flown the coop and all that remained was the need for valor.

I strode boldly with my weapons down the hall. First, I tried the needle. It would have been so nice, so convenient if that worked right away. But the needle was too short, too skinny, and I only wound up dropping it, losing it down the hole.

Okay, I figured, taking a deep breath. It was the expired Amex or nothing.

I slid the credit card down the seam of the door, at the same time turning the handle, just as I'd seen detectives do on TV. Apparently, I wasn't quite as slick as Columbo or Dennis Franz—well, they'd have probably just shot the lock out anyway—because it took me three tries before I heard the magic click that told me I'd achieved sleuthing success.

I'd never understood much about physics, having never understood much about math, but I knew enough to know that it was the counterforce created by the tension of me holding the doorknob just so that caused the door to swing open with such force, taking my arm with it, once I'd freed the lock.

Gasping for breath after my exertions, as I finally burst into this room that had been secret from me so long, I saw...

A fax machine?

Oh, there was a lot of other office equipment in there too, most of it looking old-fashioned. But the centerpiece and what really drew my attention was that fax machine.

Why did Edgar keep office equipment up here, I wondered, when his embassy office was downstairs? And why hadn't he told me what was in this room? Why, above everything else, was that fax machine so *old?* Couldn't the U.S. government afford better? Or was it just that Iceland was considered to be such a lesser embassy posting, not being as important as either Paris or London or Bonn, that it got dumped with all the leftovers?

For, surely, this ancient fax machine I saw now was the source of all the weird noises I'd heard. I saw that now, because I heard it make the very same noise as a new message came in, adding to the one I'd heard come in just a short while earlier, the paper scrolling out to add some more to the scroll already there.

I tore the sheet off, feeling Drewishly curious to see what had disturbed my sleep, what was so important it had to be communicated this way in the middle of the night.

The "From" part of the first fax read "Robert Miller." The body read:

Edgar: our suspicions have been confirmed

It ended there. Apparently, the earlier transmission had been cut off.

What had been confirmed?

I scanned down quickly to the second fax to find out.

This one also started out "From: Robert Miller"—must have been a permanent letterhead, I thought. But then my blood froze, clichéd as it may sound, my blood froze as I read the contents:

> Bebe Iversdottir is a spy with the Russian mafia. You must protect Annette from her at all costs.

The words danced in front of me, as though I were trying to make sense out of some foreign language. I couldn't believe what I was reading. How was this possible? What was going on here?

But I realized there was no time for me to question the how or why of anything. So what if I felt like Nancy, jumping the shark in #56, the final book in the original series, *The Thirteenth Pearl.* I had to assume the paper I was holding was the truth, in which case Annette, having gone willingly with Bebe, whom Annette believed to be her future mother but who was in fact a spy with the Russian mafia, was in grave danger. I had to find her before Bebe did whatever she was going to do to her for whatever reason. It might not make much sense to me, none of it, but I had to save Annette.

Bebe had told Mrs. Fairly she was taking Annette overnight to do something "spiritual." What could she have meant by that?

Making the same kind of leap of logic I'd read about Nancy Drew making countless times, the kind that made the reader think, *Whatever made her think of that?,* until she proved to be right, I thought of the only spiritual place I knew of in Iceland: the church.

I raced down the hall, down the stairs, had the door open and was outside before I realized I was barefoot. This wouldn't do at all, I thought, going back for my boots that were near the hall tree. I wouldn't get very far if my feet got frostbite. Nancy Drew might be impulsive, but she was always prepared.

And my feet wouldn't do, either, I realized.

The church was far enough away that it was too far to walk. And, anyway, enough time had been lost already. Annette had been gone for about eight hours, I figured. The thought of taking any more time to get to her than was absolutely necessary made me want to scream.

That was when I did the bravest thing I could remember ever doing in my entire life.

I hurried to the kitchen, where there was a wooden board on the wall with keys hanging from it. It was where Lars Aquavit kept the keys to the car. Without a second thought, without thinking once about how scared I was to drive that car alone, that car I couldn't even drive when someone was with me and telling me what to do, I reached for the keys, snagging them in my hands.

Then I was back in the hall, almost out the front door a second time, when Nancy Drew screamed in my brain, "A weapon! How are you going to defend yourself, if the need arises, without a weapon?"

Gee, she'd never talked directly to me like that before. And who would have imagined her voice would be so deep? She sounded just like Adriana Trigiani. She was an alto!

She was right, of course.

But, I wanted to scream back at her, I didn't have time for this! There was a little girl who needed saving. I didn't have time to pretend I was a young sleuth, going through the house stealthily to see if Edgar had conveniently left a gun or a sabre lying around that I could use in an emergency.

And then there it was.

On the same rack, from the bottom of which I'd grabbed my boots, Mrs. Fairly's black umbrella hung from a hook. I had never bothered to get my own umbrella, a fact Mrs. Fairly endlessly teased me about every time I got wet, which was often here. And whenever she used it and I saw her coming up the walk, I thought of Mary Poppins, about to fly away. I could probably poke someone in the eye or stomach with it if need be and, in a pinch, I could always just open it up; the sheer size of it popping open would confuse anybody.

I snatched it off the wall, sending up a prayer of thanks to Mary Poppins, the Patron Saint of Nannies everywhere, as I finally made it out the door.

I may have been in a rush to get to where I was going, but with my limited driving skills—okay, my nonexistent driving skills—it would have been foolish to rush too much and take the risk of killing myself before accomplishing whatever good I was supposed to accomplish in the world on this night.

Plus, I still wasn't sure how to get the damn car out of the driveway.

"Come on, Charlotte," I said, pep-talking myself, "you got the key in the lock, you got the door open. It's a start."

My fingers trembled a bit—from the cold? From fear?—
as I fit the key into the ignition.

"Cut it out!" I yelled at myself. "You're supposed to be
being brave and intrepid right now. So stop being unbrave
and unintrepid."

I turned the key, trying to remember everything Lars
Aquavit had tried to teach me about forward and reverse,
and when to do those things, about all the different gears,
about the gas, and especially about the brake.

Please, I thought, getting serious as I backed the car
down the drive, *just let me be competent long enough to do
what I need to do.*

Being competent lasted just long enough to get me the
rest of the way down the drive, turning the car around and
heading for the church at a snail's pace in one of the lower
gears.

"At this rate, it would probably be quicker if you
walked," I told myself.

"Oh, shut up. Whose side are you on?" I told myself
right back.

Yes, being competent lasted as I drove through the streets,
passing the occasional cars of intrepid Icelanders who'd
probably been out late partying. It lasted right until I got
to the church.

That was when, seeing the finish line right there ahead of
me, perhaps due to my overeagerness, I did the same brain-
dead thing I'd done on the first day Lars Aquavit tried to
teach me to drive. Pulling up, confusing the gas for the brake,
I hit down hard on it, slamming into the side of the church.

Crap!

There went the front end of the car again. Having been

healed once by mechanics already, it was once more crumpled up like an accordion at a bar mitzvah.

But there was no time for that now. Fuck the car.

I pushed the door open with my boot, grabbing the umbrella as I exited.

Then I raced to the door of the church, praying it was unlocked, since I'd forgotten my sewing needle and expired Amex card back at the embassy.

The door pulled right open. Maybe in other parts of the world, sanctuary had to be limited to business hours due to vandalism and violent crime. But here in Reykjavik, where the most likely criminal thing to happen was whatever was going on here, sanctuary was just as convenient as slurpies at a 7-Eleven.

I rushed into the church, trying to be as quiet as a rushing person in winter boots could possibly be, so as not to alert Bebe.

But the church was empty. I could see that, as I zigzagged in and out of the pews, checked out the altar. Empty.

Had I been wrong?

Oh, crap! This was just the kind of thing that would never happen to Nancy Drew—wasting time by going to the wrong place, chasing phantoms. All of Nancy's phantoms always turned out to be real. Well, except that they were all fiction.

Think, Charlotte, think!

The stairs!

The stairs in the entryway, the ones that led up to the bell tower!

Moving quicker than I'd ever moved in my life, I ran to the entryway and up the winding stairs, pushing aside the feelings of nausea and dizziness brought on by a full day of not eating anything.

As I came through to the top that overlooked the city, the freezing top where the wind whipped around, I saw by the light of the stars a huddled something in the corner: Annette!

Guarding her, of course, was Bebe Iversdottir.

She no longer looked beautiful to me, not even icily beautiful.

"You *bitch!*" I screamed at her, unthinking, as I pointed my umbrella at her.

"You...*governess!*" she laughed back at me, raising her gun in frustration. "You're too late."

"What?"

I looked more closely at Annette. It was then that I noticed for the first time that her eyes were closed. She hadn't noticed my loud and clumsy entrance. Was she asleep? Was she...dead?

"What have you done to her?" I demanded.

But before she could answer, we both heard the sound of more than one pair of feet echoing up the long stairwell.

Bebe glanced over the edge. Then she turned back to me, horrified.

"The *police?*" she said, no longer laughing as she trained her gun on me. "You called the *police?*"

I was as surprised as she was. And I didn't like to be talked to like that.

"*No,*" I said just as scathingly, "*I* didn't call the police."

Of course I hadn't called the police. I'd figured: Who would ever believe me? Who ever believes anyone about things like kidnappings and the Russian mafia until afterward?

But then I realized that gun she had trained on me was no laughing matter. In her desperation, who knew what she would do? It would be convenient if she hurled herself over the side of the tower, falling to the concrete and ice down below, but I wasn't counting on it.

So I reverted to plan.

Thank *God* I'd made a plan!

I hit the release on the umbrella and as it popped open wide, I swung it two-fisted like a Louisville Slugger, connecting the silver tip clean with the deadly gray of the gun and sending it sailing out into the night.

"Okay," I heard the Icelandic-accented voice behind me. "Which one of you crashed the embassy car?"

chapter 12

You could say that it was my lousy driving skills and not Nancy Drew at all that saved my life and Annette's. After all, the cops never would have found us if I hadn't crashed into the side of the church. And who knew what Bebe might have done then? True, I was ready with my umbrella. But there was no guarantee there would have been the same happy ending.

Of course, the happy ending was a while in coming. First, Annette had to be revived. Only, it turned out she didn't need to be revived at all. It turned out she was only sleeping. That child could sleep through anything!

In the meantime, Bebe had been trying to persuade the cops that I was some kind of lunatic—"Just look at how she is dressed!"—who'd kidnapped the two of them at umbrella-point.

She was just backing toward the stairwell, as though the cops might just let her go, when Annette woke up.

She looked around the bell tower, confused, wiping the sleep from her eyes.

"Miss Charlotte!" she cried with joy when she saw me. Then she looked accusingly at Bebe. "That woman is awful," she told me. "She promised me we were going someplace special, but then she brought me to this cold place and told me to go to sleep. I definitely do not want *her* to be my mother."

Now that she was awake, the cops immediately recognized the ambassador's daughter and they began to take matters more seriously.

If this really were a Nancy Drew book I was living, they would have let me grill Bebe myself. The police always let Nancy question subjects and after a few empathetic words from her—"We all make mistakes at times"—they were always ready to tell her the whole story and go straight. Perhaps I could be that persuasive, too?

Well, of course *that* wasn't going to happen. And when I told them Bebe was a spy with the Russian mafia, they became very skeptical.

See? I knew that would happen.

But I had the presence of mind to have them call police headquarters and have someone else sent to the embassy to retrieve the fax from Robert Miller fingering Bebe. They called another car to take Bebe away for questioning and then they took Annette and I home. It was all so confusing, and I still wasn't sure exactly what was going on, what had gone on, but at least Annette was safe and in my arms.

It wasn't until late the next day that I learned the whole story.

I hardly could believe the truth when I heard it.

★ ★ ★

Apparently the urgent call for Edgar, summoning him to the States, had all been another ruse of Bebe's and he came rushing home on the earliest flight.

He hugged Annette so hard, crouching down beside her, I thought he was never going to let her go. But then he stood and hugged me, too.

"Thank you, Charlotte," he said, tears in his eyes. "If it hadn't been for you…"

He left the sentence hanging. We both knew it didn't bear thinking about.

Previously, when I'd wanted to learn the answer to a mystery, I'd played Nancy Drew, sneaking around the house. But now I realized the best way to learn what I wanted to know—and there was a lot!—was to just be straightforward about it, ask a few questions. If I was lucky, I might even get a few answers.

"Just what the hell has been going on here?" I demanded once Mrs. Fairly had removed Annette from the room, promising her extra cake. Everyone, the whole household, was about spoiling Annette for the time being.

I suppose I could have phrased my question more delicately, but I was through once and for all with being subservient. Whatever was going on here, it had almost gotten people killed.

"I suppose I owe you an explanation," Edgar said.

"And *how*," I said. "By my calculations, you owe me about fifty-six explanations, but I'll settle for one at a time."

"Which would you like me to start with?" he asked with rare contrition.

"Bebe," I said, certain that would answer a lot, "anything to do with Bebe."

"Well," he said simply, "she works, or I should say *worked* for the Russian mafia."

"I know that," I said, exasperated. "I saw the fax."

"Yes," he said, "and it was a good thing you did. It's also a good thing you told the police here about it. When Bebe realized she'd been identified, she immediately caved under questioning."

"You've spoken to the police here already?" I asked.

"Yes, I called them repeatedly from my cell whenever I could while traveling. You don't think I was going to wait until I got back here to find out what was going on, do you?"

"Well," I said, "you do have that outdated fax machine upstairs, so who knew you could be so modern as to carry a cell?"

"That's right," he said ruefully. "You saw the room, finally learned your madwoman was really my old equipment in the communications room."

"Communications room?" I echoed. It sounded so ominous, so…CIA. "Why would you need such a thing?"

"To keep nosy people like Mrs. Fairly and you from reading things you shouldn't. We'd been suspicious of Bebe for a long time but hadn't any proof."

"Well," I said, "it was a good thing I was nosy this time, wasn't it?"

"Yes," he said, getting serious, his voice soft, "it was."

But I didn't want to hear that softness in his voice. I certainly didn't want to respond to it.

"Back to Bebe…" I suggested.

"Yes," he said, getting businesslike again, "Bebe. Once she saw the fax, she fingered everyone else in the organization. This is great news," he said, looking a trifle sad, "because it means that very soon Annette will finally be able to go home."

"Go home?" I echoed his words once again. "But this is her home," I said, "here, with you."

"Not exactly," he said. "You see, Annette's not really my daughter."

"What?"

That was when he explained to me that Annette was the next in line of a country with royalty whose current royal was under control of the Russian mafia. Now, with the plot to snatch Annette busted up—Bebe had been hiding with Annette in the tower until morning, when she was planning to fly Annette out of the country, never to be seen again—the little girl could finally go home. Edgar himself was ex-CIA and he'd been put in Iceland as the ambassador so he wouldn't be noticeable in order to protect her.

"You mean you're not really an ambassador?"

"Oh, I'm really an ambassador." He smiled.

"How?" I asked.

"You'd be surprised," he said, "how few people want these posts, considering the vetting process. And I was qualified, sort of. I am ex-CIA, after all."

"That's a little hard to believe," I said. "It's very hard."

"Yes, well," he said, "we live in a world where skyscrapers can fall from the sky and yet, somehow, flowers still bloom, somewhere, every single day. So what's one more improbable thing?"

Indeed.

"Does Annette know about any of this?" I asked.

"No," he said sadly. "She's been with me since she was just two years old. She really does think I'm her father."

It was like Annette was the Aurora from *Sleeping Beauty*, given away for her own protection at a young age.

"It'll be so hard on her when she finds out," I said.

"Yes," he said, "but her mother is a good woman. I've met her. And she's waited so long to get her daughter back."

It had rankled me, the idea of Bebe raising the child I loved so much. This I could deal with, however: once Annette went back home, wherever home was for her, I might never see her again. But she'd be going to a mother who loved her.

"It'll be hard on you, too," I said, realizing it even as I said it, "letting her go like that, after all this time."

"Yes," was all he said.

"So," I said, sucking it up, "back to Bebe."

"Yes?"

"Were you really ever in love with her?"

"God, no!" he said, clearly horrified at the prospect. "That was just all to trap her. The only woman I can ever remember really loving in my life now, truly loving, is you."

And then he kissed me.

It was the kind of amazing kiss that heals everything, erasing all the bad, leaving only good.

I couldn't believe how good it was.

Finally, I forced myself to draw away from him, looked up at him with hopeful eyes.

"Then we can be married now?" I asked.

Now it was his turn to draw back.

"Well," he said, "there's a slight problem. You see, I'm already married."

"What?"

I drew back farther.

"It's not what you think," he said, reaching for me, but I pulled back even farther, out of reach, crossed my arms.

"Explain," I said, hiding behind sternness, refusing to give in to the tears that threatened to form.

God, I was emotional these days. What was that all about?

"I've been married for a long time," he said, running his fingers through his hair as though exasperated at the mere thought of that marriage. "But in name only," he hastily added. "I was already married, and my marriage was already dead as far as I was concerned, when Robert Miller came to me with the mission of protecting Annette."

"And, what?" I asked. "You were just too busy these last few years to get around to getting divorced?"

"Essentially? Yes."

"And what of your...*wife*—is it in name only for her, too?"

"I haven't spoken to Belinda for a long time," he said. "The last I heard, she was living with some businessman in Spain. So, to answer your question, I'd say, yes."

It was so much to digest.

"I'll get a divorce," he said, "as soon as possible. But in the meantime," he added, reaching for me again, "we can be together."

"No," I said, remaining out of reach, "we can't."

chapter 13

Who should plunk down next to me on the Icelandair flight back to America but George Cranston, the same man who'd been seated next to me on my trip out there. I suppose I should have been surprised at the strange coincidence, that he should have been with me the first time and was now here with me again so many months later, but as Edgar had pointed out, so many strange things happened in the world, so many strange things had happened in my world—what was one more?

"How did it work out for you?" George asked without greeting, his words sounding somewhat surly.

"Excuse me?" I had no idea what he was talking about.

"That book you were going to write," he said. "How did it work out?"

I thought about how I'd burned the manuscript in the embassy fireplace.

"I changed my mind," I said finally. "It wasn't the story I wanted to write after all."

"Ha!" he crowed triumphantly. "See? You should have written mine."

I felt a wave of the now-familiar nausea, but I welcomed it: it was a harbinger of something hopefully good to come.

"It's okay," I said, patting my still reasonably flat stomach, "I think I'll have a new story soon."

In my bewilderment over Edgar's revelations, I had decided to do the only thing I could do: I returned to New York, back to the place where, even if they preferred not to take me in, they just had to.

Only this time, I wasn't going back to Aunt Bea. Of course I'd visit her, visit my cousins over the upcoming holidays, if they'd have me, but it was time I got a place of my own. It was time I discovered who I was in this world without the props of other people.

I hadn't been willing to accept much from Edgar when I'd finally left his house, just the money he owed me and one other thing: it would have been hard to land in the city and find a place to live by nightfall, so I allowed Edgar to use his connections to make sure there would be a place for me. If I didn't like it, I could always move once I got my bearings and had time to properly look.

I'd remained in Iceland just long enough to see that Annette had received the shocking news and taken it well. A part of me had been concerned it would be too much for her—her father wasn't really her father, her mother lived in another country, she herself was a princess—but I hadn't factored in the adaptability and resilience of small children.

Besides, what little girl doesn't want to be a princess? Annette was thrilled at the notion, particularly after Edgar promised he'd visit her and visit her often, to make sure she was doing all right. Of course I knew her future wasn't going to be all tiaras and parties—still tea parties for now—but at least as a princess she would no longer have to worry about math.

It would have been harder for me, saying goodbye to her, if I hadn't seen for myself how happy she was now. I suspected that all those years of viewing family photos that had no record before she was two may have planted the seed of suspicion in her mind, that there was another story out there. Whatever the case, she'd always been a girl badly in need of a mother and now she was going to get one.

"I will miss you, Miss Charlotte," she said tearfully.

"Same here, Your Majesty," I said, curtsying for her benefit and hoping I'd got the form of address right; no point in me messing her up with misinformation before she'd even started her new life. "But I'll visit one day, if you'll invite me."

And, somehow, I really did know I would see her again.

On the other hand, it was harder saying goodbye to Lars Aquavit and Mrs. Fairly, to Gina and Britta, than I would have imagined.

I didn't know when I'd see any of them again or even if.

Gina and Britta said they might come see me in New York sometime, but I expressed my doubts.

"Of course we will come!" said Britta.

"Perhaps in summer," added Gina, "so we can avoid the unbearable heat here."

Unbear…?

Whatever. I could explain the difference between an Icelandic summer and a Manhattan summer to them at a later date.

Mrs. Fairly and Lars Aquavit were remaining in Iceland for the time being. Well, of course Lars was—he lived there. But they were both remaining at the embassy because Edgar himself would be remaining until he'd finished his service there.

"I'm still a good ambassador, right?" he'd said ruefully. "I mean, it's not like I have to do much here."

That was true enough.

But he'd also wanted a commitment from me regarding the future and this I wouldn't make. I was too angry with him for all the deceptions.

"But I had to protect Annette!" he objected.

"But you let me fall in love with you!" I objected. "And you knew you were married!"

"But I couldn't tell you that!" he objected. "Annette wasn't supposed to know the truth! No one was supposed to know!"

"But you could have trusted *me!*" I objected. "If you loved me so much, you should have trusted *me!*"

We were both full of buts, full of objections, full of exclamation points. I didn't care if some of mine were unreasonable, given the facts. I'd been hurt, hurt too often and too deeply, and if holding on to my outrage protected me from further hurt, so be it.

"What will it take, Charlotte?" he'd asked, resigned. "What will it take to win you back?"

"Give me space and get your divorce," I'd said. "Then

come to me with the papers. If you're lucky, I'll let you court me."

"*Court* you?"

"Yes," I said, "dammit, court me."

"Okay," he agreed, "if that's what it takes."

There was one last thing I'd needed to do before leaving Iceland, but I'd put it off until I got to Keflavik Airport, having made Lars Aquavit stop at the drugstore on the way there.

For a while now, I'd been ignoring the nausea. Further, I'd ignored having missed one period and what that might mean, telling myself that it was just another one of those déjà vus all over again that seemed to keep happening to me. Surely it would turn out the same way it had with Buster: a false alarm, no child on the way. I'd put taking the test off until I'd safely left Edgar behind, because on the tiny off-chance that it should prove positive, I just wanted to deal with the news first on my own without it getting clouded by anyone else's feelings. Maybe that was selfish, but I'd been given to servitude for too many years. It was time, if only occasionally, to put myself first.

So, before boarding the plane, I'd gone to the bathroom, hoping my flight didn't leave without me as I peed on the wand, waited the requisite few minutes for the results to come through, feeling unaccountably giddy at the thought that my life was finally about to change.

Of course, I was pregnant.

epilogue

Reader, please believe me when I say, I soooo didn't marry him.

What Would Nancy Drew Do?

I know, those words have endlessly haunted this narrative. But they really are, when you think about it, the ultimate light and guide to reason.

So, then, one last time, What Would Nancy Drew Do?

I had learned, by hard lesson, that it would be easier to say what Nancy Drew would not do.

She wouldn't have gotten involved with Buster in the first place.

She wouldn't have tried to write a book, probably because she was too busy solving a new mystery every six days.

She wouldn't have gone to Iceland without researching the place first.

She wouldn't have driven a car when she didn't know

how to drive. Well, okay, in an emergency, she would have driven anything.

She wouldn't have been short or dark or Jewish, just because.

But, above all else, she would not, not ever, not even for a second, have gotten involved with Ambassador Edgar Rawlings.

Why not?

Because she would have known, instinctively, that there was something more there than what met the eye, she would have been instinctively suspicious. And, being suspicious, she would not have allowed her heart to become engaged.

And if she did by some insane stretch of the imagination fall in love with a man with a small child, whose absent wife had some kind of air of mystery about her? If she had then learned what I had learned about what was really going on?

She would not compound her previous errors by going on loving a man so obviously wrong for her. She would believe in her own self-worth enough to just walk away.

Even if she believed, with all her heart, that the man in question had really loved her more than he'd ever loved any other woman, still loved her.

She'd still walk away.

I was still walking, too.

But there was a slight hitch here, for I'd come to realize that it didn't really matter a damn what Nancy Drew would or wouldn't do, despite how much she'd taught me—about the importance of making friends; about the importance of searching for the truth, facing things. It mattered what *I* would do.

All along, through the various nanny jobs, through my whole life, really, I'd been searching for an identity. Well, I wasn't going to find it with married ambassadors and I wasn't going to find it by becoming Nancy Drew; being Nancy Drew, unless a person really was Nancy Drew, could get a girl killed. So I'd need to keep searching, I thought, but at least I now knew I was brave…sometimes. It was a start.

And what was growing inside me, the life, was a start, too.

As soon as I knew I was pregnant, I realized it was what I'd wanted all along, a child, so I could really do over the past, loving that child as I hadn't been loved. Previously, I'd settled for other people's children, with the safe buffer of their parents to keep me from loving them too much, hurting too much. But now, at last, I was ready to have my own. It might not be what every woman wanted most, but it was for me. The next child I would raise would be my own, for I could not leave any more behind.

And now for the most important, to me, question of all: What Would Charlotte Bell Do?

She'd wait and she'd go on believing. And one day, when the time was right, she'd risk walking out on that wire again. Because she believed, in spite of Buster, in spite of all the problems with Edgar, she still believed in the ultimate power of love between two human beings. And, just because it had never worked out right before, it didn't mean that it would never happen.

She'd tell Edgar about the baby, because he had a right to know, but she wouldn't let her decisions hinge on his feelings.

One day, one incredibly fine day, true love would happen for Charlotte Bell.

And when that day came, she would be ready for it.

Maybe it would be with Edgar—she kind of thought it would—and maybe it wouldn't. Only time would tell.

But Charlotte Bell still believed.

Against all odds, she still believed.

What if you could have it both ways?

New from the author of *Milkrun*
Sarah Mlynowski
Me vs. Me

Gabby Wolf has a tough choice in front of her.
Will she choose married life in Phoenix, or a
career in Manhattan? If only she could have it all.
Maybe her wish is about to come true.

On sale August 2006.

**Available wherever
paperbacks are sold.**

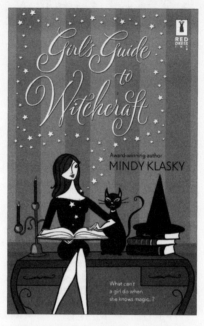

Don't miss…

A book so outrageous and addictive you
will not be able to put it down!

The Thin Pink Line

by Lauren Baratz-Logsted

A hilarious story about one woman's (fake) pregnancy.

"Here, written with humor and scathing honesty…is a
novel to share with every girlfriend you know before,
during or after the baby comes. It's a winner!"
—Adriana Trigiani, author of *Big Stone Gap*

"Jane…is so charmingly audacious, that readers will be
rooting for her."
—*Publishers Weekly*

Visit your local bookseller.

**RED
DRESS
INK**
™

www.RedDressInk.com   RDI0604TR1R